By the same author

One Just Man (Winston Trilogy Book I)
ELOHIM—Masters & Minions (Winston Trilogy Book II)
WINSTON'S KINGDOM (Winston Trilogy Book III)
ALEC (Alexander Trilogy, Book I)
ALEXANDER (Alexander Trilogy, Book II)
SACHA—The Way Back (Alexander Trilogy, Book III)
PETER AND PAUL (An intuitive sequel to Yeshûa)
THE AVATAR SYNDROME (Prequel to Headless World)
HEADLESS WORLD—The Vatican Incident (Sequel to Avatar Syndrome)
MARVIN CLARK—In Search of Freedom
THE GATE—Things My Mother Told Me
NOW—Being and Becoming
THE PRINCESS
GIFT OF GAMMAN
ENIGMA of the Second Coming
WALL—Love, Sex, and Immortality (Aquarius Trilogy Book I)
PLUTO EFECT (Aquarius Trilogy Book II)
OLYMPUS—Of Gods and Men (Aquarius Trilogy Book III)

Short stories

THE JEWEL & OTHER STORIES
CATS AND DOGS
Sci-Fi Series 1
Sci-Fi Series 2

Non-fiction eBooks by Stanislaw Kapuscinski

VISUALIZATION—Creating Your Own Universe
KEY TO IMMORTALITY
[Commentary on the Gospel of Thomas]
BEYOND RELIGION: Volumes I, II and III
[Collections of essays on perception of Reality]
DICTIONARY OF BIBLICAL SYMBOLISM
DELUSIONS—Pragmatic Realism

Poetry in Polish
[with illustrations by Bozena Happach]
KILKA SŁÓW I TROCHĘ GLINY
WIĘCEJ SŁÓW I WIĘCEJ GLINY

INHOUSEPRESS, MONTREAL, CANADA

http://inhousepress.ca

Yeshûa

A PERSONAL MEMOIR OF THE
MISSING YEARS OF JESUS

A Novel by

Stan I.S. Law

INHOUSEPRESS, MONTREAL, CANADA

Published in Canada in 2006 by
INHOUSEPRESS
inhousepress@sympatico.ca   http://www.inhousepress.ca

Design and layout
Bozena Happach

This book is a work of fiction.
Names, characters, titles, places and incidents are either the products of the
author's imagination or are used fictitiously.

LIBRARY AND ARCHIVES CANADA CATALOGUING IN
PUBLICATION

Law, Stan I. S.
Yeshûa : a personal memoir of the missing years of Jesus : a novel/
Stan I.S. Law.

ISBN 0-9731872-3-9
ISBN13 978-0-9731872-3-6

1. Jesus Christ--Fiction. I. Title.

PS8623.A92Y48 2006   C813'.6   C2006-904252-7

Printed and bound in the USA

Acknowledgment

This book would not have been possible had it not been for Edgar Cayce's comments on the activities in which Jesus engaged during the "Missing Years." It is to Edgar Cayce and all who worked to transcribe his comments that I wish to express my profound gratitude.

Yeshûa's character is further based on information gleaned from Gnostic Gospels discovered in Nag Hammadi, Upper Egypt in 1945.

And Jesus increased in wisdom and stature,
and in favour with God and man.

Luke 2:52

Prologue
The Morning of the First Day

I'd missed him by a day. A single day. I'll never forgive myself. If it hadn't been for that stupid deal when my father couldn't bear to lose a damn rupee, I would have seen him again. There I was, riding like a maniac. All for nothing.

More than three years had passed since I last saw him. I missed him from the day that we parted company. In Egypt. He was the closest friend I ever had. As a matter of fact, considering the time I spend travelling, he was virtually my only friend. And now he's gone. Dead. They tell me the Romans executed him. Like a common criminal. Why – Yeshûa wouldn't steal a crust of bread. He wouldn't hurt a fly. Not the Yeshûa I knew. Could it really be true?

They've directed me to this broken down hovel. A house, a shack really, on the back-streets of Jerusalem. Mud bricks and a straw roof. The headquarters of his followers. I just don't believe it. I can't. He was... He wouldn't let them... Yeshûa... where are you Yeshûa?

Don't listen to me. I am in a state of shock. Wouldn't you be? You would, had you known him as I did. If you knew him at all. Even if you had just met him.

I look around.
My eyes fall on a stone bench against the eastern wall. A mud brick wall like the house. All around the courtyard: drab walls, drab bench, drab, beaten down ground for a floor. Yeshûa was never drab. He was rich beyond belief. He was the perennial giver...
They let me sit here. Someone came out, told me what happened and went inside again. I've been alone since. As usual. As he was. Had been.

This is where it had all started. At least for me. On the outskirts of Jerusalem. This is where I'd met the man who now is no more. I know it. The man who came out told me. I've also heard it in town. But in my heart, in my heart of hearts, it's too much to accept. Although, on the way here, I did sense something peculiar. In the whole city. The City of Peace. Peace indeed! A city where they murder innocent people. Not the mob, not some crooks in a dark alley, but the people in power. The Romans. The illustrious noble-men.

This is a farce!

And the men inside the house aren't much help either. Or weren't to him. At least I assume there are men inside. I only met one of them. They told me, outside, before I got here, in a whisper, that his disciples are hiding here. Hiding from whom? And why? Maybe they know something I don't? They certainly didn't know *him* as I do, even if they had followed him during these last three years. Much good it did them. Or him.

I feel a pang of anger.

So much had happened during these last few years. I'd had my share of excitement, though I shared neither my father's nor Yeshûa's ambitions. Live and let live was my motto. So far it served me well. Apparently my friend hadn't fared so well. And then I'd heard, all the way home, that he was a full-fledged teacher. A Master, they called him. Like a Swami or Guru. God how time flies! I'd just returned home from China. I had dropped everything and rode all the way. I had to see him. To see if his dream had come true. He never lost hope that it would. That he would fulfil his mission. It had taken weeks to get here. It would have been many months, had I travelled with a caravan. Had I had a premonition? Had he called me to his side? Somehow?

I'd missed him by a day.

"But how exactly did it happen? I mean, he was always an easygoing fellow. At least, I found him to be so. And..." I catch myself speaking aloud.

I glance around but nobody is listening. Not to me. Anyway, they are all inside. They are all lost in their own thoughts. Apparently dark thoughts. They all seem to have crawled into their shells like a bunch of snails on a hot summer day on the shores of Tiberias. I can't take it any more. I'm going inside. It's dark. The only light comes in through the doorway I just entered. Small openings, high up on the wall, are shaded. This time I speak aloud. I want to be heard. By whoever cringes in the semi-darkness.

"Didn't you know what would happen? I mean, could you not have helped him somehow, some way?" My hand rests on the hilt of my sword. I know it's frustration speaking through me. Even anger. But after riding day and night only to miss him by a day, I have a right to be upset.

No one answers.

My eyes are getting accustomed to the dark. There are bodies everywhere. Inert. After a while, a heavy, thickset man lifts his head. As he looks up I can just see his face. It is lined as though from an intensive effort of trying to understand something beyond understanding. His hair seems prematurely gray. He looks at me as though he is emerging out of a deep, painful dream.

"No."

That's all he said. No. No we couldn't. No, we tried, and we couldn't. No. No one could help him, not even He whom he called his Father. It took a long time before I understood what he meant. It was all there. Stated as clearly as though he'd spoken all the words out loud. What really showed in his eyes was pain. Such pain, as I'd never seen before.

There are eleven of them sitting on the floor, their knees gathered under their robes, their heads bowed, or hidden in their hands. In the other room I can just see three or four women, huddled together as though trying to avoid the sand carried by the desert wind. Only there is no wind. The air stands still. In abeyance. Waiting? There is not even any noise. Not even a whimper of discontent from Mother Nature. Nor from people in this room. These people might as well be dead.

"Come!" A hand taps me on the shoulder. A young face is peering into my eyes. Asking. The same pain. There is a great deal of pain here. "Come outside," he repeats.

I gather my cape and satchel and follow the young man into the courtyard. He points to the sole stone bench against the east wall. The courtyard is awash with early morning golden-pink warmth, somehow out of place in the atmosphere of gloom. Of desperation.

"They are lost. All of them," the young man says after we sit down. I pull the cowl over my head to protect my eyes. After the darkness inside, my eyes hurt. Even in the shade. Only then I look at my companion.

"I am Satya," I say. "Satya Bihari." My name means nothing to him but it seems polite to introduce myself.

"My name is Yôchanan. People call me Yôna."

"You knew him?" A stupid question. Right now I feel pretty stupid.

A sad smile confirms my suspicions. His smile says: I knew him and I loved him.

"Yes," he nods. "We all did." Then he catches his breath. "We thought we all knew him. But we didn't. Nobody really knew him. Nobody... He was all alone," this last in a barely perceptible whisper.

My host is a young, smallish man, no more than twenty. He does his best to look happy, to maintain an air of equilibrium, even of serenity. It doesn't quite work. His features say one thing, his eyes another. I feel his anguish.

"Can you tell me what really happened?"

He looks at me for a long time. A few times he opens his mouth to speak, and his lips move up and down, as though by their own volition, and then hang open. Gusts of breath escape his heaving chest. And then, without warning, a guttural sobbing spills from his open mouth. Sobbing that shakes his insides while his body remains stiff, rigid, unyielding, refusing to let go. I move closer to the young man and put my hand on his shoulder. For a while he doesn't react and then he seems to melt, collapse in a heap. I catch him as he's slipping to the ground. I catch him and hold him as a father would hold a distraught child. Gradually his chest relaxes; his heaving becomes easier, less tortured. I can do little but wait. It doesn't last more than a few seconds. He dries his eyes with his long flowing sleeve, clears his throat and offers me a distorted facsimile of a smile.

"He told us to be happy," he says.

I let that go. "What did people say about him?" My young companion regains control of himself. "I mean, what..."

"They said that he was the king who didn't make it."

"King?"

"King of the Jews. Of Judea. They said he would set us free..."

"From the Romans?"

It's hard to believe this young man. I'd first met Yeshûa when he was a twelve-year-old boy. I'd spent years travelling with him across the continents. We went as far north as Palmyra, as far west as Memphis, and as far east as my own home, Benares. I'd slept in the same tent with him on a hundred occasions. We talked until the first light dimmed the stars over our heads. I'd known the man. He was not a king. He'd never had any ambition of becoming a king. He had as low regard for the power wielded by man, any man as... well, as I did. Only more so. Yeshûa was a vagabond. A homeless hobo. He was a seeker of truth, of the secret of life. He was satisfied with fewer creature comforts than any man I'd ever met. The nearest he'd gotten to the concept of an ego was to try and find out who exactly he was. King? These people must be crazy.

"That's what they thought."

I look at Yôchanan with closer attention. There is something he is not telling me. "But you don't, Yôna?" I ask not knowing quite what to expect.

Once again it takes him a while to reply. He seemed to be looking for the right words. It was as though he'd never spoken on the subject before. Almost as though it was all new to him. Then Yôchanan leaned back against the adobe wall.

"He didn't talk about us, here, " he started, choosing his words carefully. I nod my encouragement. "He said," the young man hesitates then seems to gather courage. "He said that His kingdom was not of this world."

I want to shout "What!?" but his hand silences me with a strange authority.

"He always meant what He said."

There is steel in Yôchanan's tone. Confident, unbending. A strange change sweeps over him. He wasn't offering an opinion. He was sharing a statement of fact.

Yeshûa imparted strange respect among his closest friends. Disciples, I think they call themselves. Or something like that. This last statement did sound like Yeshûa talking. The Yeshûa I'd known. Only the Yeshûa I knew didn't teach. He was always learning. More so than any man I'd ever met. But he did have that power of persuasion. He didn't talk much, not in public, but when he did speak, he sounded as though he was beyond being challenged. It sounded as though what he said had to be said, and he simply vocalized the truth in a manner in which people were likely to understand it.

"You loved him very much..." I speak softly, really thinking of myself.

I did love him very much. Yeshûa was not a man who was easy to love. Oh, he was complacent enough towards most, towards the masses, but when he befriended you, there were no more compromises. It was all or nothing. You cannot serve two masters, he'd told me. So many years ago. So many times. We were discussing loyalty to the government versus your own family. He was arguing for total commitment to the idea. Or ideal. We also joked a lot.

"Wait until you get married," I quipped. "Then you'll see what master you must serve. At least if you want your supper!"

I recall his eyes. He laughed more than any man I'd met in all my travels. He had a strange capacity to see beauty in virtually everything. And when he became aware of it, he laughed. "Just look at these," he'd say pointing at some flowers, "or those," his hand followed the contour of the desert dunes afar, "or the riches we are given to witness," he'd say pointing at the night sky. He seemed to live in constant awe of the world around him. It was all beauty for him, all perfect, all an inscrutable gift made exclusively for our pleasure. For our joy. If he were a Greek, he would have been a follower of Epicurus. Both he and Epicurus denied the existence of gods. It sounded strange coming from one raised in the strictest observances instilled in him by the Essenes. Maybe that's why he'd run away. For years. For so many years. And yet?

And yet he came back. How I wish he hadn't.

"I'm sorry," says Yôchanan. "There is little more I can tell you."

And with that Yôna rose slowly and half walked, half staggered towards the dark opening in the wall. A moment later the darkness embraced him with a merciful blanket. He will hide in it, as I now wish I could hide. Hide from memories that fill the emptiness with such vividness before my eyes.

Once more I am alone. More alone than I have ever been in my life. More alone than on that first caravan, before I met him. With suddenness that jars my raw nerves, memories flood my mind. My eyes are filled with images — long and short, snippets of events, of journeys, words, fragments of discussions, arguments we'd had over the years. The pain that I detected in the eyes of the men in the darkened room is now my own. I simply cannot accept that I'll never speak to him again. I shut my eyes. I would give all I have to shut out the whole world. It seems empty now, devoid of life.

The next instant I see a scruffy lad hiding behind a sun-drenched stone wall. A lad who would grow into a man like no man I'd ever met. My eyes burn from recent lack of sleep. I'd tried so hard to get to see my friend. I close my eyes again. My young friend's face is still there. He is smiling...

* * * * *

Part One

Rebellion
The First Day and the Night

1

Escape

I remember it all as though it had happened yesterday. I remember how I felt. I remember the camp we struck at the foot of the hill, just outside Herod's wall on the road to Shechem and Damascus. I remember the guards, and the men giving us a wide berth. I even remember my own tent and the weather. It was hot. Really hot. So hot I preferred to stay in my tent. But what I remember best of all is that playing on my own is no fun at all. Not when you're fourteen and filled with more energy than you know what to do with.

I couldn't really blame my father. After all, it was I who had begged him to let me come. My hometown was fine, but... well, there was something that was calling me to far away places. And so, after long arguments with the whole family, this was to become my very first trip. My mother was dead set against it, but dad overruled her. Good for him, he'd said. And for me, I thought. Only I never realized that for months on end I wouldn't see anyone remotely my own age. And when I did, within a week or two, we moved on. At the latest. We would be on our way again.

And then I saw Yeshûa.

I found him hiding behind the corner of a building, as though running away from some invisible enemy. I beckoned him to come and hide inside my tent. After a single glance in my direction he sprinted for the open flap and dove headlong onto my bunk. I'd never seen a boy run that fast. He must have had plenty of practice.

"What's up?" I asked, as curious as I was startled. I'd learned some Hebrew over the last year or so. My father made a point of making me learn the languages of all the countries we were going to visit. At the time, I had no idea that the local people spoke mostly Aramaic.

"If you start now, by the time you're my age, you'll speak them all with ease," he assured me.

Just then, six or eight men appeared from around the building, wielding sticks, spitting into the sand and wiping their foreheads. They were all dressed in black, had long beards and looked angry. They looked this way and that, but didn't dare to approach the caravan. My father had guards posted at the four corners and some extra ones on the lookout as well. Yeshûa only got through by his extraordinary burst of speed. Or maybe the guards were looking the other way.

"What's up?" I asked again. Yeshûa did not inspire trust. His clothing was torn at the elbow, his face smudged, there was blood on his left knee. Only his head made me smile. It was a bobbing halo of reddish, curly hair. More like a girl, I thought, till I met his eyes. There was nothing feminine in those eyes. They were steely blue, looking straight at you. In fact, they were looking straight inside you. Or through you. Instinctively, I lowered my own eyes. When I looked up again, he was smiling

"Thanks," he said. "What is your name? I am Yeshûa."

He spoke with a northern accent, drawling like the people from Galilee, from around Lake Chinnereth. I think the Romans called it the sea of Tiberius, after their emperor. Romans liked doing that. Renaming things, I mean. They preferred their own names. When you do business, it's good to know such things. But for the sake of local people, you had to remember their own names. If you wanted a good trade, that is. Anyway, when you travel as much a we do, you also learn a lot about accents. You learn to distinguish between slight variations, changes in modulation. I didn't know it at the time, but later, dad told me that I have a musical ear. I can imitate various dialects at will. It seemed easy to me. Natural. I know this was only my first trip, but we've been on the road for the last fourteen months. That's a long time to practice.

"Why were they chasing you?" I prodded again.

"Your father is an important man," Yeshûa said, peeking out of the tent and completely ignoring my question. "Do you travel a lot?"

"The last fourteen months!" I said proudly. Not many boys had seen what I had seen. "Does your knee hurt?"

Yeshûa glanced at his knee. Blood was beginning to coagulate in two narrow streamlets. He straightened his leg in front of him and wiped the blood with his sleeve. "I'll live," he said, in a tone that dismissed the inconsequential. Then he asked, "are they gone?"

I raised the flap an inch or two and peered out. Then I opened the front leaf wider. There were no signs of any men wielding sticks or of any suspicious marauders. Father liked to camp a little beyond the beaten track. It was safer, he said. He would move out only such goods to the *maarah*, the local market place, as deemed suitable for local appeal. I tied the flap up to let in more air.

"They're gone," I assured him.

"They won't do that again," he said. "Not for a while."

I had no idea who wouldn't do what to whom, but I let it go. For now.

"How do you do your schooling?" Yeshûa asked, changing the subject yet again.

"Father says travel broadens the mind. You learn as you go. I can speak four languages and I can describe the route, in detail, from Benares to Jerusalem," I told him. I wanted to ask if he could do the same but he beat me to it. The expression on his face spoke volumes. He was impressed. "One of father's men is teaching me numbers and astrology," I added. For some reason I needed my unexpected guest's approval.

"Would you teach me?"

I was stunned. No one had ever asked me to teach them anything. They were always teaching *me*. Always. And now I could be... And then I looked at him with suspicion.

"You're kidding, right?"

"There is so much to learn. Only they don't know it. They think you can find everything in the Scrolls?" He shook his head.

"The scrolls?"

"Torah," he smiled again. "You know, the scriptures." It would be proper to say that he was smiling all the time, only sometimes his smile was broader. "My mentors feel that if I learn the Torah by heart, I'll know everything. Only I already know it by heart, and I know nothing. Nothing at all."

This time he laughed outright. For the want of something better to do, I joined him. We sat cross-legged opposite each other, swaying backwards and forwards, laughing. Finally, Yeshûa wiped off his tears of merriment and for the first time the expression on his face got serious.

"Do you think you could ask your father if I could join you?"

He is asking me if I could have my dream come true. If I could have a companion on my travels, a boy my own or nearly my own age, to play with, to talk to, to argue with, to conquer....

"What about your parents?"

"You need not worry. I am twelve now." He said this as though this proclaimed his well-earned maturity. "And I must go," he added quietly. It implied, with you or without you, but I must go. And then he looked at me at some length. "Don't worry," he reassured me again. "I am neither a thief nor a robber. I knocked over some tables of some traders in the Temple. They shouldn't..." He stopped short. "I'll have to do it again..." he stopped again. Then he appeared to have changed his mind. For a while he just sat there, something churning in his mind.

"Will you speak to your father?" he asked again. His tone was controlled but urgent. Yeshûa seemed to be in a great hurry.

I must have been crazy. Thief or not, I hardly knew this boy. Correction. I didn't know him at all. But where would I get another chance like this? When we pulled in for overnight stops, the men sat together around the fire, chewing hashish and talking about women. I stopped listening ten months ago. On and on they talked. Women this, women that. It was as though they hadn't seen a woman for months. Even my father joined in. What was so special about women? They stopped talking about women only to talk about money. As if that was so fascinating.

"I'll speak to him," I said. I had no idea why but I knew I was doing the right thing. I also had no idea what a fateful decision I'd just made. The next few years were to become the most memorable years of my entire life. Just those next few years. Eighteen, to be precise.

Waiting was the worst. I spoke to my father the next morning. He said he'd think about it and he went about his business. I didn't even know if he'd taken me seriously. I killed time. With one of the guards, I wondered about Jerusalem, looking at nothing in particular, hoping to see Yeshûa pop up from around the corner. Three days had passed before I saw him again.

"Well?" he asked without any preambles.

"I spoke to him."

"And? What did he say?"

"Not much. He said he'd think about it."

Yeshûa looked around as though making sure he wasn't followed, or if the coast were clear, and turned to me again.

"Take me to him." He was a very direct boy. "Please," he added belatedly.

"I don't even know where he is right now," I pleaded. It didn't do to pester my father.

"He'll be having food about now," said my body-guard, who watched our interchange with detached interest.

"Why did you let me dive into Satya's tent?" my young friend asked, looking the guard in the eye.

"I couldn't let those men get to you, could I? You didn't look as though you were about to do Satyajit any harm." He used my full, unabbreviated name. It was more formal.

"You knew that he knew?" I asked in disbelief.

"I didn't. He just... Never mind. Will you take me to your father?"

I shrugged. It was his funeral. My dad was a very important man.

When I introduced Yeshûa to my father, he pulled me by my sleeve.

"Leave us alone," he whispered. And then there was that belated, and this time urgent, "Pleeeease."

"I have to wash my hands," I said in order to save face as I ran off.

Two days later, it was all arranged. At first light Yeshûa's parents escorted him to my father's tent. I didn't even have a chance to meet them. From a distance, they seemed shy, reserved. They talked for a short while. Then his mother embraced Yeshûa. I remembered my own mother hugging me before my first departure. This seemed a little different. His mother embraced him lovingly yet she seemed to hold him as though she were handling something precious and fragile. They looked more like brother and sister. His mother looked almost as young as Yeshûa himself. And she was about his size. Tiny. Tiny and delicate. The same blue eyes. Then she stood back while his father gave him his paternal instructions. I know. I'd been given mine on the day of my departure from home.

Yeshûa gave the appearance of listening politely, even attentively, though I was sure his mind was already way out over the deserts sands. Finally his dad also embraced him, took his mother by the arm and led her away. From afar, she glanced back. Just once. By the time she looked again, our caravan turned the corner. Minutes later we were in the open desert. Well, it wasn't a desert but it was the dry season. Things looked pretty bleak. They stayed greener closer to the Jordan valley. Yeshûa was walking by my side. We were together. Or better still, I was no longer alone.

And this is how it all began.

Memories flood my mind as I sit, outwardly detached, inside seemingly empty, stunned, without feeling, just like the stone bench beneath me. It is a small courtyard. To my left there is a small wooden gate which opens outwards. On my right, a simple hole in the sun-dried brick wall leads to the inner chamber where the disciples are gathered, trying to escape their anguish. Perhaps misery does like company, but not mine. I'd rather be with my memories. So many of them. So many years when he and I were alone, away from the world, just together. For the most part, my thoughts are completely disorganized. Like a stream meandering through a desert, turning and twisting, looking for some sense in the river of life. When I try to dismiss them, they only come back with renewed force. Some are just feelings, some are vivid, even as the hot sun is vivid above me. Perhaps that is why my eyes hurt so much. I forgot to pull the cowl over my head to shield them. I am not quite myself.

A young woman brings me a small skin of water. I drink gratefully. She leaves without a word. Her eyes are red. I don't even know her name.

It is as if I am intended to review the years I'd spent with Yeshûa. As if it is meant to be. Perhaps one day I shall write

*them down. Only not yet. They hurt too much. They say
there is a destiny defined in the stars for all of us. Perhaps
they are right. But if it is so, then what is my destiny to be?
Now that Yeshûa is gone?*

What was the destiny written in the stars for Yeshûa?

A t first, we hardly talked. I mean we didn't discuss
anything. Yeshûa's eyes were darting this way and
that. Each time he saw something he hadn't seen
before, he would ask me what it was. It could have been
some rocks, or a desert plant, or anything at all. He had to
know. If I couldn't supply an answer, he would look around
to see if he could bother someone else. Usually he didn't,
but he wanted to. At least he didn't until he'd met Sri Arum
Singh.

But that was only a week later. For now I was his only
source of information, no matter how inadequate. The
funny thing was that I hadn't noticed half the things that fascinated him. Which was just about everything. And that included the nights. I told him that Sri Singh taught me astrology, not astronomy. But it was no good. He would suck
out of me any information I had, good or bad, profound or
of no consequence. He was like a leach in the pond at the
bottom of our garden. Back home, that is.

After three days, I couldn't hold it any longer. I had to
ask him.

"What did you tell my father? I mean, to let you
come?"

"It was nothing," he replied. "Nothing of importance."

"Come on. My father doesn't give anything away he
doesn't have to. Did you use magic?"

"What!? Why would you say such a thing? Don't you
know that magic is evil?"

I didn't, actually. Sri Singh and I didn't get to discuss
magic as yet.

"So what did you say to him?"

Yeshûa was evidently uncomfortable. I had him trapped and he knew it.

"I told him that your mother would like you to have a companion."

"And he bought that?"

"Why not? It's the truth." He sounded pretty confident.

"And what did my father say?"

"Nothing."

"What?" He was talking in riddles.

"Nothing at the time. I stood before him while he ate. Then, when he finished, he said that I was a very smart boy. That I was probably right. And..." Yeshûa was speaking haltingly, seemingly unsure of himself.

"...and?" I wished he would speak faster.

"And then he asked me when I could be ready."

"...and?" He needed nudging.

"I said I would have to ask my parents."

"And that was that?"

"Pretty much. What else could there have been?"

"Didn't he talk about money?"

"No, of course not." Yeshûa looked surprised.

But not as surprised as I was. My father didn't become the richest man in Benares by offering free rides to stray lads. On the house. Or on a camel, so to speak. But this time he did. Yeshûa must have done or said something else. But I never found out what.

Within a few minutes, we went back to him asking me questions and me trying to answer them. In other words, the usual. Somehow, in spite of his questions, perhaps because of them, it was the first time I thought of home since I'd met him. And of the pond. And the beach. I could picture both of us jumping into the river from an overhanging branch.

It was good not to be alone.

In a way, Yeshûa had been lucky. Normally, my father didn't take caravans all the way to their final destinations.

We, my father's men, that is, would take the goods a certain distance to a trading post, where they would exchange their wares for others, with which they would then return home. The goods left behind would find their way further along, carried by other camels or other beasts of burden, in turn bringing other goods back with them. That way no one had to be away from home for long. Only every ten years, or so, my father would travel the whole distance himself, to check on new markets, new political systems, or just out of sheer interest. No matter how much my father loved my mom, he loved travelling too. Almost as much.

It was then, thinking of my father's lengthy journey, that I guessed why Yeshûa had chosen the particular gambit to be invited to join the caravan. Somehow he must have guessed that my father would do almost anything for mother. Anything to make her happy. Even if he did take me on this trip against her wishes. Perhaps he'd felt guilty about it, and when Yeshûa suggested that mom could be happy with my having a companion, he practically jumped at the opportunity. There was something very clever about Yeshûa. He was certainly smart well beyond his age.

There was one subject matter, I soon found, which Yeshûa covered with a cloak of silence. It was his childhood. Whenever I would ask him about his parents, his friends in school, or his teachers, his lips tightened, as though the subject was not to be pursued. His eyes would look away and, without answering my question, he would point to something and change the subject. I couldn't figure out what it was that kept him so tight-lipped about his youthful past. His eye and facial expression did not reveal any pain. If there were any feeling that I could detect I would call it a sense of rebellion. A hard, adamant, unyielding rebellion.

It was a while later, I forget exactly when, that Yeshûa told me more about his rapid retreat from Jerusalem. Apparently, sometime after his twelfth birthday, his parents, together with a number of friends from Nazareth and Capernaum, came to the Temple to celebrate the Passover. And some Temple it was. Brand new. Gleaming white marble and gold everywhere. And during the Passover there were songs and dance, and psalm singing by the Temple choir. It was fun.

After the ceremonies and the attendant festivities were over, his parents, together with their friends as well as a number of members of a sect from some sort of monastery on Mount Carmel, prepared to make their way home. For reasons I didn't quite understand at the time, there had been quite a crowd of them. His parents, just as the members of the sect, who apparently had been there to look after him, assumed that Yeshûa had made his own travelling arrangements. His parents thought that he would be travelling with his own friends and the monks from Mount Carmel thought that he would be with his parents.

"It wasn't so difficult to confuse them, just a little," Yeshûa said with a mischievous boyish grin. "I've waited for a breath of freedom..." he cut himself off, as though having already said too much.

I'd also learned later that, at the time, Yeshûa had no personal friends. For that matter, he hardly knew his own parents. I'd also learned that he took the first opportunity he had, ever, to spread his wings. To test some of the knowledge, which had been pumped into his poor head from the day, he'd learned to walk. Yeshûa waited for the homebound procession to leave before doing his own thing.

What he did exactly, I didn't quite understand, but whatever it was, it precipitated his rapid, and none-too-elegant, departure from Jerusalem. Out of sheer politeness he'd waited for his parents, who he knew would return to Jerusalem in search of their only son, to ask their permission to join my father's caravan. I got a distinct impression that his parents had been conditioned, at least to some degree, not to deny Yeshûa's requests. It had something to do with the monks from Mount Carmel.

Years passed before I'd learned what lay behind it all. If Yeshûa hadn't become my best friend, I would have never believed it myself.

* * * * *

2

The Desert

I forget where or when the following event took place, but it couldn't have been more than a few weeks, months at most, after we first left Jerusalem. We followed the main road to Shechem, then took the right fork, bearing northeast towards Scythopolis, and finally crossed Jordan just south of Lake Chinnereth to take the mountain road to Damascus. It wasn't the best road, but my father deemed it the safest. There were too many riffraff in the lower, richer grounds, where bandits could hide in the thick bush that covered most of the ground. The desert was safer. It was here, in the vast expanse of rocks and sand that, for the first time, Yeshûa raised a tiny edge of the veil that obfuscated from me, and I should well imagine from the rest of the world, his most secret thoughts.

It was a moonless night, and thus stars that salted the sky seemed to have multiplied a thousand-fold from one horizon to the other. Against their background, the River of Light, known to the Hebrews as *N'har di Nur*, and to the Arabs as just *Al Nahr*, was as vivid, bright and sparkling, and as clearly defined, as ever I'd seen it on my travels. Back home, we knew it as the Bed of Ganges, the most holy of rivers.

Until this night, Yeshûa hadn't talked much. He preferred to listen. This was the beginning of what became an almost nightly congress of thoughts that we, two lads in their early teens, chose to share. To date, his interests lay only in learning the intricacies of caravan life, of commerce and other aspects that to a merchant were of great value. His past was his own. His inner life remained safe behind those steely irises of his, which absorbed with insatiable hunger, but, until now, didn't give anything away.

Later, as the moon came out, I found him standing alone on the top of a rock outcropping, some two hundred steps from our camp, overlooking the arid ocean. His head was held high, waving from one side to the other, as though it were swayed by the non-existent wind. I recall that we had both been entranced by the intensity of silence. If you've never spent a night in the desert, don't pretend that you have. It wasn't the real desert, forbidding in its vastness, which we would cross on the way to Palmyra, but the essence was the same. A night in the desert is unlike any other experience. You may be as tall as an oak, as important as a minister in a Persian court or a Roman tribune, yet out here, in the vastness of this endless expanse of rocks and sand, amid the grotesque shadows cast by moonlight – you feel small. Tiny. Completely insignificant. Even the mountains shrink under the grandeur spanning the horizons. Yet, at the same time, you are not dwarfed by the exuberance of the starry splendour. You are absorbed by it. It is as though the sky inhaled you with every breath you took. You become part of everything. Part of the Whole. Part of the sand and the rocks, the hills and the air, the sky, the stars... You become a pebble on the Bed of Ganges. You are like the breath that enters your lungs and then floats out mingling with the invisible currents in the vastness of space.

And every night was like that. Night after night.

I wasn't aware of it then. He taught me. Perhaps the first lesson he taught me was to appreciate beauty. In all its forms. In all things. All places.

So many years ago, yet it seem as though...

"What is your name for Yahweh?" he asked me without turning his head. He must have sensed that I followed him out of the tent we shared. I was surprised he used the name Yahweh. The orthodox Jews were not allowed to use the name of their god. I could have sworn Yeshûa had been raised as an orthodox Jew. My father had said as much.

"Brahma," I replied. "We have many gods in India. We have Brahma who created the universe, Vishnu who sustains it, and Shiva is the Destroyer. But they are all aspects of the same deity."

He didn't say anything. I too had been swept off my feet by the magic of the desert night. I felt the need to share my wonder with him. "This is where Brahma says to you 'I OWN YOU'," I said quietly.

He remained silent. For a time I thought he hadn't heard me. Then, as though emerging from an ocean as deep as the desert was wide, he turned his eyes toward me. They shone like the stars above. "No," he said. "This is where Brahma says 'YOU AND I ARE ONE'."

Yeshûa had experienced the enigmatic draw of the desert before, when he'd been little, he said, but this was different. He took a few steps toward me and grabbed me by the hand as though to assure himself that he wasn't dreaming. I was more used to this inexplicable mystery, although one can never really take it for granted. Once you experience Brahma's Splendour, you smile not out of fear but in gratitude. And this is not because, as Yeshûa implied, you become like a god, only because you become absorbed by the Creator.

I have but a vague memory of the rest of that night. We talked till dawn, resting enough atop the camels swaying in their rhythmic gait. They really were the ships of the desert. Some years later, we talked like that virtually every night. But then, it was an exception. When we first met, in the first few months, Yeshûa didn't share his inner thoughts easily. He had been brought up to listen, not to talk. I hadn't yet learned that a deep, smouldering anger churned in Yeshûa's heart. He had been angry with his people. He had been angry with the priesthood and the lawyers and even the Essenes who'd reared him. He was angry at the depth of depravity, at the dismissive attitude his people had toward the wisdom of the ages. They had forced him to learn each word of the Torah by heart, but no one ever attempted to understand what the words meant.

"Oh, they thought they did," he told me on one occasion. "They thought it was the word of Yahweh. And the word of Yahweh is not to be questioned but obeyed. There were moments when we were allowed to dig after some hidden meaning, provided that we didn't even dream of putting our conclusions, our findings, into practice. It was like reciting a codex of laws, and assuming that once you knew it, you were absolved from having to live by it."

When anger stirred him, it poured out like a flood.

"They are like guard-dogs protecting a garden of delicious vegetables. They don't eat any of it themselves, and they will not let anyone else even taste its bounty."

Young Yeshûa was not a boy capable of compromise. He tolerated it in others, provided that it did not encroach on his budding belief system. He couldn't remain with his mentors. He felt stifled. He said that back home, he could no longer breathe.

"Either they hammered line after line into my brain, or else they indulged in speculations, which in no way advanced my knowledge of who I am. And after years of this, there had been moments when they treated me like a cross between a scholar and the incarnation of... of Buddha."

He chose words that made some sort of sense to me. I am a Hindû, but Buddha's teachings were known to me. You can't help it when you are raised in Benares. It is the home of Shiva Visweswara. It is also a place of pilgrimage for the Buddhists and Hindûs alike. What mattered to my father was that my hometown was also a great trade centre.

Even then, in those early days of our friendship, I noted that Yeshûa rebelled against any imposed obligations. He loved the world. He loved it with the passion of youth. He celebrated each sunrise and every sunset. He cut down on sleep to the absolute minimum, lest he miss something life had to offer.

Yeshûa was an uncompromising, implacable lover of life.

I shake my head. The sun is now high in the sky. Must be close to noon. I move to the south side of the courtyard to sit in the shadow of the wall. A sliver of shade about a step wide. Later I shall move again against the shadow cast by the wall on the west. It'll offer more protection. There is no bench here, but I can rest my back against the wall. My legs also feel good stretched straight in front of me.

The moment I close my eyes, images of long ago force themselves before me with uncanny vividness.

My back hurts. It must be the long ride. A very long ride.

There is no sound coming from the dark opening leading to the inner chamber. Even the women had stopped crying. Then I hear a dog barking in the distance. There is a painful yelp and he stops. There is silence again.

Snippets of memories flit across my mind without any chronological order. One moment I see a lad of twelve, through the eyes of a fourteen-year-old, the next instant I hear his words as though he spoke them right here and now, slowly, thoughtfully, coming from a man who'd spent his life trying to bridge the great divide between his outer shell and the innermost secrets of atma. In my language, atma is the real you, your true self. All else is maya. Illusion. Or so I'm told.

As I sit alone, I am losing all sensation of time. I press my back against the hard wall. It keeps hurting. Pictures, fragments of the moments we shared, float before my eyes even as clouds that cross the serene ocean above; uncontrolled, detached, elusive, often only just grasped, torn out of the fabric of time and space. The next instant, the inexorable movement of time goes on, again, unwinding, uncaring, arranging events in a sequential order. At the time I thought I understood his words. At the time...

A t first, the reason behind his sudden departure from Jerusalem remained elusive.

"I want to see the world," he'd told me. "Don't you?"

There was no arguing this logic. My father didn't mind either way. He found Yeshûa pleasant, courteous and, as such, suitable company for his son. He was told by Joseph, Yeshûa's father, that he can send him back at any time, with any caravan heading for Judea. Apparently, Joseph offered dad some money, but my father had refused. Dad was a complex man. He loved making money, but he felt no need to remain attached to it. He taught me that. He told me that it is the process which matters, more so than the result. I always listened when my father spoke.

Yeshûa confessed the real reason for his departure much later.

Initially, he seemed a little standoffish. It turned out to be shyness. He hadn't met many boys his own age. He'd spent most of his time among women. Over time, I grew to like him, then to love him as a brother. It would seem that even during those early months when we spent nights gazing up at the dark sky, as clear as on that night on the way to Damascus, that we were passing innumerable hours talking about his inner life. But we didn't. We talked mostly about everyday events, about my own boyhood, back home in Benares, of my early schooling, of my aunts and uncles, of family life in general.

"You have brothers?" he asked. His eyes lit up when I'd told him.

"Three brothers and two sisters," I confessed, taking full credit for my parents' virility.

"I never had a family life," he'd said. And then, momentarily, though barely visible in the starlight, I noticed that his near-constant smile left his face. "Poor mother," he added, but would not explain any further.

I've learned not to probe. He would talk freely when he wished. At other times he seemed as distant as the mountain peeks I'd left behind at home – those toward north. In those moments I'd learned to let him be, to let the moment pass. And it did. Quickly. But even in those early days, I'd sensed some deep and troubling enigma fomenting in his young mind. At those times, I thought I'd detected hints of irrepressible loneliness taking hold of him. A loneliness not resulting from the growing distance from his family, but rather from something much more intangible, yet, seemingly, very real to him.

During those first few years, Yeshûa seemed to have been freeing himself from a burden imposed on him by others. By his past. It sounds silly, even now, to talk of the past in someone so young, but Yeshûa's life had been so controlled, subjected to such discipline that at no time had he been given a chance to be a boy, let alone a child. Even on that first leg to Damascus and later on the way to Palmyra and Babylon, he filled his days with apparent hunger for the simplest of things. He would rave over the beauty of a common cactus squeezing life out of a crevice in a rock, a strand of grass, incongruous in the desert, springing from a seed blown by the wind, a flower that grew, as he said, for no other purpose than to bring heaven to earth.

And this hadn't changed over the years. Even years later, in India, when we met only for a few days at a time, his awe of the world remained unshaken. His eyes sparkled, his joy remained ebullient, his heart seemed open to the wonders around him.

But nights had been different.

At night, especially during those first few months, perhaps longer, he spoke to me in words of rebellion. He thought that the Essenes, who controlled every minute of his young life, wanted to lumber him with all of the frustrations which they'd accumulated over the years, and to deny the beauty of life by the exigencies of their own aesthetic existence. He didn't say all that in those precise terms. He was a mere boy then. But that was the import of what he'd said. Yeshûa, although subjected to it himself, or perhaps because of it, dismissed monastic life as unnatural. He thought that turning one's back on the world was turning one's back on the creation of the Almighty.

"If Yahweh didn't want us to see the world," he'd once said, "he wouldn't have equipped us with eyes."

Yeshûa thought that everything had a purpose, and our job was to uncover what it was. No matter what it took. We had to learn who we really were.

"Two boys enjoying a ride...?" I quipped. He ignored me.

"And man's purpose is to learn about Atma by studying His creation." When he'd said it, Atma sounded as though spoken with a capital A.

He liked using Indian terminology. It was his way of showing his respect for other people's faiths. He never said nor implied that there is anything superior in the faith in which he'd been brought up. If anything, he thought his own religion was stifling. He thought that the essence of his own faith had been buried under a complex system of laws and regulations that made it impossible for men and women to really enjoy life. I recall being amazed and a little abashed by the scope of his knowledge. I'd been brought up to grab all the living that life had to offer. My family was rich, but we also enjoyed the simplest of things. Like diving in a river, or climbing a tree or just playing games on the lawn in front of our house.

"The Torah was written to show us how to best enjoy life," he said during one of our nightly discussions. "Instead, people use it to strangle themselves into submission to our priesthood. To place us all in irons of our own making. If only someone would show them the way...."

Apparently, many years later, someone did.

Even as I think of my parched throat, a girl, perhaps a woman, appears from the dark frame of the doorway leading to the house. She carries a jug on her shoulder that is nearly as big as her head. How did she know I felt thirsty? Perhaps Yeshûa taught them all to be mind readers. He was certainly proficient at it himself. In later years.

As she comes closer I see that it is a woman, though very small. When I get up, she barely reaches my chest. She stands before me in silence.

"Shalom," I say in my best Hebrew accent.

"I brought you some water, sir," she says.

I wonder why she called me sir. I am certainly not looking very notable. Not after all the riding I had just done. I am covered with dust from head to toe. I make a mental note to get washed at the first opportunity.

"Thank you," I say in Hebrew. The Jews have so many ways of saying thanks and I hope I used the right one. I can't wait. I grab the jug from her girlish hands and draw deep on the water. I feel as though I hadn't drunk for years. Actually, on my last leg I hadn't taken time to drink or eat. There had been an inexplicable force nagging me to hurry. Hurry, hurry, sang the wind in my ears. Hurry, hurry, the horses hoofs had stomped a hollow tattoo on the rocks, roads and the beaten down ground. Hurry, croaked birds rising with mad flapping of wings to get out of my horse's way.

She smiles and leaves with tiny, child-like steps. I wonder what her name is. I forgot to ask.

She looks and walks like a child. But her face is a mask of frozen pain. She cannot even hide it. At least, not very well. Perhaps the pain is too great.

"He would have made her smile, " I think aloud. "He could make anyone smile."

Only he isn't here. Not anymore.

That day, for the first time, he'd spoken to me about his mother. Just a few words. He said that his mother's name meant many things in Hebrew. That many people thought that it meant 'bitter'. But if taken from an Egyptian root *mryt*, it could mean 'the beloved one'. The Greeks changed the name to Miriam, meaning fat, thick and strong. Or... rebellious, as in insurrection or against limitations. And some say that it comes from *maya* meaning an illusion. He said that it may well be up to him, which of those names will come true. Which name would best describe her.

And then he told me that it was unfair that he was supposed to decide such things. That he loved life. That he wanted to just live. Not decide on his mother's future. Or anyone else's.

I hear him as though it was today...

* * * * *

3

Damascus

I forget how long it took us, but some time later we arrived in, what many call, the oldest city in the world. The city of Sham, or Dimashq. As usual my father set up camp on the periphery of the city. This time it wasn't just a question of safety. Mostly, he didn't want to interfere with anyone's land rights. People were beginning to realize that land, which heretofore lay free, was of value. They staked out claims and then charged daily fees if one wanted to camp on their property.

After the days we'd spent on the arid terrain, the richness of the verdant land was almost overpowering. The streets, full of traders, their carts replete with fresh fruit, vegetables and grains held all of our attention. My father's men immediately began restocking with fresh provisions for the next leg of our journey. Yeshûa and I hadn't been needed. We enjoyed the invigorating experience of skinny-dipping in the cool Barada river, which fed the city with its pure waters. Yeshûa never swam before in his life. Once learned, it became a passion for him. Boy, was he a quick learner!

"I feel free!" he shouted with joy. "I feel free like a fish," he continued diving indeed like a fish only to come up for air some distance further. Apparently, even by Lake

Chinnereth, close to where his parents lived, people didn't swim much. In Nazareth, Yeshûa's hometown, village really, water was precious. They had to reach deep into the ground and hoist it up a jug at a time. But even those who washed with water from the lake carried it in large clay ewers to their homes. Swimming was not in their nature.

"Lake is for fish," he mimicked in the authoritative tone of an elder. "And for us to fish in. Fish swim, men walk on land." Yeshûa's father was a simple man. Yeshûa respected him for his honesty, his kindness and for the way he treated his mother. Not for his intellectual capacity. And anyway, there were many restrictions with which Yeshûa was encumbered. The Jews took life very seriously.

After the swim, Yeshûa and I took a lazy stroll through and around the city. Everywhere we looked there was something that seemed ancient. It was like walking through various eras, through thousands of years of history. Yeshûa was rapidly infecting me with his desire for knowledge. His curiosity was contagious. He had stopped strangers on the street and asked them, with a broken accent, about whatever he saw and didn't understand. He never felt embarrassed. When people laughed at his inability to express himself, he shrugged, smiled and tried somebody else. And there was a vast choice of people. We heard a dozen languages and twice as many accents. And anyway, people who lived in Dimashq seemed to speak half a dozen languages each. Dimashq is an ancient city, but the trade in it is very modern.

Halfway through the second afternoon after our arrival, I managed to get hold of my teacher to fill us in on some of the background. As usual, whenever time permitted, my teacher was glad to see me. Usually I listened attentively to his words, but lately I had been awestricken by the fire in Yeshûa's eyes whenever he had a chance to learn something new. And all this, all that was outside the confines of the Torah, was new to him. His eyes shone as though he was alleviating a hunger gnawing at his young heart.

And there was a great deal to learn.

The history of Dimashq reached further back than the beginning of the world. The Hebrew world. Yeshûa was stunned to hear of numbers like 6000 years before he was born. Some 2000 years before his own teachers said Yahweh created Adam. Could it be that the Essenes were wrong? Yet there was also a link with the Torah. Some said, recounted our teacher, that the old name of Sham – the alternate name of Dimashq – had been derived from Shem, the eldest son of Noah, the ancient who saved us from extinction. Not for the first time since our arrival in this archaic city did Yeshûa wonder if history was fact or fiction.

He loved sitting at the feet of his new teacher, the elderly Sri Arum Singh, who on occasion looked as old as the stories he recounted. Sri is a title of respect, like Mister, I told him. The hired hands address my father as Sahib, meaning lord or master. After all, he was their boss, virtually the master of their lives. Sri is more like a title of respect rather than authority. Unless you mean moral authority. Back home, we address the Yogis and Swamis with Sri.

Arum Singh's gray beard cascaded down his meagre chest, his eyes were red rimmed from constant study. He was small, seemingly feeble, but no man would dare to raise his hand to him. He was the sage, the authority, second only to my father.

It was he, the ancient Sri Singh, who planted the first seeds of doubt in young Yeshûa's heart. It was he who un-wittingly forced him to interpret the writings of the Torah, not as an infallible history, but as a document of life's lessons, given to the Hebrews in an allegory and parable format. But the depth of this realization came to my friend much later. This was but the first seed. What it did accomplish, more than anything, was to fuel the rebellion that Yeshûa felt towards all that he'd been taught at such length. He told me some time later that, at the time, he'd been ready to reject all he'd ever learned, all he'd ever heard from the monks at Mount Carmel, all he'd ever read in scrolls, including the Torah. He wanted to start from scratch, turn over a new leaf. Rejuvenate himself. It was almost as though he wanted to be

born again. He wanted to incorporate in his life whatever
he'd learned and deemed good. Except for his parents no
one seemed to have done so. And, sadly, he hardly ever
thought of his parents as paradigms to be emulated. Perhaps
they were too close to his heart. Perhaps he resented having
been passed on to the monks, like a prized goat. Or perhaps
he just resented having been sequestered in a cave to study,
and study, and do more study. He wanted to live.

"I didn't have a chance," he said. "I was the new reincarnation of Buddha, remember?" Only this time he didn't
laugh. There was too much anger in him. Mostly at himself.

The Syrians claimed thousands of years as their history.
In this cradle, they said, man discovered the secrets of agri-
culture. He developed the first mastery of metallurgy. Here
was the seat of ancient religions, philosophies. Here they
invented the first alphabet, systems for planing cities. Here
the ancient forefathers gave birth to cultural and even diplo-
matic exchanges. They were the initiators of civilized life on
this earth.

"So they claim," said Sri Singh, his Hindû accent in
Hebrew more pronounced than mine. Arum Singh was more
than just my or our teacher. He served my father as the official translator and negotiator when deals had reached a certain level of complexity. My father relied heavily on his
abilities on such occasions. "Written history starts only
some hundred and fifty years ago with the Amorites. It
doesn't compare with our Vedas," Singh continued after
some thought.

"Vedas?" Yeshûa jumped on the word instantly.

"They are the writings of our Hindû tradition. Rather
like your Torah, only much older."

I could see Yeshûa's eyes growing wider. He'd been
taught for years that nothing is older than the Torah. That
nothing can reach further back than the history of mankind
as recorded in the Holy Book of Genesis. And now this? I
could see the struggle in my friend's heart. The condition-

ing of years being assailed by this elderly man, sitting cross-legged on a small pillow, a gentle smile on his wide mouth. Sri Singh didn't force whatever he said on his pupils. If anything, he told them to question the facts, to dig deeper, to reach out, or in, on their own.

"This is not like the Essenes," Yeshûa told me after the first real session with Sri Arum Singh. "He makes you decide what is right and what is wrong." His smile got broader. "Or what is true and what isn't," he added after more thought.

"Sri Singh seldom shares something which he doubts himself. If he does, he says so," I confirmed Yeshûa's conclusions. Sri Singh was, still is, a very honest man. I recalled what my father told me some time ago: "A man can fool another man, if he's clever. But he can seldom fool a child." Of course I wouldn't dare to call Yeshûa a child. Like he'd told me. He was already twelve.

"You can never tell a man what he should believe in," Yeshûa continued thinking aloud. "To do so would be like telling his Atma what to do."

Already then, I knew what he meant. But only later I'd learned that in his own language, in Hebrew, it would be like telling Yahweh what to do. The Jews have a strange religion. They believe that there is The Existing One, or the Self-Existent, who nevertheless strikes an echo of His Presence in every man and woman. They abbreviate this deity's incommunicable name with the letters YHWH which, when pronounced out loud, which is strictly forbidden, sound like Yahweh. The tetragrammaton stands for the Hebrew letters Yod, Hé, Wau, and Hé, which represent the masculine and feminine universal principles.

It was this divine principle extant in every man, every woman, which weighed heavily on my young friend. At some time or another, during one of those long, balmy nights, when he wasn't so angry, he told me a beautiful story of Jacob who became Israel, by conquering his lower nature.

"But it's an allegory," he said sadly. "Like everything else in the Scrolls of Moses."

Arum Singh told us a great deal more about Dimashq. Long stories, full of intricate details unfolded every day that we stayed there. When we were lucky, he joined Yeshûa and myself to share some more legends after the evening meal.

"Some seven or eight hundred years ago, the original Aramean city became buried under repeated armed incursions of the Assyrians. Then came the Chaldeans under Nebuchandnezzar, until the Persian king, Cyrus, took over the city. But it was still later, under the Macedonian general, Alexander, that Syria became the hub of a huge empire that reached as far north as the Afghan and as far west as the Tarus Mountains. Some of it is confirmed in your Scriptures," Sri Singh said looking at Yeshûa. My friend nodded.

"Yes, Sir. I do remember," he affirmed quickly. Evidently he didn't want to interrupt the lecture.

"Only recently Rome moved in on the ancient cultures. The Romans came half a century ago and made Syria their own. The men of Dimashq became valued merchants of the Roman Empire. Your father," the sage turned towards me, "is benefiting by distributing the wares between Europe and the Orient. As for Dimashq, what we see here is an entirely new city, built on the ruins of the past. Yet even now, the local cloth and glassware and particularly swords are renown throughout the Roman Empire. We have a lot to be grateful for."

Yeshûa listened spellbound. The scholar's words tasted like water to a man dying of thirst. Only Yeshûa was not yet a man. He was a strange amalgam of boyish emotions mixed with a mature desire for knowledge. This is why he'd escaped. This is what he came for. Perhaps, by some strange quirk of fate, he'd known that he would find Sri Singh here, along the long trek that would eventually take us all to India.

"And even as Rome conquered the land, the philosophers of Rome began to supplant the earlier thinkers. Even so there is a veritable whirlpool of ideas fighting for supremacy. The Greek thinkers embodied mostly by Socrates, Plato and Aristotle of some centuries ago were later challenged by their Roman successors."

"Socrates? Plato?" Yeshûa couldn't help himself. His mind had been sheltered from any ungodly influences. For his own good, no doubt. To protect the purity of Jewish thought. As I watched his face, it once again registered a pang of anger. "How could they do this to me?" he muttered under his nose.

Arum Singh smiled. "It is rarely that someone so young would have such wide interests, my boy. Satya, here, no more heard about them than you did," the old man was trying to placate my friend. You have a whole lifetime to examine your life. You have to get a life first, though. Otherwise...?"

It is late afternoon now. I drag myself up and move again, this time against the western wall, which offers the most shade. I have no idea if I've been sleeping or dreaming. But whatever tricks my mind played on me, the images were real. They were taking place here and now. They were so much more than just memories. I wondered, how was that possible?

Soon the first stars will begin to show their light. But this is not the desert. The air here is neither as pure, nor as cool. The stones and bricks of the buildings amass a great deal of heat during the day. They retain their warmth almost until dawn. I get up again; I stretch my legs, and go outside the courtyard to relieve myself. Then I sit down again. I still haven't washed. Now, I couldn't go indoors even if invited. I can't go anywhere. My brother who'd left four weeks before me, to go as far as Alexandria, or maybe Memphis, will only get here two weeks from now. I have nowhere to go. I came to see my friend...

Even as I think of him, Yeshûa's face is again displacing all other images. I can see his eyes staring at Sri Singh. There is both admiration and hunger mixed in equal meas-

ure. I think he would give his right arm to possess Arum Singh's knowledge. Why is it so important to him, I wonder. And why is there such a hurry to learn now, or rather there and then, in each moment, as if even then he was running out of time.

It is cooler now.

Even as I look up towards the eastern sky, a dark cloud obscures the horizon. It might rain, I think hopefully. At least the rain would wash off dust and grime from my whole body. They might even let me go inside, afterward. But only if it rains. No matter. It certainly wouldn't bother me. I've weathered many a storm in a camel's saddle. A small houdah, actually, but the effect was similar. And then I see his eyes again, staring into mine.

"What is it that you want from me?" I ask. But there is only silence.

Yeshûa's eyes demanded an answer. "Socrates? Plato? Aristotle?" he repeated. He was rapacious for knowledge. He simply had to know.
"Many scrolls had been written already, many more will be written by our children's children. You cannot abbreviate the endowment those three men had given to the world and do them justice. Socrates became what he was, chiefly to combat the Sophists. And who were the Sophists, you'll ask? The Sophists had been led by Protagoras, a native of Abdera. He taught that man is a measure of all things. He rejected absolute truth, but related truth and beauty and even goodness to the needs and interest of man."

"He rejected Brahma?" Yeshûa cocked his head to one side.

"He didn't get involved in theology. There had been too many gods in his day. Just too many. What he preached, really, was that all things are relative. And the measure of that relativity is man. Who else could it be?"

"Man is a measure of all things...." Yeshûa repeated. It was obvious that Sophistic thought made an impression on the young scholar. "And Socrates objected to this?" he asked, his penetrating stare boring into Sri Singh's eyes.

"Socrates didn't think we could rely on our senses. He thought we were too fallible. He wasn't really interested in creating a new school of thought, but rather with defining the ethics. Plato followed in his master's footsteps and went further by proposing that the universe was essentially spiritual and purposeful. Thus, he refuted the relativism of the Sophists. To affirm his theories, he developed his doctrine of Ideas. And so on, and so on, and so on...."

"How do you know all this?" Yeshûa was in awe.

The old man smiled. "When you get to be my age, what else can I do. I sit and read, and try to be useful. To lads such as you and Satya. If it weren't for you youngsters, I would feel pretty useless."

I recall smiling at Arum Singh's humility. I knew well of the high standing he held with my father. And my father had clout inside and outside India. He carried his reputation with him. People listened whenever he talked. Yet they listened even more when Sri Singh talked, though the old man preferred talking on matters other than my father's.

"And Aristotle?" Yeshûa wouldn't let go.

"Aristotle came last. Although he was Plato's pupil he became more pragmatic. More practical in his approach; less spiritual, you might say. In a way, he combined Plato's universal Ideas, or forms as Plato called them, with material forms – or matter itself. He thought that evolution springs from the interaction of form and matter upon each other. He, you might say, was more down to earth...."

"And what of Rome, of Roman thought?" Yeshûa would not be denied.

"That, my young friend is quite another story. We have plenty of time to learn the heritage of human thought. Plenty of time...." And the sage rose lightly and went about his business.

Two days after this discussion, we veered off the Fertile Crescent and entered the real desert. No more periodic rests in the shade of palms. No more water within a shouting distance. Sand, rocks and desolation. And then, when we accepted that one day we shall inevitably die of thirst, we saw birds flying over the horizon. Soon after, when crossing over a hill, we saw the palms of Palmyra.

Palmyra – the 'place of palms.' Palms grow there because the whole settlement had been built around an oasis – in the middle of a hilly desert. No one can avoid stopping in Palmyra. Not if they or their camels need water.

Until recently, Palmyra had been called Tadmor. The locals still use the old name. Although thriving for some three hundred years, it is only now, since the Romans took over, that the settlement has became a town. When we passed through it, the Romans had been busy building a magnificent theatre.

"Strange," said Yeshûa, always observant, always ready to add to his knowledge. "So far the Romans have contributed little to architecture, sculpture, or culture, other than their legions. But they do like the theatre. Sri Singh says they have an abundance of poets and writers."

"Just why is this so strange?" I asked. He was always finding things that left little mark on me.

"It seems that we all have different elements to contribute to the jigsaw of life."

He was twelve years old when he said that.

There was another reason why no trader could avoid visiting Tadmor, or Palmyra. It lay on the crossroads of the two major trade routes. One from the Far East and India lead to the head of the Persian Gulf. The other, known as the Silk Road, stretched from the Eurasian continent all the way to China. No wonder Emperor Tiberius wanted to control it. To control Palmyra. Yet, for some strange reason, the Arameans and Arabs managed to remain semi-independent for the last half century. Perhaps they found a way to make

themselves indispensable to the invaders. Such things were
of interest to my father and, by succession, to me.

Yeshûa was developing quite different interests. The
most important god of Palmyra was Bel. At least until Roman influence relegated him to a lower status. But it was
here that I discovered Yeshûa's primary interest. Whatever
gods existed, anywhere, he had to study them. Study the
gods in relation to the people. Or so I thought at the time.

Here, for the first and I hasten to add the only time,
Yeshûa got lost. We were to stop in Palmyra for three days,
and I was hoping to have some fun running around town
with my friend. Alas, look as I might, Yeshûa was nowhere
to be seen. I didn't want to land him in hot water with father,
but in shear desperation I confessed my concern to Sri
Singh.

He nodded his head a few times as though confirming
his suspicions.

"Ask the people at the Temple of Bel."

Sri Singh was right. I found Yeshûa sitting on the steps
of the Temple, deep in thought. When I got to him, I was
ready to tell him off for giving me so much trouble. He beat
me to it.

"I've been waiting for you for at least an hour," he
said. When he saw my stunned expression he added, "I was
sure Sri Singh would know where to find me."

I thought it best to say nothing. After all, he was right
and I didn't like confirming this to him or to anybody else.
There is such a thing as pride.

"The Greeks call him Zeus," Yeshûa continued as if
nothing had happened. The Romans, Jupiter. Here, he is
Bel."

He talked for half an hour. I must say, some of the
things he said sounded pretty interesting. Not at all like
talking about trade and negotiating prices. There seemed
more to it than that. It was years later that I realized that the
Temple of Bel was the beginning of what would prove, later,
to be Yeshûa's passion. The study of countless, inimitable as

well as superfluous and temperamental gods of affectation, jealousy, presumptuousness, pomposity even as gods who seemed caring, full of concern, helpfulness, even compassion and love. A plethora of gods. Gods of every size, sex, power, specialty, allegiance ... gods galore. Yet at the time, in Palmyra, I had no idea why. Gods were gods, to me at least. If you left them alone, they left you alone. And the more you were left alone the better off you were. Except for Krishna. He was different. But Krishna wasn't really a god. He was an incarnation of god. He was, is, all pleasure.

See? I told you He was different. But at the time, Yeshûa hadn't met Krishna yet. No wonder he had so much to learn.

It wouldn't hurt till the next day. I fell off my bench. Luckily it is less than a cubit above the ground. For a moment I considered staying on the dirt – it seemed softer. Then I changed my mind. Who knows what creepy-crawlies might take advantage in order to make a meal of me? I climb back on the slab, only this time I lay on my back. The stone is just wide enough. It is good to stretch my back. It got really stiff from sitting around for hours on end. I've sat many a time, even longer, on a camel's hump, but the camel moved. It swayed from side to side. I had no chance to stiffen. Here? Here I felt as if all life had left me. Just my body remained frozen into immobility.

Again I look up at the sky. Time seems to stand still. I must stop those memories crowding my mind. I must get some real sleep.

And then a question invades my tired awareness. It carries a bitter taste. It asks, "Why bother?"

* * * * *

4

Change of plans

I must have dozed off. A dreamless, void kind of sleep. A sleep as though I'd never been born.

As I sit here, Yeshûa's face repeatedly forces itself before my eyes. I can see him regarding Sri Singh with surprise, admiration, and just a hint of impatience. After Singh's assurance, I remember Yeshûa's face clouding over. It was as though he didn't expect to have much time to live.

It is completely dark now. No sound comes from inside the house. Not even a snore. Incongruously, I wonder if the disciples are sleeping. Does it matter? Perhaps they are subjected to more pain than I am. They were there, I suppose, when Yeshûa was executed. Murdered. By the Romans – with his own people's willing participation. They must have taken him to be some sort of homeless hobo, perhaps stirring people to take responsibility for their actions. He did that, even when I knew him.

"Whatever you do take, you pay for," he'd said when I stole an apple from a street vendor and ran for my life. He said that but couldn't help laughing when the angry woman threw an apple at me, in an attempt to hit me. He caught the apple with one hand turned round, bowed low and thanked the livid trader. She shook her fist at him. Then he too joined me in rapid withdrawal.

"What about your apple? I asked.

"That's different," he said. "My apple was given to me."

In a way he was right. I suppose.

As for his admonishment to me, he claimed this sentiment even before he'd studied the Law of Karma. I guess, there were things that were innate to him. He was born with certain knowledge, even if others are born with the ability to run fast, or be a good cook. Maybe this is what the cast system in my country is all about. It didn't matter, as long as you did the best you could. He also said that. Seems so obvious, and yet I've met so many men who did their utmost to avoid their responsibilities. To avoid doing their best.

I turn on my side. The wall in front of me is just a dark shape within a dark background. I turn my eyes to the sky. The same stars, the same firmament stretches overhead. Nothing has changed. All is as it should be. The world continues to unfold itself in an orderly fashion. Only he isn't with us. He is gone. Forever. I find it hard to accept.

I close my eyes to dismiss pangs of pain churning in my chest. I felt similar pain when my mother died. Only this is different. My mother was well over fifty. You expect elderly people to die. We all die, sooner or later. But Yeshûa was too young. He still had a lot of living to do. I wanted him to visit my hometown once more. My friends were waiting for him.

Why did I love this man so much? We played, we argued, we laughed, we even fought, once or twice. We certainly travelled a lot together. But there is something more. Something intangible which seems to radiate from his eyes. Even now....

Two weeks had passed before Arum Singh had time to talk to us again. He came twice to set exercises for my friend and me. Exercises in Sanskrit. Sanskrit and Latin. We had to read and write in both languages. Singh believed that any intelligent man must know Sanskrit to develop his understanding of the mysteries of life.

"But Latin you need to make a living, while Sanskrit is the language of atma. It is the mother of all languages," he told us. I thought that a bit funny. Some time ago Yeshûa said the same thing about Hebrew. And, although only with his own people, I'd heard him speak Aramaic.

Sri Singh came early, bowed low with hands held together, and muttered the traditional Indian greeting, *namaste*. After we returned the salutation, he lowered himself with an impressive agility – for a man his age.

He always assumed the same posture. His legs crossed, one heel below the perineum. It is as many yogis sit. In India we know it as the pose of the Spiritually Enlightened. The *Siddhasana*. To this day I really don't know if Sri Arum Singh is a spiritual man. He shared knowledge with us, but not his private life. He was not a man easy to fathom. Smiling, seemingly sedate, invariably polite yet maintaining a certain distance. I recall wondering if it could have been due to his cast, back home, but I never had the courage to ask. My father belonged to the few Hindï who thought the cast system was a lot of hogwash. But there again, my father was a very materialistic man. He valued knowledge for the wealth that it could bring him. If he could make money from spirituality, he would probably do so. We never talked about this subject. Neither with Sri Singh nor with my father. But whatever Sri Singh's inner convictions were, he sure knew a great deal about virtually everything else.

"So what about the Roman influence?" Yeshûa asked as if we were continuing the discussion of two weeks ago.

A man came demanding Sri Sigh's attention. He left with a slight bow.

And then came the surprise. When a caravan is as big as ours, with so many short-term traders taking advantage of the safety we provided, we were all accustomed to not seeing my father for days at a time. But this time, two weeks passed by without seeing him anywhere. During that same time, Sri Singh had been unusually busy. I began putting two and two together. Then I went to Sri Singh and stuck to him like glue until he told me the truth. Finally Sri Singh came back to talk to us both.

For a short while Sri Singh sat gathering his thoughts. He had to tell me what was going on with my father. Not that I was really worried. They say that bad news travels fast, but I was curious.

"Three days before we left Dimashq for Palmyra, your father, Satya, also left Dimashq but he rode in the direction of Antioch," Sri Singh said in a measured voice.

There was much more to the story.

Originally we were all going to proceed directly to Mesopotamia, but dad heard from some merchants arriving from the west of a new consignment of goods arriving from the west. An abundance of interesting wares were more than he could resist. He knew he would trade them at a good profit further east. The East was hungry for the articles of western culture. The reverse was true also. That's why my father is a rich man. Dad could wait for the goods to arrive in Dimashq, but by then the best of the pick would be gone, or spoken for. We were told to abide in the camp on the periphery of Dimashq, then to continue at a leisurely pace to Palmyra, while he and a dozen camels sped westward to meet the oncoming convoy. He told Arum Singh to stay with us and we, Yeshûa and I, were to accord him absolute obedience. This was no hardship, nor was the assurance necessary. We both respected the sage, and we had no desire to provoke his anger.

"The Roman influence...?" Yeshûa prompted again as though the conversation we had yesterday hadn't been interrupted at all.

"Where's the fire?" Singh asked.

"What? Oh, I'm sorry. But we've waited two weeks for your lecture."

"Fifteen days," Singh corrected. "And I don't lecture. I share with you lads what little knowledge I have managed to accumulate." He then beckoned us to sit down and relax. "We have plenty of time. I don't expect your father to catch up with us before at least another month."

"But he didn't even say good-bye!" I couldn't help challenging the master.

"Such are the exigencies of caravan life. Sometimes one has to make a decision and act on it immediately. About a month. Do you mind so much?" There was humour in his gaze as he directed his eyes at Yeshûa.

"No, Sir," my friend muttered. And then he got the message. "Oh, nooo, Sir. I'm sure Satya also doesn't mind, do you Satya?" He looked at me, daring me to contradict him. I wouldn't give him the pleasure. Anyway, we wanted to hear Sri Singh speak.

"So, where were we?" The sage was ready to start. "Ah, yes. The Romans." Sri Singh turned his head toward the west. "The Romans were no match for the Greeks. Not in the field of philosophy. Romans are soldiers, administrators, even engineers, rather than thinkers. Thanks to the Greeks, they had their successes in literature and poetry, but they committed one cardinal sin. They completely subordinated the individual to the good of the state. They displayed utter contempt for the Stoics...."

"Stoics, Sir?" This was Yeshûa.

"They were the followers of Zeno who, already some two hundred years ago, was concerned not so much with the welfare of the society, but with the good of the individual. While normally taken to have been a Greek, he was in fact a Phoenician Cypriot. Although he denied the existence of atma, unless it be made of matter, his greatest contribution was to affirm the universality of man. He believed in equality. He refused to recognize the difference between the Greeks and those they called the barbarians. He also proclaimed the predisposition of good within the universe. He thought that all contradictions would ultimately resolve themselves and contribute towards ultimate good. Evil, he said, was relative and even evil was instrumental in the ultimate perfection of the universe." Arum Singh stopped to take a sip of water.

I recall glancing at Yeshûa. His face, a mask of concentration, was cast in granite. His eyes didn't blink nor stray from Arum Singh's face. He seemed transported to some other reality where knowledge was the price of entry.

"He was preaching the omnipresence of..." Yeshûa whispered. Then he asked aloud. "And you say his philosophy was materialistic?" There was incredulity in my friend's tone.

"By the day's standards. Remember that the Greeks espoused a whole Pantheon of gods and goddesses. Rather like they accuse Hinduism of having." This time the old man's smile broadened as though he were sharing some secret joke. "But it is also a philosophy which offers guidance in everyday life. A philosophy very close to the Hindû thought. They regarded personal courage in the face of danger and suffering, indifference to material circumstances, and particularly detachment, as the highest traits to be sought by mankind," Singh concluded.

"And the Roman's rejected his teaching?" The same incredulity.

"Well, he wasn't a Roman. Romans, like all people of inferior intellect, regard themselves to be superior. Only their definition of superiority was different from the Greeks. It was a question of state versus individuality."

My own eyes alternated between Singh and Yeshûa's face. This time I glanced at my friend and noticed unmistakable signs of anger. He confirmed my observation later. "I felt great anger, right then. Why is it that people don't go forward? They seem to be walking in circles, like a chicken with its head cut off."

At the time, Arum Singh continued his comments.

"...and whatever we may think of others, and there were indeed many others, too many to discuss, the Stoic philosophy was the most noble that came out of the Hellenic world. Whatever their shortcomings, the Stoics have been great humanitarians. You might say that Socrates was the forerunner of the Stoics. We give credit to Plato and Aristotle for their Ideas, but it had been the Stoics who developed the theory of Innate Ideas, as they did of Harmony, as in living in harmony with the world. Noble sentiments indeed..."

"And the Romans...?" I could see anger rising again, this time even in Yeshûa's tone.

Sri Singh immediately noticed my friend's anguish. "Don't be quick to judge others," he said. "It is easy to be right in hindsight."

"But the Roman's came later!" Yeshûa wouldn't give in.

For a while there was silence. For some reason Singh was delaying giving his opinion on Roman philosophy. He kept veering off on a tangent, as though delaying the inevitable.

"You are not angry at the Romans," Sri Singh said at length. "You are angry at your own people for withholding the truth from you."

This time my friend said nothing. His head bowed to his chest. Anger seemed to be evaporating, turning itself into sorrow. It seemed as though emotions were getting the best of him. It was also apparent that the lessons the Stoics had to offer were dear to him. That he took them to heart.

"There is so much to learn..." he said under his chin. "So much to learn...."

"For what it's worth, my young friend," Singh said, seeing his charge's continued anguish, "Roman culture was peculiarly barren of original thought."

At the time I didn't understand why Singh, who never seemed to say anything negative about anybody, chose those particular words with which to finish his lecture. Much, much later I understood. That last sentence was directed solely at Yeshûa. Arum Singh sensed that my friend compared the Romans to Yeshûa's own teachers, buried in the caves of Qumran. Or even Mount Carmel. Both suffered from inexplicable infertility of philosophical concepts. Both closed their hearts to the influx of creative thought, to new concepts, new ideas. Both even destroyed the old concepts if such didn't fit into their desired effect. Philosophically as in the practical sense, though quite differently, they were centred on results, not in the way of obtaining them.

My friend understood that, there and then. It took me many years...

For some reason, since Yeshûa joined us, Sri Singh chose to speak mostly about subjects touching on philosophy, ethics and even about subjects dealing with human relations. It hadn't always been so. When I was his only student, he lectured mostly on economy, astronomy and mathematics. For some reason this changed. Perhaps it was just as well. Had we been listening to a lecture on mathematics, Yeshûa would have learned that the Romans not only lacked originality but also destroyed what they couldn't understand. I'd learned from my mentor that there is a single point at which philosophy, theology and mathematics cross axes of interest. This point is Infinity. And Infinity had been defined, mathematically, by a single man, some two hundred years ago. That man was Archimedes.

This man from Syracuse was not only a brilliant mathematician but also a great physicist and engineer. He could have done so much for the Roman Empire. But a soldier of the glorious legions didn't understand what the mathematical genius was doing. So he killed him. He stuck a sword in his back. Soldiers are like that. They kill. It is their job.

Or perhaps, we weren't quite ready for Archimedes, back then.

Or now.

We don't seem ready for so many things. Why was my mind wondering like that, even then, only a few months after I'd met him? Why am I wondering still?

* * * * *

5

The Crescent of Fertility

I'd never slept on a surface as hard as this. Did you ever try tossing and turning on a stone slab? Perhaps there are softer surfaces, a mat or a bit of straw, inside the house, but I can hardly barge in and trip over a dozen sleeping bodies. I presume there are still a dozen of them. I think Yôna said eleven. And some women.

I look up. Some clouds are now building up from the west. The one I saw earlier over the east horizon is gone. If it starts raining, sooner or later I'll have to go inside, scattered bodies notwithstanding. After the grime is gone. The clouds look dark, foreboding against the otherwise clear sky. The leading edge of an approaching front, the one facing east, displays a slightly brighter contour. A single stroke of a brush. It gives the clouds a three dimensional appearance. Like a giant pillow I wish I had to put under my head. The stars toward the east are already paling. It will be dawn in a few hours. I'd hardly slept. Just ran a stack of memories through my mind. Not that I wanted to. They came and demanded attention. Complete attention. They were all so amazingly real.

There is so much we shared – he and I. Over so many years. What else can I do?

Since I had pinned down Arum Singh about dad's whereabouts, he'd given us lectures daily. He had more time now, less work. Not all the camels in the caravan belonged to my father. There were always a number of hangers-on, men, traders, who paid a percentage of their business for the protection a large convoy had to offer. When dad, Sahib Bihari, left for Antioch, all the men who joined the caravan for security stayed behind.

I'd spoken to some of them.

They all hoped to continue with us along the Crescent of Fertility. This is a large strip of land that stretches from Jerusalem along the Mediterranean coast to the north, then extends eastward between the northern edge of the Syrian Desert and the mountains from the north all through Mesopotamia, and finally turns south, towards Babylon and Ur. All along this fertile land people are wealthy and ready to part with their money, gold and silver, in exchange for foreign products rare or unobtainable in their part of the world. Once we got to Ur, we would follow the coastal road, such as it was, along the Persian Gulf, then we would bear east, ever along the coast, towards India, in the direction of my home. By then all those who came for the ride would have dropped off.

Periodically, we changed the animals. They would make their way back carrying return trade, while we would transfer our own goods to new camels, horses and, later, elephants and continue on our way. Father had been thinking of owning a 'fleet' of camels and other beasts of burden, but it was just too much trouble. There were specialists who did nothing but cater to the tradesmen, supplying the means of transportation. One could hardly compete with their prices. Sri Singh once told me that we have entered the age of specialization.

The men, who remained in our camp during dad's absence, continued to indulge in some fairly brisk trading. Smaller dealers had to go down the river to the market place, to display their wares. But even the remaining camels, which

my father left in Singh's charge, carried enough goods to
attract traders as well as the local people to come visit us, in
our camp, north of the settlements. And there were many all
along the river. We invariably stopped north of the trading
centre, so as not to allow the prospective buyers to assess our
wares. We wanted to keep control of the timing and information. Yeshûa and I helped by fetching various items,
packing them safely back if not required, and generally trying to make ourselves useful. We didn't have to do that, but
one of the lessons Sri Singh imparted on both of us was to be
as useful as we could.

"Always make sure that you don't owe anything to
anyone," he once said, virtually in passing. "It would be a
shame to have to come back just to pay back a rupee." He
was talking about the Wheel of Awagawan. About Reincarnation.

I clearly recall that occasion.

The moment Sri Singh said those words, I immediately
thought of the apple I stole, and Yeshûa confessed later that
he had thought of the meals he'd enjoyed since he'd joined
us. We both squared our shoulders with renewed energy. As
time went by, Arum Singh imparted a peculiar influence on
us both. He never forced us to do anything. Never attempted to impose his will. All he did was to nudge us to
think along certain lines. He pulled rather than pushed, like
a current of a vast river that wins by gentle persuasion.
Arum Singh was a great teacher.

I wondered why he'd never travelled with father's caravans before. When the opportunity presented itself, I asked
him.

"The time wasn't ripe then," he replied enigmatically.
And then he added: "I wasn't needed yet."

If that answer was meant to satisfy me, it didn't work.
At the time I wondered if he was referring to my own presence, without which he would have no one to teach. But if
so, then how come my father placed so much authority in his
hands? Teaching was really carried out only in his spare
time. No, he was hired for his skill with languages. And for

his ability to negotiate deals using complex mathematical formulas. His teaching seemed almost an afterthought.

And then I thought of Yeshûa. If it hadn't been for Sri Singh, Yeshûa would have had no one to learn from. Frankly, I could pick up a few languages and get some rudimentary mathematics even from my father. But Yeshûa? He needed Arum Singh. He needed his knowledge of philosophy, of religions, of subjects that were, at least at the time, of little interest to me. Did Sri Singh know something no one else knew? Was his fate written in the stars?

My father caught up with us vaguely disappointed. He'd gotten what he'd wanted, but it wasn't the bonanza he'd expected. Nevertheless, the camels he had taken with him returned fully loaded with goods. He couldn't have bought, or traded, any more. Frankly, I think he was just tired.

We took some rest.

Two days later I had discovered a facet of my father's character I'd never seen, or in this case heard, before. During his absence, Sri Singh allowed me to negotiate some trades. It was not as simple a matter as it seemed. I had an added disadvantage of not being taken quite seriously because of my age. But, I was well prepared. When the traders saw that they could not take advantage of my youth, they began taking me seriously. At this point the advantage turned in my favour. While they were attempting to ridicule me, I'd been learning of their weaknesses. In no time I had bettered the prices outlined by Sri Singh.

Later, my old teacher praised my acuity, and that was that. I thought I would hear no more about it. In a way, I didn't. But at an after dinner session, which my father held with other men, I've overheard him bragging about me.

"He could outbid anyone of you," dad boasted quite shamelessly. "Why, he could sell an ivory comb to a man as bald as an elephant's backside!" he added standing astride, his hand on the hilt of his sword, daring anyone to contradict him.

No one dared.

It so happens that, at the time, I had no idea how bald an elephant's backside was. What was more to the point was that dad never spoke a word about my apparent prowess to me. I remained the son of Sahib Bihari – in for the ride. I felt a little hurt, a little proud, but not really sorry. It turned out that this was not only my first but also my last free ride.

The usual trade route would have taken us further north, along the northern part of the Parthian Empire, then through the Kushan Empire toward my home in Benares. But this time we took the lesser known road. When my father took part in the caravan himself, he liked to open new territories. It was his decision to veer south and follow, as much as possible, the water's edge. We were coming back lighter than we had been on our way out. It seemed like a risk worth taking.

Ten days later we were ready for the next leg of our return trip. I was looking forward to the fabled valley of the lower Tigris-Euphrates. Sri Singh had already told me some stories of the ancient Sumerians who had laid foundations of culture in this region. I was certain he would repeat some of them for Yeshûa's sake.

On the eve of departure I had my first of many, progressively more unusual if not actually mystifying experiences with Yeshûa. I woke up that night and noticed that my friend was sitting in *Siddhasana*, the pose he'd learned from Sri Singh. He was perfectly still, giving an impression of being absorbed in peculiar affinity with the rock upon which he was sitting. To an outside observer he might have seemed idling. Doing nothing, or wasting time. Someone once said that idle time is a devil's playground. Just then a cloud moved on, and I could clearly see his features in the light of the full moon. His face was cast in ivory marble. His eyes were half-open, his chest moved effortlessly with regular if slightly shallow breathing. Yeshûa was not idle. I suspected that he must have been meditating on some of Arum Singh's words.

"Not so," he interrupted my speculations. Only then had I noticed that his eyes, concealed by the long, almost girlish eyelashes, were directed at me. Somehow he knew what I'd been thinking.

"You were not thinking?" I asked when I recovered from my surprise. My suspicions of idleness returned.

"Most of the time I'm listening," he replied.

"Even when no one's talking?" I felt I had to say something. We seemed lost in an ocean of silence. Not even the fairest wind stirred any leaves on nearby trees.

"Particularly then," he replied in a tone of grave reassurance.

Somehow I knew he wasn't joking. It came to me, there and then, that the devil had no access to Yeshûa's mind. It was never idle. Sometimes it was just intensely receptive. It was disposed to listen. I felt too embarrassed to ask him, but a strange thought crossed my mind. I suspected he was listening to his *atma*.

Once we were on our way, Arum Singh brought his camel to ride with us. Yeshûa and I walked on either side of his beast, hoping to hear him talk. Even I found our teacher more and more interesting. Yeshûa's thirst for knowledge continued to be contagious.

But Sir Singh didn't begin lecturing until after the evening meal. He rode glancing at us, as if expecting either one of us to do something peculiar. Later I suspected that he was mostly studying my friend. Finally, at the next overnight stop he asked us if we wanted to hear about the land that we were crossing.

"Mesopotamia?" I asked.

"Persia," he replied. "Mesopotamia was but an insignificant portion of the vast Persian Empire. The Parthians are horsemen while the Persians had been empire builders. At the time of King Darius I, only half a millennium ago, its span was from what would later become known as the Persian

Gulf to the Red Sea, along the Mediterranean to the Aegean
and eastward all the way to the Black Sea. Then it continued
along the Caucasus around the southern part of the Caspian
and then along the Oxus river up north to the sea of Aral. Its
east boundary runs along the Indus river down to the Sea of
Arabia. By far the greatest Empire the world has ever
known."

As our teacher spoke he slowly unfolded a tightly rolled
scroll, and then proceeded to outline, with his finger, the
contours of the empire. I followed this movement, spellbound.

I could see, however, that Yeshûa was not impressed. At
least not overtly. I, on the other hand, could hardly believe
my ears. Nevertheless, my young friend bowed in traditional
Hindû fashion and waited for Sri Singh to sit down. He
knew that sooner or later Sri Singh would get to the parts that
were of interest to him. The master returned the greeting
and sat facing both of us.

"I'd better start at the beginning," he said, looking
around as though gathering his thoughts. "To find the first
settlements along the lower valley of the Tigris and Euphrates, we must go back some five thousand years. The people
who settled here were known as the Sumerians."

We both glanced at Yeshûa. Singh knew that Hebrew
Scriptures state that God created Adam around four thousand years ago. He'd told me that already, before Yeshûa
had joined us. The Sumerians, according to local tradition,
prospered for thousands of years before Hebrew history had
even begun. On hearing these facts, Yeshûa didn't bat an
eyelid. But there was a reason why Sri Singh chose his words
so carefully. I'd learned of it before the night was over.
And we did talk deep into the night.

"I mention them, because their language resembled
somewhat that spoken in some of the earliest civilizations of
India ... well before it was spoken in this hub of civiliza-
tion."

"Wow!" I couldn't help myself. Somehow I felt proud of my Indian heritage. Sri Singh smiled but ignored me. His next sentence put me in my place.

"But the Sumerians didn't last long," he said, and I could swear there was a twinkle in his eyes when he looked at me. "They were annexed by the Elamites, only to be conquered by Amories, the Semitic people." This time he glanced at Yeshûa as if to say "your cousins." My friend, however, remained completely passive. I was right. "Your cousins," Singh said, "came from the fringes of the Arabian Desert. They developed the village of Babylon into their capital, and thus became known as Babylonians. Old Babylonians, to be more precise, as their later successors in the same district were known as the Chaldeans."

This was too much to remember all at once.

"But like all civilizations, not to mention empires, they didn't last long. A wave of barbarians, devoid of culture but more dexterous with the sword, had overrun them. There is nothing you need know about them, the Kassites, except that your father, Satya, should be grateful to them to this day."

At this I held my breath.

"The Kassites introduced a horse to this valley."

My father was the only member of the caravan who rode a horse. Not all the time. Horses were much less sturdy than camels. Less disposed to difficult, desert terrain. They could also support less weight. On occasion we even had to carry extra water with us, just for their sake. But father felt like the leader that he was, when he mounted his steed. I was very proud of my father.

"Some two thousand years after the original Sumarians, some three millennia ago, another Semitic people founded a tiny kingdom along the Tigris river. They were the Assyrians. For a long time they lived in peace until, over a millennium later, they began to expand. Syria, Phoenicia and even your kingdom," Singh looked at Yeshûa, "the Kingdom of Israel, as had Egypt, had all fallen to the Assyrian army."

"Not the Kingdom of Judah," Yeshûa added with bowed head. His pride must have suffered.

"How so?" Sri Singh asked. I could swear that he knew but was testing my friend's knowledge.

Yeshûa waved his head as though unwilling to share his knowledge. The silence lengthened. Finally he spoke, his voice a little shaky, as if expecting to be contradicted. He spoke in Hebrew, citing his Scriptures verbatim: *"And it came to pass that night, that the anger of the Lord went out, and smote in the camp of the Assyrians an hundred fourscore and five thousand: and when they arose early in the morning, behold they were all dead corpses."*

Again, there was an extended silence. Finally Sri Singh continued.

"Quite right, my young friend. A great pestilence must have smitten the Assyrian army. Great pestilence indeed..."

Yeshûa didn't say anything, but his head hung a little lower.

"But even victories are not meant to last, least we grow proud. The Chaldeans, another nation of Semites, captured Nineveh, less than a century later."

Sri Sigh sipped some water. He got up, stretched his legs and looked down at us. The first stars were already twinkling over the eastern horizon. Then his old face broadened in a kind smile.

"Do you want more? Tonight?"

I recall looking at my friend. Slowly he raised his head and looked up at his teacher. "Please, Sir. I must... " He didn't finish. For some reason Yeshûa found this lecture particularly painful. Arum Singh nodded and sat down again.

"What the Romans call *lex talionis*, or the law of retaliation, became an aspect of Sumerian law." Neither of us understood what he said. Singh smiled. "An eye for an eye, a tooth for a tooth, a limb for a limb..." he recited softly. Then he added, almost in a whisper. "This law came into being some four and a half millennia ago."

Yeshûa caught his breath. He seemed to be losing something, as though it were slipping from his grasp. His face remained facing the master, but it seemed frozen as on that occasion when I saw him in the moonlight. There was no expression on his face all.

At long last Sri Singh continued.

"While there was some modest achievement in their law, by the time the Old Babylonians took over, hordes of monsters and demons enforced by evil spirits went under the guise of religion. They did not invent witchcraft – just elevated it to new heights. Or sank to new depths, depending on your point of view. In their literature we find a precursor of your Book of Job, the Babylonian Job, as it is sometimes called."

There was no reaction from Yeshûa.

"As for Assyrian supremacy, well, it had risen and was maintained by the use of unspeakable cruelties. They impaled their enemies on stakes, skinned them alive, cut off their noses and ears, and worse. But their karma caught up with them quickly. Seldom empires fall as fast as theirs did. And their conqueror, in turn, took vengeance upon them according to *lex talionis*."

The stars were now covering the whole eastern segment of the sky. Even the western part of the nocturnal dome was nearly dark enough to display its jewels. Yeshûa's eyes seemed to wander the far horizon, the sky, or infinity itself. One could not tell if he was still listening.

"But let us not forget that Sumerians gave us their cuneiform writing of some three hundred and fifty syllabic and phonetic signs. It was the Persians who devised an alphabet of only thirty-nine letters. And that was a mere half-millennium ago. At least in this area...."

Both of us looked up. Yeshûa had his Hebrew and I had my Sanskrit. Both languages were a lot older than the Persian contribution. It made me feel good. I'd hoped Yeshûa also derived some satisfaction from his heritage. If he did, his face did not register any.

"And this, brings us back to the achievement of the Persian Empire. I already told you about its extent. King Darius I brought it to its greatest glory. It was resplendent, magnificent, and it lasted about thirty-five years."

Arum Singh let that sink in. This time there was some movement in Yeshûa's face. He was evidently drawing some conclusions.

"His culture was eclectic. He borrowed from everyone. From everyone he conquered. There is no stimulus to create when you can steal." A smile accompanied this assurance. But the great king had built a Royal Road. It stretched from Susa near the Persian Gulf all the way to Ephesus in Ionia. They say that travelling day and night, a courier could deliver a message along its total length in less than a week. Communication is of vital importance when you're running an empire."

"For thirty-five years." Yeshûa murmured.

"Yes, young man. In this glorious universe, all that has a beginning must have its end."

"And what of their religion?" Yeshûa asked.

Sri Singh nodded. It was as though he had been expecting this question.

"It had a much more enduring influence on the ancient Persians. Some six centuries ago there was a prophet they called Zarathustra. He inherited a society steeped in superstition, in animal sacrifice, magic and rampant polytheism. He was more interested in a higher ethical plane. The religion he'd created was strictly dualistic. Ahura-Mazda ruled over all the good in the universe; his counterpart, Ahriman, presided over the powers of darkness. Even as Ahura-Mazda was incapable of any wickedness, Ahriman was by nature treacherous and malevolent. In Zarathustra's view, the world, what we would call reality, was a struggle between these two opposing forces. Ultimately Ahura-Mazda would win, but only after the coming of the messiah, who would be born miraculously, and bring about the resurrection of the dead and, ultimately, after some twelve thousand years, the last judgment. The good would be rewarded with immediate bliss, the wicked would be cast into the fires of hell. Luckily, the Persian hell did not last for ever."

I remember glancing at my friend. This time his eyes have been drilling holes in my master's irises. There was such concentration on his face, as I've never seen before. Perhaps, even since. Yeshûa was absorbing every fragment, every single letter of Sri Singh's dissertation. I would wager that a year later he would be able to repeat it word for word.

It was getting late. Singh adjusted his position slightly.

"There is only a little more," he said. "I must tell you about Mithras."

By now my back was curved. Yeshûa's remained ram-rod straight. He'd sensed what was to follow to be 'his' subject matter.

"Over the years, there sprang up a long list of cults, but the oldest of these was Mithraism. Mithras was said to have been Ahura-Mazda's chief lieutenant in the struggle against the forces of evil. He is said to have suffered greatly in his earthly form, before being raised to a deity. He performed miracles, saved lives by feeding the masses in days following a great drought, as after a disastrous flood. He fed them bread and wine. He proclaimed Sunday to be the sacred day of the week, and December twenty-fifth the most sacred day of the year. It was near the day of the winter solstice, when the sun was born – once again on its journey from the Southern Hemisphere. The poor people identified with Mithras, not just in Persia, but his worship reached out as far as Rome."

There ensued a prolonged silence. It was the first time since I met Yeshûa that he didn't rise to bow to Sri Singh, and our master left, softly, without making a sound. It was as though the old man knew what was going on in my young friend's mind. Although I've never learned just how.

Yeshûa sat for a long time. For hours. As usual on such occasions, he remained completely immobile. As though he crossed over to a different reality, a world where

others had not been permitted to enter. He seemed to dwell
in his own realm.

Yet it was then and there that I just noticed something
traumatic in Yeshûa's eyes. A certain phase, which began on
that day I first saw him hiding behind the wall in Jerusalem,
was over. It was complete. It marked the end of his rebellion. He only confessed this to me some time later. I'll
never forget his words.

"So far," he'd said, his eyes scanning the horizon, " I
have learned two things from the mouth of Sri Singh. The
first is that every empire the world has ever known has over-
reached itself. And that is why it fell. For the same reason
all the future empires will fall. It is the nature of the beast to
go beyond its assigned purpose. And why? It is because
power corrupts. As empires continue to expand, they ex-
ploit, and finally dominate, with brutal force if necessary.
Their destruction seldom comes from without. It is the poi-
son within which ultimately destroys them."

And then he looked me in the eyes. His stare seemed to
penetrate my whole being. This was no longer the boy I
played with, with whom I climbed trees and threw stones in
the river. This was a youth, not a year older than when I met
him, yet mature beyond his years. There was wisdom in his
eyes that was impossible to question. It took all my will
power not to look away.

"All that we build in this world is transient, my friend,"
he said with a sad smile lingering on his lips. Then he
seemed to cheer up. "And the second lesson which Arum
Singh conveyed to me is that it is not Yahweh nor Brahma
nor any other god who creates religions. It is man." And
then his steely-blue eyes again drifted to the far horizon.
"We are gods," he said, "even if we die like men."

* * * * *

6

The Roots

For the next few days, even weeks, Yeshûa behaved like the boy I knew and loved playing with. He seemed to enjoy, and be amused by, the simplest of things. He turned back to the companion I saved from a fate worse than death, on that first day in Jerusalem. He was a boy, a little less than thirteen years of age, willing to learn all he could about everything and everyone around him. His passion for knowledge, which till recently had been centred on the weighty words of our teacher, was now, directed at all the men we travelled with. He walked or rode next to a different man virtually every day. Then he would come back to my side and invite me to play whatever tickled my fancy.

Yeshûa was taking a rest. He was recharging his energy.

On the other hand, now that I saw the other side of his personality, I could never treat him in exactly the same way. He was a boy, seemingly carefree, filled with the joy of living. But I never knew when he would become still, detached and tell me something that I would remember for the rest of my life. There was something very elusive about my young friend. Only two years my junior, but also many years ahead of me in certain matters. In short, Yeshûa had become, at least to me, an enigma.

Days turned to weeks, weeks into months, and finally we arrived in Babylon. There was little to show for its purported earlier glory. Empires seem to bloom, open like a Chinese rose greeting the morning sunshine, and then, by early dusk closing its petals with hardly a scent left behind. So short seem their moment of glory. We all felt tired. It was good to make camp.

That evening, relaxing in our tent, I asked Yeshûa to tell me more about his own country. He seemed reticent. Then it came out without much enthusiasm.

"Sri Singh could tell you more than I," he assured me.

But I insisted. Finally he acquiesced.

We never strayed too far from the river. We needed water for the animals, and men too wanted to wash away the dust of the journey from their bodies and clothes. Yeshûa got up from his bunk and walked out to the embankment. I followed him wanting to pursue my question. We sat facing the quiet current making its unrelenting way toward the ocean.

"We are like the water you see in this river," he said at last. "We think we know where we are going but, to be honest, we are carried by events from one misfortune to another. You could say that has been the history of my people. Sometimes I wonder if we are going in the right direction. Or if we should or would turn, given a chance."

There was no pleasure in the words he'd spoken. There was none of the usual joy. I began to feel sorry I'd asked him, but I was truly curious about what kind of people my friend had come from. He was certainly different from any boy, or man, I'd ever met. Since the last lecture Sri Singh had given us, Yeshûa seemed as carefree as the wild birds frolicking on the riverbank.

"Since I heard Sri Singh speak, I sometimes wonder if anything I've learned back home is of any value. They taught me history as described in the Torah. Now ... well, now I wonder if Torah has anything to do with history. It seems to me as though some fragments of our past may have been used to illustrate profound, spiritual truth. But not in their definition of spiritual truth. There is so much to learn..."

His voice trailed off as though loosing confidence. Once again I felt really sorry for my friend. No longer for having asked him about his country, but for his visible inner torment. Whatever he was feeling, it seemed extremely painful to him. He looked and sounded as though he'd lost his home, his country, his established terms of reference. It also seemed as though he was very lonely. I didn't realize it at the time, but that was the moment Yeshûa had become aware of being truly homeless. A homeless hobo, without a place to put his head. I hardly knew what to say.

"Yeshûa, you'll never be alone... not as long as I live...." It seemed like a lame affirmation of friendship, but when you're fourteen years old, you are not endowed with an appropriate turn of phrase.

"And that is why I shall always love you," he replied simply.

I had to turn my head to hide tears welling in my eyes. I have no idea why his simple statement had such an effect on me. After all, I too was still only a boy. A lad not given to emotional behaviour. If I were older, I would have taken Yeshûa in my arms and hugged him as I've seen men hug each other after a successful repulsion of bandits attacking our convoy. They didn't seem embarrassed nor effeminate in this display of affection. Yet, I was still just fourteen, of an age when boys don't yet know how to act like men.

"I know," Yeshûa said. "It's all right."

I had no idea what he was talking about. He couldn't have detected my emotions. Nor my thoughts. Yet he'd said the right thing at the right time. The absurdity of it was that it was he, Yeshûa, who was cheering me up. Not the other way around.

It was later that evening when I asked Yeshûa to tell me what he'd learned from Sri Singh on the subject of the Hebrews. My friend had a session with him while I rode ahead of the caravan with my father, who was teaching me how to locate a good camping ground for that evening's sojourn. I suspected they had talked about Yeshûa's people.

Again, my friend didn't seem overjoyed at the prospect of talking about his kinsmen. But the last time I'd asked him, we hardly talked. I wanted some more general background.

"So what can I tell you about my people?" He finally succumbed to my request. "I suppose we must have originated somewhere in the Arabian Desert, although our first recorded leader, Abraham, appears to have settled in northwestern Mesopotamia. This must have been... less than two thousand year ago. About that same time Egyptians and Cretans developed large-scale industries, while the Babylonians wallowed in their worship of demons. It was a crazy mixed up world. According to Sri Singh, at that time the Egyptians had already believed in personal immortality for the last five hundred years and it was a thousand years since they had espoused an ethical religion. That's right, my friend. That was two thousand years before my people began to worship Yahweh."

"But I thought..." I bit my tongue. It must have been difficult for Yeshûa to point out a number of vastly advanced nations – well ahead of his people.

"Yes," he guessed the reason behind my hesitation. "It is hard to admit that we were a bunch of nomads when others had already been building cultures, civilizations and making advances in science. It is even more difficult when you've been taught that you should accept the Torah literally. Nevertheless, perhaps it is not so important when you start, but rather for how long you can go on..."

This time I kept quiet.

"Anyway," he continued with resignation in his voice, "Abraham's grandson, Jacob, later called Israel, migrated westward and attempted to occupy the Land of Cannan, later called Palestine. Some two hundred years after that, his people met with famine. Some of my forefathers tried to escape drought by moving still further west, settling in the vicinity of the rich land of the Delta. The Delta of the Nile. Alas, the Pharaoh had other plans for this land so... he enslaved them. It was only some one thousand two hundred and fifty years ago that Moses, the new Hebrew leader, led them out to the Sinai Peninsula. It was also he who taught them to worship Yahweh... the deity who till then was only revered by Hebrew shepherds in the vicinity of Sinai. What mattered was that Moses succeeded in uniting the tribes sufficiently to conquer, or really re-conquer the Land of Cannan."

"I thought it was called Palestine...?"

"Only later. The name Palestine comes from the Philistines who came down from Asia Minor. But that too came later. The land, supposedly flowing with milk and honey, was a dry and inhospitable place, but a lot better than the wastes of Arabia. The problem was that the Cannanites already occupied it for centuries. Eventually, after many wars, the Israelites won. After all, they were more primitive, they had nothing to lose." Towards the end, I could hear bitterness in my friend's voice.

"They were all like that. It was dog eat dog – the world over." I tried to cheer him.

"Will it ever change?" Yeshûa wondered aloud. "Is it really impossible for people to share their wealth with each other? Is it so hard to love one another, even one's enemy?"

As I open my eyes, the sun kisses the top edge of the wall directly in front of me. I hardly notice. My mind, my heart, are firmly anchored somewhere in the vicinity of Babylon. My young friend's words are still ringing in my ears. "Is it so hard to love one another, even one's enemy?" What strange notions he'd had. His exact age was always a mys-

*tery to me. He must have been thirteen, at the most. Perhaps
less. A mere lad. We never talked about age – his or mine.
It did not matter. Then or now.*

*I wonder what the disciples are doing. It is the second
morning since Yeshûa was murdered. That's right. I cannot
think of it as an execution. When you kill an innocent man,
that's murder.*

*I feel really thirsty. Thirsty, hungry, cold and miserable.
But I am alive. He's not.*

"The Philistines were a good influence on the tribes.
They'd helped to unite us. We even elected a
king. Before this time Judges ruled, but they
were really glorified priests. That was little more than a millennium ago. But King Saul did not see eye to eye with the
last of the Judges. It was only his successor, King David, who
bathed in blood to the detriment of others. One success followed another. For forty years he ruled. He brought glory
to our chequered history. He conquered the Philistines. He
united the tribes. But great glory takes great money. High
taxes and conscription followed. His son, King Solomon,
continued for a while. My people think of him as a great
and wise monarch. I disagree. Any man who keeps a harem
of seven hundred wives and three hundred concubines,
builds for himself sumptuous palaces, and for his god an ex-
orbitant temple, must pay for it from his own pocket. Only
his pockets were empty. Every three months he drafted
thirty thousand Hebrews and sent them as slave labour to
work the forest and the mines of Phoenicia. King Hiram of
Tyre grew rich. Solomon grew poor. He'd learned his lesson too late. Vanity, 'tis all vanity, he realized. Too late. At
the time of his death, the country was in open revolt. You
sure you want to know all this?"

I didn't. But I didn't know I didn't until I'd heard it.
Like the proud king, I'd learned too late.

"The kingdom broke up. The glory was over. Like all worldly glory. It passes."

His voice, still steady, got more and more quiet, until only a whisper left his lips. I had no heart to make him go on. He was my friend, and he was hurting.

"It wasn't really the politics of your people that led me to ask you..." I lied. But I knew that philosophy and culture, even religion, was closer to his heart.

"Ah, yes. Religion. Well, I mentioned its origins when I talked about Moses. As for what can be derived from our scriptures, you have to ask Sri Singh. I believe that virtually the whole Torah and a great deal more of the ancient, and some not so ancient, writings are given to us in allegory. It is up to each individual to find his own truth in them. If you take them exactly as written, you do not do them justice."

"But, surely..." I tried hard to cajole Yeshûa to raise an edge of his own personal veil. He wouldn't. No matter how I coaxed him, he would not say another word on the subject. I did get him to mention philosophy, however. But even then he was equally terse.

"It would take a much older and wiser man than I to analyze Judaic philosophy. And anyway, I wasn't really taught much about it. But from what I have learned, they do not indulge in excessive optimism."

Soon after that assurance, we went to sleep.

For some reason, this lengthy confession put a lid on our learning. Arum Singh was preoccupied with other matters. The only thing he conscientiously supervised was our study of languages. Apparently Sanskrit and Latin no longer sufficed. We were to indulge in Hindi, some Arabian dialects, and then, to our surprise, Egyptian as spoken in the Delta Valley.

"A time will come when you'll need it," he said. I wasn't quite sure if Sri Singh was referring to Yeshûa or to myself. "And trust me," he added, "whatever language you can learn while young will save you many an hour of study later."

We both trusted him. He was a man who inspired trust.

As for Yeshûa's roots, for some reason I couldn't let
go. I had to know what made him the way he was, the way
he appeared to be. In spite of all his playfulness, the boyish
pranks he played on the members of the caravan, there was
something mysterious about him. It must have originated
way back, in his home, in his upbringing, perhaps instilled by
the mysterious Essenes whom he'd mentioned but never explained. Finally, a few camps down the river he let me in on
a subject he admitted he'd never talked about to anyone.

"Well, my friend," he accentuated this appellation
making me feel very special, "there was Judith. She had
more influence on my life than anyone else. And that in-
cludes my mother and father."

He stopped as though still unsure if he should go on. It
was self-evident that some things are harder to share than
others. Even with a friend. I did not prompt him. When
travelling with a caravan, you learn patience. A lot of patience. No matter how much you wanted to be already
home, often there have been months, sometimes years between you and your destination. Some people were not
meant to be vagabonds. Others, like my father, couldn't stay
in one place for long. I wondered to which group my friend
belonged. So far he fit very well into the daily routine. As if
being homeless were part of his nature.

"Yes," he repeated after a long pause, "there was Judith."

"Yes?" By now my curiosity was peaked. I've never
heard of any mysterious Judith. In fact Yeshûa had never
mentioned any names from his past. I knew neither his father's nor any of his family's names. I still didn't know if
he had any brothers or sisters, any aunts or uncles. Once he
tried to explain his mother's name, but even then he sounded
enigmatic. Regarding his private life, he was very private
indeed.

"I could never quite figure her out," he started, having
at last decided to share his innermost secrets. "But, I suppose, I'd better start at the beginning."

There was another pause as, apparently, Yeshûa wasn't quite sure where exactly the beginning was. When he finally started again, he talked slowly, pensively, as though he himself was trying to figure out what might have happened.

"You recall Sri Singh telling us about Mithras, Mazda's lieutenant? Well, from what our teacher told us, and from what I've read myself, Mithras had started out as a relatively minor figure in the religion introduced by Zarathustra. But sometime during the fifth century before our time, he progressed to become the principle god of Persia. About four hundred years ago his teachings had reached my people. Mithras, by the way, in Old Persian means 'Friend', an appellation dear to all who felt lonely and forgotten. That is how many of my own people felt. They couldn't let go of their own traditional teachings, but the idea of a messiah was dear to people who, at the time, were going through a period of vigorously searching for their own identity. Some two to three hundred years still earlier, our great prophets, Amos, Hosea, Isaiah and Micah had broadened our outlook...."

"And you remember all that?" I couldn't help interrupting.

Yeshûa smiled. "I've never suffered from a lack of memory. Remember, though, I'd only just turned ten years of age when I was taught all that. I may well have coloured the information with a youthful, immature slant."

"Not you, my friend. I'm sure you did them justice!" This I said with utter conviction.

As for my prodding him for details, it was not just a question of learning about my friend's past. I felt, rightly or wrongly, that Yeshûa had to relieve himself of the pent up knowledge that was fomenting in his young mind. For the life of me I had no idea how I, myself, was capable of such mature perception. I was but two years his senior. Obviously, I wasn't capable of analyzing his psychological problems. My questions resulted from my love for him. My intuition guided my words, not my mind. They say that travel makes for strange bedfellows, and Yeshûa and I shared a tent. Some of his precocious wisdom must have rubbed off on me. Anyway, I loved him then, as I do now, and love feeds solutions to difficult problems.

"To continue," he said bowing his head in gratitude, "the prophets I mentioned had lifted our religion to a belief in a single god. Before them, the various tribes already believed in Yahweh, but each clan had its own version of the deity. Now, finally, Yahweh became the Lord of the Universe. Also, as with Mithras, Yahweh became accepted as a god of righteousness, of justice and goodness. Such an image of god seems obvious to us now, but before their time, before the time of the prophets, the Yahweh of Moses had been more concerned with ritualistic sacrifice and observances than he was with the purity of heart of his people. Or so it seemed to me, based on the writings of the Torah."

Yeshûa picked up a stone and threw it into the river. The flat pebble skimmed the flat surface six or seven times before sinking. "We were like that. Skimming the surface. We still didn't dare to dig deeper into our... our atma. Even El, our popular name for God, was little more than a guardian, protecting places from evil. We were, for the want of a better word, quite primitive."

At least on this occasion, he and I being alone, Yeshûa didn't seem unduly embarrassed by such an admission. He knew I would never take advantage of his frankness.

"And what happened then?"

"As I've said, by the fourth century before our time Persian influence reached not only our cities, but our minds. There had always been many sects among my people, but one particular group formed a brotherhood evidently determined to adapt the teachings of Mithras to their own needs. Particularly, as I've already mentioned, they had been quite taken by the Mithran concept of a messiah. But while the Persian version called for thousands of years to bring about such a...

"...an avatar?" I tried to help.

"Yes, the messiah – the brotherhood sought to accelerate the process by extensive studies of prophesies, astrology, numerology and reincarnation. Apparently for the first time,

Jews formed a loose organization dedicated to go beyond our own teaching, and even to reach out to other countries, other cultures, to gain knowledge. They studied the philosophies and religions of Persia, India, Greece and Egypt. And their own, of course, in a very dedicated fashion. Don't forget that Mithraism was a very powerful force. According to Sri Singh, it reached your own country and spread with considerable success."

"And what of this Judy?" I wanted him to get to the point.

"Judith," he corrected. "Judith in Hebrew simply means a Jewish woman. But to the initiated its meaning goes further. It is the feminine form of Judah. It means: 'let God be praised." An apt name for her purposes. Anyway, she, Judith, broke with tradition. To my knowledge she was the first woman, ever, to have become the head of any sect. We were, I suppose still are, a very paternalistic people. Anyway, apparently she'd earned her right by displaying gifts of prophecy and healing. She also wrote extensively and kept detailed records of all her own and the whole sect's findings."

Gradually I felt drawn into the story. I could picture an old woman, her long gray hair flowing down her back, writing on a rough-hewn table with an oil lamp casting grotesque shadows on the walls of a damp and dank cave. At least I suppose it must have been a cave. Yeshûa intimated that the sect was on the fringes of respectability. They'd probably spent most of their time in hiding.

"There was one purpose which drove Judith and her Essenes. She believed her principle, her sole mission was to bring forth conditions in which the messiah would be born among her people. Preferably, among the members of her brotherhood. With this thought in mind, she set about gathering a group of young girls who might prove suitable to bear, to bring forth, the... ah, the avatar."

With that Yeshûa shook his head. He moved it from side to side, as if trying to deny everything he'd just spoken.

"Imagine," he said at last. "They thought that they could take Mithras' idea and use it to their own advantage...."

It was then that I began to suspect what was coming. I first rejected the idea, but it kept returning with renewed force. Like waves building up on an angry ocean. I looked around. It was already getting dark, but I could still see the fire stirring in the eyes of my young, rebellious friend. And then I blurted without conscious control.

"You're the messiah," I said softly. "You are the one that has been chosen...." It wasn't a question. The answer had been staring me in the face for some time. I just couldn't accept it. Apparently, nor could my friend.

"There is so much to learn," he said after a long pause. "So much to learn, and so little time...."

He must have known something I didn't. Even then.

It was a week later when Yeshûa finally finished his personal story. Apparently his mother, Mary, had been one of twelve maidens selected. They had all been dedicated to the concept of becoming channels for the coming of the messiah. All of them had been sequestered into the monastery on, or inside Mount Carmel. Luckily for Yeshûa, Mount Carmel was in Galilee and not far from Nazareth where his parents lived.

"If only it were true," Yeshûa's tone hardened. "Later I learned that they were mere children, as young as four and five, willingly given up by their parents to be reared by Judith. Imagine, children who were no longer children but objects of one woman's ambition. They lived for the sole purpose of satisfying the dream of one Jewess."

"I thought there was a whole brotherhood..."

"Well, yes. But Jews take good orders. And Judith was a boss incapable of tolerating compromise or dissent. No matter what, no matter what the children had wanted..." He then stared at me with fire flickering in his eyes. "Did you ever play in a cave?"

It was the first time that I'd heard my friend really angry. I strongly suspected that Yeshûa experienced the will of

the woman in charge on his own skin. No compromise. The
end was all that mattered. Never mind the means. And suddenly I understood why he had to escape from the influence
of those people. They wanted him to fulfil not his dreams
but theirs.

A moment later the anger was gone. The tone of his
voice changed to one of sadness.

"Poor mother... She had no say in any of it at all.
They even made her marry a man she'd never met. A good
man. A man kind and honest. But what of love? What of
her own youth, her girlish desires, her absence of friends of
her own age, of toys and.... Poor mother. She never even
once complained. It was as though she had no mind of her
own...." Yeshûa's eyes drifted to a distant star, indifferent
to his or anybody's fate. The sky looked cold and forbidding. The stars turned into diamonds fashioned from pure
ice. Hard and unforgiving. Indifferent. The beauty we both
always saw was conspicuously absent. It was held in abeyance. Could it be that it is we who create the realty we perceive? I asked him.

"Always," he replied instantly. "Always," he repeated nodding vigorously. "And this is precisely the problem!"

Later he told me that he'd once heard his father, Joseph,
talking to someone about his mother's training. Chastity,
purity, love, patience, endurance had all been taken for
granted.

"Yet the way my father described it, it sounded more
like persecution than like tests of mental and physical
strength. It was oppression. And when she became the cho
sen one, they found her an instant husband. A man twice her
age. I am not blaming father. Mother was, is, a beautiful
woman. But at the time, she was a mere girl. About the age I
am today. Perhaps younger..." There was both, sorrow and
anger fighting for control of his features. "And they only
released her from her prison after the wedding. At Carmel,
of course."

It sounded as though Mary, Yeshûa's mother, had been dealt little choice in her life.

"And what happened to Judith?" I asked.

"She continued to manipulate reality to justify her prophecies. She was very good at that. She directed the visitors from Persia, or maybe your country, seeking the birth of the supposed messiah, to seek directions at Herod's palace. She knew what reaction there would be from Herod once he'd learned about a 'King of the Jews' being born. In no time at all, we had to run for our lives, all the way to Egypt. But she had it all planned. She had already sent some of the brethren, the Essenes, to get there before us, and some more to follow. She'd also appointed her spy, supposedly a servant, a girl whose name sounded like Josie. I'd learned later, that she was the girl who purportedly took care of me when I was a child. Like an nanny. But I wouldn't trust her. I'd been too young then, of course, to have anything to say. But they told me later that they used my garments to simulate miraculous healing. I'm sure that too had been orchestrated by Judith. She had to make sure that prophecies would be fulfilled."

And then, for no apparent reason, he started laughing. For a moment I thought he'd gone over the line, but his laughter was so contagious that I could do no more than join him. Finally he wiped his eyes.

"You will love this!" he cried out. "Me, miracles! Then!" He was again trying to control another attack of gut wrenching chortle. "Imagine! That was some twelve years ago, and to this very day I cannot perform a single miracle on my own. And don't think I haven't tried!"

W̱e were already relaxing on our bunks when he raised himself on one elbow.

"I didn't tell you this..." he said in such a tone of voice that I could imagine a mischievous grin lighting up his face. "I didn't tell you, but when I was running away from the Temple in Jerusalem that day we'd met, I didn't just knock over the tables. I also showed up a bunch of pompous gentlemen who thought they knew all the answers. They didn't like that."

Again I could swear I could see a rueful smile in absolute darkness. "No, Satya, my friend. They didn't like that at all."

I always suspected there was more than one reason for Yeshûa's sudden departure from his own country. He wanted to stay alive. Even according to Sri Singh, the learned scholars of theology, apparently specializing in prurient demagogy, did not like competition. They hated even more being ridiculed by a twelve-year-old. In public.

I was right. It was some time later, months rather than weeks, that I learned that Yeshûa did not particularly like the scribes and Pharisees, to whom I assumed he was referring at the time.

Next morning Yeshûa looked and sounded like a new man. Man or boy, but new, at any rate. He looked and sounded as though a great weight had been lifted from his shoulders. It seemed that I had been right. After we bathed and ate, he put his hand on my shoulder.

"Thank you my friend. You probably saved my life," his face was smiling but his tone of voice was deadly serious. "A few more months and I would have gone crazy!"

I never realized just how heavy his burden had been. I didn't know what to say. Boys are not very good at this sort of thing.

"As for my sudden departure, I also left Judea to free my mother," he added, almost as an afterthought. "For as long as I was there, she would be treated as a curiosity. Once I left, she would be free. As Judith would say, she'd done her job. Now she'll live a more normal life and have other children. And she'll be a real mother to them. And a great mother, at that."

A mother I never really had, he seemed to be saying. I read it in his eyes. And then he looked away, his gaze following the ripples on the river. Ripples getting wider and wider, even as my friend's life had been destined to become.

* * * * *

Part Two

The Awakening
The Morning and the Second Day

7

Detachment

It is a wonderful feeling when, sitting on a slab of stone, lips parched, stomach growling, someone brings you food and drink. It is a little after sunrise. Through half closed eyes I see a young woman, her long robe flowing gracefully in the air. As I lower my eyes again, I see her bare feet. She's no apparition after all. She stands in front of me, as though waiting for me to speak.

"Shalom," I greet her. I assume she's an angel or else one of the women tending to men inside the house.

She doesn't say a word but puts a metal tray on the bench beside me. Then, with a slight bow and still without a word she retreats. For a moment I think I imagined her. But the tray besides me gives her reality. I eat and drink slowly, trying to fill as much time with food and drink as I can. I really don't know why I am still here. I seem as lost as the men and women inside the house.

Some undefined time later Yôna comes out and greets me with a bow.

"Have you slept well?" he asks. If it weren't for genuine concern showing on his face I would probably think he was being facetious. He wasn't. I smile, pointing to my back. He nods his head.

"We have some straw inside. You're welcome to it. Here," he looks around, "the wind would blow it off...."

"Thank you," I say and he leaves without another word. I call after him.

"Yôna?" I'm desperate. He turns. "Yôna, I need to wash...."

He tells me where I can go to get cleaned up. It is a public place. I might have to pay a shekel or two. He turns to go and stops again. "Or you could ask our women...."

"No! No," I interrupt him. "I wouldn't dream of it. They are already so kind." I point to the food tray.

He smiles and disappears inside the dark opening. I finish eating and go to where Yôna said I could get cleaned up. An hour later I am sitting again in the same spot.

What am I doing here?

"Veda means knowledge," said Sri Singh, after we'd all settled in our usual postures. He and Yeshûa in *Padmasana*, the Lotus seat, I cross-legged. "The four Vedas, the Rig, Sama, Yajur, and Atharva Vedas have been passed on orally from times immemorial. Once the wisdom flowed in great abundance. Over millennia, under the influence of Kali Yuga, the flow diminished, as men could no longer comprehend their import."

Yeshûa looked up.

"Yes, Yeshûa. In India we believe that only individual souls are capable of advancement. The world at large falls into disrepair. Like any machine, no matter how magnificent. There have been four Yugas or Ages, the Golden, Silver, Bronze, and now the Age of Iron. We live in a time wherein the spirit is supplanted by lower energies. We call it the age of Kali, the goddess of death."

Here Arum Singh turned to me.

"Go and make yourself useful, Satya. These matters are not new to you...."

I recall being grateful for being excused from this lecture. Already back home I'd spent months reciting the long, sweeping poems of the various Vedas. They were all filled with gods of all description. Under the powerful Indra, other gods held humanity in an iron grip of faith and superstition. Rather like in Babylon. The fire-god Agni brought wisdom from other gods. The god of the night sky, Varuna, struck echoes of the Greek Uranus, while Mitra, the god of the day sky resembled the Persian Mithras. The Greek Zeus had his counterpart in Dyaus. There were many others. When I'd been taught the rudiments of Vedas, before my first journey, I'd counted thirty-three gods in Rig-Veda alone. I had no desire to hear the lectures again.

My father didn't really approve of religion. He said that I must know it, but it was up to me to find things to believe. He tended to rely more on his intuition than the teaching of priesthood.

But the teaching got stuck in my young mind.

The Sama Veda, I recalled, is credited with the origins of Hindû music. Its chants and melodies refer back to Rig-Veda, praising Indra, Agni or Soma. They said that singing the verses resembled Greek choruses. Their influence had become strong as far back as one millennium ago, when trade with Babylon already grew in scale.

And then there was Yajur Veda. It sounded rich in sacrifice formulas while the Atharva Veda, dealt with magic and secret incantations. It was, my teacher told me, by far the oldest, reaching back to pre-Aryan India. It is filled with black magic, powerful spells with both good and evil consequences. But it wasn't all frightening. It also gave instruction in shamanic healing, the use of herbs and even healthful cooking.

I wondered what reaction Yeshûa would have to the ancient Vedas.

"...after the decline of the Mauryan Empire, the Satvahan Dynasty became established in Deccan. Now this is very recent, my friend...."

As I peeked from a safe distance, Sri Singh was still lecturing Yeshûa, this time on the political climate of India.

The Deccan district was well south of our present itinerary. But it paid to know who your friends might be.

S omehow the next two or three years, the years following that night north of Babylon when Yeshûa had unburdened himself from the stored up emotions of his childhood, my memories became fragmentary, disjointed, as though not our relationship but his progress became imbedded in my mind. With the exception of Sri Singh's lecture on Vedas, I do remember that, for a long while, we hadn't talked about any subject remotely related to any religious tradition. It was as though Yeshûa dismissed all of his past, all of the responsibilities which the Essenes had tried so hard to place on his shoulders. I had no idea, at the time, if his newfound freedom would last. Whenever Sri Singh mentioned some aspects of the Hindû thought, almost immediately Yeshûa held him back. I recall his measured tone as he made his desire known to Sri Singh. I had never heard anyone telling Sri Singh what to do.

"You cannot put new wine into old skins," he said. I had no idea what he'd been talking about, but Sri Singh appeared to have understood. He smiled, placed his hands together and withdrew to his other duties. It struck me, at the time, that Singh had a peculiarly respectful attitude toward my young friend. To me Yeshûa was just a pal, a good companion in play and in argument. To Sri Singh he seemed to be more. Only much later did I become aware of what it was that Sri Singh saw in him.

Toward the evening of the next day, Yeshûa tried to explain to me his allegory about the wine. "Apostasy," he'd said, "is not for the purpose of forgetting or discarding previous knowledge or beliefs. Its purpose is to rid oneself of the past's emotional content."

Whatever that may have meant, I understood, there and then that, at the time, Yeshûa has been dealing not with his knowledge but with his emotions. I can't say that this made me much wiser. I was still at the stage of acquiring my own knowledge, not at the phase of standing apart and watching it wither in memory. My knowledge, of course, was much more mundane in character.

At any rate, those next three years seemed carefully erased from my memory. Perhaps there was nothing my mind deemed worthy of recording. Oh, I remember, vaguely, our trials and tribulations associated with travel, but those were not directly related to Yeshûa. As for my connection with my friend, it was as though those few years hadn't happened at all. I vaguely remember Arum Singh during those years, growing more distant. Aloof is perhaps a better word. There is one fragment I recall rather well. I seem to remember the old teacher surreptitiously turning his eyes whenever I espied him looking at Yeshûa.

Funny that. I didn't dare to ask why he did that, of course.

Later, much later, I asked myself what was it that drew the old scholar's attention to my friend. Normally Arum Singh was reserved to the point of shyness. On the other hand when he felt his duty to do something there was no question of hesitation, nor excuses. Also, there was neither sign nor regress when he did what he felt was necessary. It was as though there were two men, or at least two personalities inhabiting the same body. A man of strong convictions, and a man who preferred to remain invisible.

Just before the years seemingly evaporated from my memory like smoke from a ritualistic burning of some sacrificial goat, I recalled another fragment of our stay on the outskirts of Babylon. It was the rainy season which, to the delight of most of the men, held us there for nearly three months. The men had been delighted because Babylon was renown for its pleasures of the flesh. Food, a variety of fermented drinks and particularly ladies of pleasure abounded in great profusion. Men, having earned some gold, had been in a position to taste lavishly of the forbidden fruit. Al-

though, at the time, no one thought of it as forbidden. Most
of it was amply displayed on the streets. I recall my father
giving me a few coins to visit, what Yeshûa called, the dens of
iniquity. I also recall having had a big verbal battle with him
on the subject.

"If we didn't enjoy sex, Brahma would not find any
human expression," I argued steadfastly. I had gotten
mixed up. It is Krishna whose name in Sanskrit means "All
Pleasure" and Krishna was the incarnation of Vishnu, not
Brahma. I confused, or at least commingled, pleasure with
creation.

"Are you suggesting that Brahma's sole expression is
centred between your legs?" He was a little angry. A rare
moment indeed. "Be serious, sex is meant to be fun. Like
all Brahma's gifts. As for practical aspects, sex is indispensable for procreation, but it does nothing for atma."

"No," I said holding my ground. "But if Krishna is
the only source of all that we have, then I refuse to exclude
any gifts which He has conferred upon me." Or something
like that.

It's hard to remember the exact words. All I know is
that I'd won the argument, but I suspect only because
Yeshûa had not yet learned about Sri Krishna. That came
much later. I do hope I'll remember more of our friendship. Perhaps it was the irritation in both of us that erased
some of our memories from our minds. At least from my
mind. I wonder if he would have remembered. If only he
were here....

But apart from the mundane, Babylon no longer had
that much to offer. I sat next to Yeshûa when Sri Singh was
completing his lecture on the city with such an illustrious
history.

"Once Alexander entered its walls, some three hundred
years ago, the Persian and Mesopotamian dominance waned
rapidly. It was the beginning of the end, even as all triumphs
must end in failure. Three hundred years further back,
Nebuchadnezzar the Second had ruled the Neo-Babylonians.
He also razed Jerusalem, and brought your forefathers here,

into captivity. He built his main temple, the Esagila, in honour of god Marduk, whose monumental ziggurat became known as the Tower of Babel."

Lectures like this took place almost daily. And then, one day, we left.

There had been other fragments.

The face in front of me was that of a young man between sixteen and eighteen years of age. Definitely young and definitely mature. He was sitting in *Padmasana*, his legs twisted in a most painful fashion. His long arms were gripping his bare knees. He was doing the *Loukiki-mudra*, an exercise that consists, at least outwardly, of rotating your body in a clock-wise movement. His stomach, alternatively, contracted and was thrust forward. Doing all this, he was smiling and regarding me with, what I can only describe as, infinite patience. I recall shaking my head in disbelief, for when I told Yeshûa that while I am here, surely he can relax his stringent posture and simply sit cross-legged on the pillow, he laughed.

Then I told him that Loukiki-mudra is normally practised with legs in a cross-legged position, not with legs tied in a pretzel.

"You must believe me that it is no hardship," he said. "It is as natural to me as walking or standing." A broad, carefree grin confirmed his inexplicable sentiment. At least, inexplicable to me.

Two years have passed since we arrived in India. Two years since Yeshûa went off on a tangent, seeking his own place in our strange world. He possessed an amazing affinity for a variety of languages. After a mere two years he must have spoken a number of our native tongues flawlessly. Perhaps with a tinge of an accent, but then, my country is so vast, that anyone who travels always speaks with an accent. Hindî, various Dravidian dialects including Telugu, probably for its beautiful poetry, and obviously Sanskrit – to name just a few.

"Why do you do this?" I asked pointing to his stomach. I rated the exercises, which were part of Hatha Yoga, as refined self-abuse. At best, as a mild form of torture.

"It is no more than the Greek athletes do before their Olympics.

"And just who told you about that?" I was beginning to be jealous of his scholarship. Particularly when it had nothing to do with religion or philosophy.

"I meet people," he said still grinning. He was always grinning. His days of pensive facial expressions had dissolved into the hoary past. "Oh, all right!" He let go of his knees and threw his hands up in mock desperation. "Sri Singh had visited me last month. He stayed a few weeks and, well you know Arumji, he is a veritable gold mine of information."

"Last month?" I saw Sri Singh only two weeks ago. I didn't know he'd been away from my hometown. I also noted that Yeshûa substituted the more affectionate form of address when talking about Arum Singh. The suffix -ji, as in Arumji, expressed both respect *and* affection. It was apparent that Sri Singh and Yeshûa have progressed from a teacher-pupil relationship to that of true friendship.

"He visits me periodically. I think he feels a little responsible for my state of mind."

"And why would he feel that?"

"Actually, he told me. He said that as he had removed the old wine, he felt responsible that the new wine would not intoxicate me too quickly."

"Am I supposed to understand what you are talking about?"

Yeshûa looked at me for some time. As he kept staring at me, I began to feel the power of his gaze. I felt there was no way I could turn my own eyes away from his. We were locked like this for a time I couldn't define. But when he finally released me, I knew exactly what he meant by his previous statement. The next moment he laughed pointing at his stomach, which was reaching a protrusion bigger than ever before.

"I bet you couldn't do that," he exclaimed rotating his stomach in a most revolting manner. That's right. Not revolving but revolting.

"Nor would I want to," I confirmed. "You look horrible."

And somehow, as I said that, the magic moment was gone. It had nothing to do with neither our sparing nor his exercises. I recalled it after I got home. There was something strange going on with my friend. Perhaps he'd been studying some magic, I wondered. But almost immediately I dismissed this notion. Whatever Yeshûa did was not magic. It seemed that his actions or abilities were more natural in this world than what we all seem to think of as natural. It was as though we were all half-asleep.

He, my dear friend, was in the process of awakening.

I get up to stretch my legs. It is already getting hot. In spite of the drink I had at the well where I'd washed, my throat already feels parched.

It is my second day of painful, or at the very least incredibly absorbing, memories. Actually, that is not true at all. The memories are, for the most part, joyful. In fact, it is this process of thinking of my friend that brings him back to me. There are moments when it seems that he had never left.

It feels as though he is still here. With me....

"The purpose of all Yogas," he said, "is the extinction of suffering. You achieve this by faith, understanding and realization. There are many schools, but your Vedanta and certain sections of the Upanishads written after the Vedas are helpful. The Nyaya, Vaise-

sika, Samkhya and Mimamsa taught me a lot. They taught
me to rely on my intuition, more so than my intellect. It
gave me a great sense of belonging...."

Again he was leaving me behind. He sounded like Sri
Singh, only more difficult to understand. He made no al-
lowance for my ignorance. Arum Singh did.

This time Yeshûa was fully dressed, looking like a typi-
cal Hindû, with only his hair setting him apart. And from
nearby – his eyes, of course. No Hindû man or woman I had
ever met had eyes quite so blue. Like the sky on a hot
summer's day. Otherwise, he would be quite invisible in a
crowd.

"Why are you telling me all this?" I asked.

"Because you are my friend," he replied simply.

"So? Are you suggesting that I should stop suffering?"

For once he looked serious. "It takes time to learn to
suffer, it takes time to learn to overcome its asperity. Ideally,
one should learn to rise above suffering before it really
starts. If we become immune to suffering, then, in a way, we
become immortal."

As usual, or at least of late, my friend was talking in riddles. He saw through my discomfort.

"Buddha equates life with suffering. Obviously, by
physical standards, if you die you no longer suffer. But is
the reverse also true? If you no longer suffer, would you
ever die?"

"I never thought of immortality in those terms," I confessed. I recall hoping that he wouldn't ask me in what
terms I have thought of it. It would be embarrassing.

"Life is not a biological function," he said after a
pause. "Life is a state of consciousness. If you study the
words of Sri Krishna: life Is. It has Its being only in the present. It is also omnipresent. We must learn to identify with
that presence, and we must do so in the present tense. It is
the beginning and the end of all things."

I wasn't sure he was really speaking to me. There had
been moments when he seemed to listen while he spoke, as

though he was voicing something passed on to him from his unconscious. I remember Sri Krishna's words recorded in the Bhagavad-Gita: I am the Self, seated in the hearts of all creatures. I am the beginning, the middle, and the end of all beings." The beginning and the end of all things. Was Yeshûa quoting Sri Krishna, or did this knowledge come from a different source. Could it have originated within himself?

"And in what way can I benefit from this knowledge?" I felt a bit flustered at asking a question that might well be obvious to my friend. But I could not allow him to drift so far apart from me that I would lose his friendship.

"That would never happen," he said.

Was he reading my thoughts again?

Yeshûa smiled. "You must stop being so surprised that I've gained some powers which you call magical. They are not magical at all. Any man, you for instance, who would devote his life to my particular pursuits, would attain equal abilities. Perhaps greater. Not that they are anything special. Many men will come who will do much greater things than I. Remember, you only live in the present. You never stop growing."

It sounded to me like a bit of a contradiction. But, what do I know?

The strangest thing I noticed about Yeshûa was that from an angry young man he metamorphosed, in very quick time, into a man of quite exemplary aloofness. He treated knowledge as my father would treat pointers from experienced travellers from far away countries. Yeshûa studied new cultures, religions, philosophies, even some political systems, but he never seemed to espouse any of them. They became a storehouse of information to be incorporated into his own particular reality. And his perception of reality was more and more that of complete detachment.

* * * * *

8

Mahabharata

"**N**inety thousand couplets, usually some thirty-two syllables each. It tells a story of a dynastic struggle in the kingdom of Kurukshetra. Inspired poets composed it less than two hundred years ago, yet it is at the root of a profound advance of Hindû thought from the days of the early Vedas. We call it the Mahabharata."

Sri Singh's hands were opened wide as if they were holding a scroll as thick as any I'd ever seen. His gesture was so expressive that even Yeshûa, used to ongoing studies that the Essenes had forced on him, looked surprised. He couldn't quite picture ninety thousand couplets.

"And what of the Bhagavad-Gita?" he asked. Apparently the fame of this poem and its beauty had reached Palestine.

"Ah, yes. The Song Celestial. The poet was inspired by Lord Krishna. We think of him as the Supreme Personality of the Godhead Himself. Lord Krishna speaks of himself as being one, yet present in every man. It is a book whose wisdom is as deep as the heart of the listener, or reader, who pursues Truth."

Even as Sri Singh was speaking, I moved closer to listen. I've heard the story of Indra many a time, but Sri Singh always managed to add a new slant, a new understanding to the words of the Bhagavad-Gita. Sri Singh acknowledged my presence with a nod and a smile.

"Welcome my old friend," he said addressing me. "It is a while since you've graced us with your presence."

I wasn't sure if he was being sarcastic or paying respect to the son of Sahib Bihari. Sri Singh was well capable of blending one with the other. He respected all man equally. If he disagreed with my father, he said so. Others, all others I had ever met, never dared. They valued their life too much....

Yeshûa ignored me.

"And what of Brahma, Arumji?" he asked. His face was a mask of concentration. He seemed to exclude all external vibrations having ears only for the old teacher.

"Brahma is not the ultimate creator. He's the original living being, in some ways like your Adam, only on a universal scale. He too had been taught Vedic knowledge by the Personality of Godhead. The supreme intelligence behind all creations is Lord Krishna, who is the sole source of the creative energy, *prakriti*, through which all things are made. Thus it is not Brahma we should worship, but Sri Krishna. Brahma, you might say, is the universal engineer. He constructs the universe from the countless stars, adorning our heaven, to the most insignificant insect. But the life force behind is...."

"So Sri Krishna is pure energy?" Yeshûa's tone was quiet but there was a sense of expectation in it, rather like that of a long distance messenger approaching the final stage of the race.

"You cannot limit Lord Krishna," Sri Singh replied as quietly. I felt there was a certain undefined struggle between the two men. Between the old man and Yeshûa. They were both on the same side, yet testing their muscles. Mental muscles. "Yes, Lord Krishna is pure energy. But as such he has the capacity to reach beyond all limitations. The energy can incarnate itself even into a human form. Doing so, it in no way diminishes its presence in the rest of the universe."

I never realized how difficult our Hindû philosophy is. Or is it religion? If so, I've never met anyone who even thought about it. Not in those terms. Apart from Sri Singh, of course.

"So the totality of Lord Krishna is equally present in the Whole as in any of his or its parts?

Now I lost the ability not only to understand the answers, but even the questions. Only this was not really a question and Sri Singh remained quiet. I tried my best to reason it out. How can you be equally present in the Whole as in Part?

"It is the qualitative and the quantitative relation...." Yeshûa continued as though he was alone. "The nature doesn't change, only its mode of expression."

"Is a drop of water from the vast ocean any different from its source?" Sri Singh mused pensively.

"I am that I am," said Yeshûa. "Yes. I am that I am."

If this was supposed to mean something – I remained at sea. Or in that ocean they were talking about. I already had a number of sessions with my teacher on the inner meaning of the Bhagavad-Gita. I even read most of the Mahabharata. But whatever they were talking about was as incomprehensible to me as the tongue of the Egyptians. Although, at least in that field, I was making some progress.

I tried hard not to give away that I'd given up. I was there only as a passive listener. Perhaps, in time, some of their wisdom would rub off on me. Yes, *their* wisdom. Yeshûa was no longer a lad sitting cross-legged at the feet of his master. He was an active participator in the discussion. In a way, he'd come of age.

I looked at the two men I most admired. Apart from my father, of course. But father, well, that was a different kind of admiration. My father represented all that was good in this world. Or rather, in the world of business. But these two men, my Jewish friend and my old teacher, they always took me beyond the horizon. When I was sure that I'd learned all that I needed to know, they showed me that I'm still less than a beginner.

They sat opposite each other, each perfectly balanced in the Lotus Seat, an *asana* that I still haven't mastered. Yet they looked comfortable, perfectly at peace with the world and even with themselves. The latter, I learned later, was much harder to achieve.

After that particular session, whenever the two men met, I made myself scarce. They didn't push me aside. In fact, on many occasions they welcomed me. Somehow I couldn't remain. Not now. Perhaps a time would come when I would be able to sit with them. But I did stay within earshot of their voices. For a while now I wasn't able to participate in their discussions. I felt left behind. And yet, when Yeshûa and I were alone, there was no detectable change in him. He was the same reliable friend, still full of laugher, still willing to play practical jokes, with what looked like, total involvement. It seemed that Yeshûa was more than just one man. His personality expanded or contracted, virtually at will. He didn't prepare himself for his talks with Sir Singh; he just lowered himself into *Padmasana*, and switched to a different mental vibration. His thoughts must have flowed within those vibrations with equal alacrity up and down the stream, expanding into pools of greater involvement, meandering through some intricate landscapes, and, on occasion, rushing headlong towards a cascade of discovery.

There were times when the two men shared amusing moments. I suspected that they were exchanging a few jokes. Not so. They continued to exchange *slokas* from the Bhagavad-Gita, quoting them from memory as though they both read nothing but that particular Holy Scripture. I knew the truth to be otherwise. Whatever scrolls, or tablets or any form of writing Yeshûa could get hold of, he read. Sri Singh paved the way for him. For many years my old teacher has been recognized in the whole of Northern India as a scholar, and, I only learned later, as a holy man. It was both his reputations that opened the doors for Yeshûa to writings inaccessible to mere mortals.

The next time I saw them nothing had changed. They seemed to be swapping yarns, only the words were apparently inspired by Lord Krishna Himself.

"So who is this Brahma? Surely, it is Lord Krishna!"

This was Yeshûa in his usual posture, a broad grin on his handsome face. His eyes were shining with an extraordinary light. More so than usual. "Even as Brahman is the indestructible eternal form, which you call soul, so it is one with Vishnu, the redeemer. As also is Lord Krishna. Is he not omnipresent?"

To me it sounded as though they were interpolating the Hindï and Sanskrit meanings, and rolling them into one. Or else, they were talking about something quite different. Arum Singh remained silent, as though expecting Yeshûa to continue. He did.

"The wise man sees Brahma in a cow, an elephant, an unclean dog, even a dog eater... They are all one...."

I may have been wrong. But I suspected that now Yeshûa was not speaking of a personification but of the divine essence, the absolute, self-existent eternal presence. The source of all things in the universe. I think Yeshûa called it the spirit.

There was wonder in my friend's voice as if he was discovering something he'd always known yet had never brought to the forefront of his mind. I had quite different problems. A dog eater? I rebelled against such concepts. The dog-eaters were regarded as unclean in my country. But I had no time to dwell on my doubts. My thoughts had been interrupted by Sri Singh who joined his hands and bowed before Yeshûa.

"Such knowledge is reserved for those who attain Brahma realization. We also call it self-realization. When sustained at all times, it is the realization of Krishna."

I could only just hear the last words uttered by my old teacher, yet, for some reason, my spine tingled with a mixture of admiration and apprehension. And I had no idea why. Sri Singh had been speaking of my childhood friend. The lad I stole apples with. Actually I did the stealing, but, well,

he was there. He was speaking of *my* Yeshûa. And suddenly
I felt very possessive of my friend. I didn't want to share
him with Arum Singh, nor with Brahma nor even with Lord
Krishna. Nor with anyone else, for that matter. I wanted to
get on a horse, or an elephant, with him, and just ride off into
the jungle. Forever. Only I didn't.

For a long time the two men I most admired, now both
my mentors, sat facing each other like two old friends who
knew each other's thoughts so well that there was no need
for words. How I wished, there and then, that I'd followed
my young friend's footsteps, that I'd chosen his way rather
than mine, and had grown with him to greater understanding.
Yet, even Lord Krishna teaches that we each have our own
journey to travel. Was not Indra told to kill his own kin, even
against his own will? We all journey along our own, lonely
paths, sometimes crossing paths with a kindred soul, the rest
of the time navigating our ship on the ocean of life, alone at
the helm.

But apparently not so, Yeshûa told me later. We met
some two hours after he'd sat with Sri Singh. They no
longer waited for my arrival. I felt a little jealous of
Yeshûa's preferential treatment. But Sri Singh was no longer
in my father's employ. He was a free agent, to do as he
chose. But this figment of my memory is not accurate nor
fair either, as neither of them had ever rejected my presence.
It was I who did not find comfort in their exchanges. I knew
I couldn't really participate in them. Perhaps I just wasn't
ready.

"You can walk your path, but not really be part of it.
Think of yourself as an observer. As watching yourself doing what you must. Or at least should. You'll find it easier," he told me. There was real concern on his face.

I did. Many years later.

Roused by the voices inside the house, I snap out of my ru-minations. I cannot quite discern what they are talking about. There is some kind of argument. Quite heated. I think some of them want to go out and do something, appar-ently not quite knowing what. The others want to stay put. I think I detect fear in their voices. They are afraid to be ar-rested for having been the followers of Yeshûa.

How strange this sounds. The Yeshûa I knew and loved would never allow anyone to follow him or even his teach-ing. He never tired of repeating that he had so much to learn. Always. Even when later Sri Singh confessed that he had no more to teach him, Yeshûa embraced the old man like a prodigal son. I remember tears in his eyes. But he didn't deny the old teacher. He said something quite unex-pected.

"Wheresoever I am, I shall always be with you."

Whatever that meant, the old man seemed to have un-derstood. I could see profound peace in his eyes. It seemed that Yeshûa had said what Arum Singh wanted to hear.

The argument inside the house is growing in volume.

"We shall stay here, for now."

It was the voice of command. It was also the voice that once said 'No' to me. I learned from Yôna that it belonged to the fisherman called Simon. Later they called him Peter.

The moment I closed my eyes, I was back in India, packed and ready to participate in another caravan. My father was training me to take over from him. As soon as possible, he'd said. The goods had been amassed, the elephants fed an extra portion. All was ready. We would take the elephants as far as my father's associate on the Ara-bian Sea, and once there, we would change to camels and horses. It was easier that way. More flexible. I was busy with the last minute preparations.

And then Yeshûa's face again filled my inner vision.

Over the last few days, I practically begged Yeshûa to come with us. He'd learned somehow that we were leaving and came to say good-bye. I didn't ask how he'd known. I stopped asking him questions about his knowledge some time ago. He just knew. But I couldn't shake off the sorrow of not being able to see him for a year of two. Perhaps longer. One could never be sure what happened on a long journey. I was a grown man, but somehow I was close to tears. This wasn't the first time I had to leave him behind. To pursue his studies, he'd said.

Once again he acted the same way he had done so many years ago. He held me at arm's length and gazed into my eyes. For some reason, also unknown to me, I stopped asking him why he did that. But it always set my heart at peace. Somehow.

"You have a great deal to do here," I said in apparent understanding.

"As you have at your father's side," he replied.

I forgot what power Yeshûa possessed in his eyes. A single look sufficed for me to agree with him. He told me later that this was only true if the recipient of his gaze was open.

"Only if you have an open heart," he confirmed. "Otherwise, I can do nothing." He sounded as though he'd learned that from past experience.

"Just how does it work?" I asked not imagining for a moment that he would tell me. I assumed it must be some sort of a secret reserved for men who study such things.

"There is no secret," he said, as if reading my mind. "Even if you open your heart, it would be for naught if I held mine closed. If we are lucky, for an instant of eternity we become one. Whatever I know is available to you. And vice-versa. Your knowledge becomes mine. Only it is not really mine. It is always there, available to all who are willing to open themselves to the infinite."

"I see," I lied. "Thank you." This second phrase was honest. I had been grateful. The pain I'd felt minutes ago was gone.

"Do you know, my dear Satya, that during those moments of eternity when we unite, we are both immortal?"

This time I didn't lie. I chose to believe him. It was easier than trying to understand him. And then we embraced like brothers.

The next day we left before dawn. So did he. Only I had no idea where we were going.

* * * * *

9

AUM,
The Ganga
and The Bunyan Tree

Two rows of small ceramic containers with tiny wick flames in their centre cast warm shadows deep into the long, mysterious chamber. Behind each flame hovered a thin, emaciated face, the lips pursed as though ready to bestow a kiss on some invisible object. Seconds later I realized that those immobile lips attached like funnels to expressionless faces, were the source of the single, sonorous chord that reached me even as I was approaching the Temple.

These pursed lips combined, dozens of them, to produce a single sound, which merged the various vibrations of the holy syllable of AUM. Three letters yet four constituent parts. The deep throated aaaah, the forward resonating uuuu that sounded like an elongated whoooo of a mysterious awl on a moonless night, and the final dying murmur of mmmmm.... The M, though the last sound, was not yet the final element. The final component of the holy syllable was silence. The silence of the universe which gives birth to all other sounds. Yet here, among these faithful acolytes, all four elements of the chord coexisted in perfect harmony – in a single expression of that which is, which is becoming, that which sustains itself and finally returns to its point of origin.

In the flickering light of the small oil lamps, I could just see that all but one of the heads were clean-shaven. The polished scalps reflected the mellow sheen of the yellow glow. All scalps but one. The last one, at the end of the left row seemed curiously aflame. In the semi-darkness, I could just see the red, unruly curls of my old friend. I had no idea how long he'd been sitting here invoking the holy AUM. I even had no idea how long Yeshûa was living here, in this Ashram, among the men whose sole ambition was to escape the wheel of Awagawan.

For what seemed like eternity, my presence had gone unnoticed. Sitting on their heals, their shins flat against the thin floor mats in the sacred position of *swastikasana*, the Swastika Seat, the monks attention was far from immediate reality. Later, I knew, when advanced, their joints would be loose enough to remain still, for hours, and honour the holy AUM in *Padmasana*, the famed Lotus Seat. Yet even now, the sound was all that moved. After long minutes, a shadow stirred behind the frozen acolytes. It moved toward the back of the row and, as far as I could see, tapped the owner of the curly red hair on the shoulder with a short wooden slat. The man got up, bowed to the centre of the room and withdrew backward. A minute or two later, someone tapped me on my shoulder.

"Come with me, Satya," he whispered and moved back towards the entrance of the chamber without another word.

I followed him as silently as I could. In spite of a considerable vibration set up by the monks chanting their holy vowel, there was such purity of sound here that one would not dare to contaminate it with worldly extraneous noises. Once outside, Yeshûa embraced me like a long-lost brother.

"It must be close to a year," he said, tears of joy shimmering in his eyes.

"A year and two months," I corrected. It was a rare occasion that I could correct my friend in anything.

"Time loses its meaning here," he said in a way of an excuse. "I really missed you, my friend...." And, as if for lack of words to express his friendship, he embraced me once more. I too felt moisture rising under my eyelids, which I flapped up and down furiously in an effort to dry them.

"By all the gods of India, it is good to see you," I said after freeing myself from his bear hug. He filled in considerably during these last few years. His embrace was as firm as any man's I've met, or hugged, and a lot stronger than most. Yeshûa was a man, in mind and body.

"And how is your father, and mother? Sri Singh...?"

"Whoa, now hold it. I came to see you. First you must tell me about yourself," I countered.

Now that Yeshûa was no longer under my father's protection, we saw each other only sporadically. Also my father kept me busy learning various trades routes, particularly trading itself, so that I might one day soon take over his caravan business. Yet it seemed that no matter how much I learned, there was always more, always some acquired secret that my father would only share with his first-born. I was the chosen one, and that alone kept me busy.

"There is little to tell. I am learning..." he answered, his eyes lowering to his hands that were still held together in *namaste. Namaste*, in India, is a way of greeting that which is perfect within the person you encounter. It is a greeting accorded to your interlocutor's atma. It is as much a salutation of respect as of friendship, indeed of love. At least for those who know its true meaning.

"Still humble?" I teased him. It has been a while.

"I'm serious. It seems that the more you learn, the more there is to learn. And you?"

I told him of my father's plans for me.

"Will you be visiting my country?" Did I detect or just imagine hope in his voice?

"We shall be trekking to Egypt." I couldn't help smiling at his eyes lighting up. "I'll be sure to give them your regards," I added quickly.

"You'll be passing...." We were obviously talking about his parents.

"...close to Nazareth. I presume they are still living there?"

At this he froze. Evidently he'd never thought of that. But he recovered quickly.

"People in my country don't move much. They too are frozen in time. The Romans see to that," he added with just a touch of bitterness.

"Have you kept count of the years that you've spent away from Palestine?" I asked. My father and I had taken two more trips to Persia leaving Yeshûa behind. There was also China and a number of shorter trips. On each occasion, well before leaving, we'd asked Yeshûa if he would like to join us, but he just spread his arms, palms outward as though to display his emptiness. "I have so much to learn still...." His voice trailing off in abject apology. "Really...."

Yeshûa was a very different man now from the youngster who'd arrived in India.

"Are you getting to, ah... wherever you want to...."

I didn't quite know how to ask him if he was nearing his goals. Frankly, I didn't really know what goals he held before him. I am not even sure he knew.

"Yes," he replied immediately, frankly, to my surprise.

"You are?"

He laughed. "Why, my dear Satya, do you sound so surprised? We all reach a stage when we must start giving back what we've acquired."

There was that youthful spark in his eye I'd learned to love so much. This man never seemed to take himself seriously. "And you've acquired the knowledge you were seeking?"

"I try. But," and the other, the far away look, returned to his eyes, "now at least I know where I am going."

For some reason this confession did not seem to bring joy to his usual peaceful features. But the moment passed and my friend laughed again.

"Look at that elephant," he pointed to the huge monster who approached us while we were lost in conversation. We had been sitting on a fallen log. The elephant seemed ready to step on us. Yeshûa looked up at him, and the mammoth beast let out a huge sound as though in greeting. Yeshûa laughed, got up and patted the elephant on his nose. The elephant encircled Yeshûa with his trunk and seemed to hold him close to his gigantic ear.

"I know," he said. "I will later."

At this the elephant waved his enormous proboscis and walked majestically away.

"Did I hear you speak to an elephant?" I asked jokingly.

"Well, yes. He's a friend of mine." There seemed a trace of embarrassment in his tone.

"A friend....?"

"I can talk to him and he always listens. Most people prefer to just talk..."

"What did you tell him, just now?"

"That you too are a friend of mine," he looked at the departing beast. Then he turned to me, the old spark back in his steely blue eyes. "When we hugged each other, he wasn't sure that you were not attacking me. He came to make sure that I was all right."

"You're joking," I grinned.

"Ask him!"

"I would rather not, if you don't mind. And what was all that holding you close to his ear all about?" I was humouring my friend.

"Well, you see, when elephants hear things, they assume automatically that it reaches them through their ears. And since the subliminal communication comes over as a whisper, they think that if you're close to their ear, they'll hear you better." Yeshûa replied keeping a straight face.

Another giant shadow hovered over my head. I doubted Yeshûa would have time to save me this time. As I closed my eyes, menacing darkness closed in....

I'm still alive. From half-closed eyes I see the cloud already passing. It shielded the sun. At least for a moment. It must be close to noon. In an hour or so, a girl would bring me some water. A girl, a woman, a maiden? I wonder if she's one of the chosen twelve from Mount Carmel. Ah, yes. She'd definitely be a woman by now. A mother of many children. Whoever she is, I know I can count on her. For water.

I never learned if Yeshûa had been joking or been serious, regarding that elephant. I do know one thing. I've spoken to a dozen elephants since that time. And not one, ever, embraced me with his trunk to hold me close to his or her ear. Perhaps I spoke more distinctly than Yeshûa. Or maybe the other elephants spoke a different dialect. We have so many of them. He'll never tell me. It's too late now. I suppose I'll never know.

The crowd was gathering slowly but with determination. Most of the men were half-naked, a get-up appropriate in the sweltering heat. Women didn't dare to emulate their menfolk. Their flowing saris flitted and mingled like colourful butterflies within the mahogany forest. The air seemed to vibrate, shimmering as I've seen it do occasionally on my travels, over large paved areas. Like in a Roman theatre. Only here, it was everywhere. Even the water was tepid to the touch, though still cooler than almost everything else.

The speaker was a man revered by many. Tall, his skin baked dark by the relentless sun; he was evidently oblivious to the heat. In some ways he also seemed oblivious to the crowd, which parted before him as if it were moved by a magic wand. I was reminded of Moses parting the Red Sea. Only this sea was made up of people. I've never seen so many people in one place. Finally, the sage arrived at the water's edge. He waded into the slow moving current up to his waist, dipped himself, including his head, then came out to stand with his ankles still in the water. The gray, ashy paint adorning his face was waterproof. It did not come off, nor even smear. It was his badge of office. The insignia of his profession.

He was the renowned Swami Shivananda.

Yeshûa and I managed to scale the upper branches of a magnificent banyan tree to listen. We shared the limbs with many natives, mostly youngsters, who gave us dirty looks. They evidently thought the upper branches of the ancient banyan have been reserved for them, for the youth agile enough to reach them. We may have made a mistake. Should we leave before the Swami finished his sermon, we would be forced to tread on hand and limb of those below us.

"Enjoy the view," Yeshûa said. "Never mind if we can hear him. You learn by watching the people, not just by feeding your mind with the thoughts of others."

It took a while before the swarming crowd stopped pushing and pulling for a better vantage point. They sought salvation in the Swami's words. Salvation from the everlasting Wheel of Awagawan. From the suffering imposed on them by their karma. By themselves. Only few of them realized that they, themselves, had been the architects of their fate. Of their karma. Hence, the Swami. And then the Swami raised one hand.

Like a gentle wind, the crowd swayed to face him. The sound of a thousand greetings, farewells and bickering died down to a mere whisper. Then that too had stopped.

"The Ganga was not always here," the emaciated Swami spoke at last. "She lived in Kailash, and she flowed for the pleasure of gods and no other. And if it hadn't been for King Bhagirath, she would still flow only in heaven. But the King pleaded with gods for mercy and purification. Not for himself, but for the sixty thousand sons

of his ancestor who conquered and plundered the
world, as they did even the nether regions, where
Kapila the Hermit with but a single glance re-
duced them to ashes. And thus those thousands
of souls remained beyond redemption. Bhagirath knew that only the purifying waters of the
Ganga could release the souls of the sixty thousand. He begged and prayed for mercy, all to no
avail. It was only after Bagirath beseeched Par-
vati, Shiva's divine consort that, at her interces-
sion Lord Shiva directed the tempestuous currents of the Ganga to flow through his hair, thus
causing millions of streams to descend upon the
earth. The sixty thousand lost souls could now
be revived by the reanimating waters of the goddess Ganga...."

It was about then that the branch upon which we, together with a half-dozen youth, had been sitting, began
bending downward in a grotesquely slow motion. In the
next few seconds the descent toward mother earth seemed to
accelerate, only to slow down again. A miracle, I thought.
My friend must have learned some new tricks.

I was disappointed.

It transpired that this time, twenty or so arms had caught
not only the main branch loaded with too many bodies, but
the side limbs, offshoots and twigs springing from it, and
thus sustained it at arm-length, above their heads. They did
not do so, necessarily, out of the generosity of their hearts,
but rather to protect their heads and those of their wives and
children.

For a moment I thought we might remain in this position. After all, the view was still relatively good, the seating
not too uncomfortable, and there was no particular reason to
change our vantage point.

"Brahma functions in mysterious ways," Yeshûa said,
even as the many hands below us decided that we were taking
unfair advantage of them. With a surprising unanimity they

all stepped aside and allowed the branch to complete its way down with a single motion.

"Wowww, aaaah, oh noooo..." resounded all around us. It wasn't just a question of our own bones, but of the scores of people heretofore below us, who were now pushed one onto another, indeed one over the other, in a single instant.

"I think it may be wise to make a strategic withdrawal," Yeshûa suggested, and not waiting for my answer, he got down on all fours and made his way between people's legs until he reached space enough for him to get up.

"I've tried it before," he said when we both recovered our vertical position. "It is the only way to make oneself invisible in a crowd." His broad grin accompanied this declaration. "Seriously though, are you all right?"

I wasn't. As I landed on the ground, there was a sharp and none too thin twig that wedged itself in the portion of my anatomy I usually reserve for evacuation rather than absorption of extraneous matter. Although I managed to free myself almost instantly from the offensive tail-like prominence, I still felt sore. A hole in my outer garment also advertised a most unstrategic location.

"Get me somewhere where I can rearrange my clothing," I told him. When his face displaced a supercilious grin, I added, "NOW!"

This worked. Some minutes later we were sitting a good distance from the swaying crowd, enough to enjoy our relative solitude. The soreness in my rear quarters seemed to have subsided sufficiently to allow me to sit down in reasonable comfort.

"Why did you take me to that circus?" I asked at long last.

"I told you. I also study people. Their needs and their behaviour."

"Couldn't you read about it?"

Yeshûa smiled. "Can you read about how to conduct a caravan? How to conduct a good negotiation with another trader? You deal with goods and money. I'm... I am learning how to deal with people. I must be among them. Touch their bodies, their auras. Believe me, your people need knowledge no less than my people. But my duty lies elsewhere."

As usual, he'd lost me half-way through his answer.

"What people do you deal with." I never suspected that Yeshûa would be interested in slave trade.

"I touch their bodies, but I try to reach their souls. Their atma. Only our concept of atma is a bit different than yours...." He looked at me as if to check if I was at all interested. "If you attempted to understand our scriptures in its allegorical context, then you'd learn that we have two names for atma. Or at least the entity you call atma is our El. The individualization of Yahweh. But there is also *nephesh*, you might call it an animal soul, which, at least the way I see it, we should attempt to raise to the level of atma. We must bathe it in the Ganga. Purify it. We must raise it to the presence of that within us which is immortal, indestructible, eternal."

I let that sink in. I still had problems with the concept of eternity as against immortality.

"You are quite right. Whatever is immortal cannot have a beginning. What starts must have its end. As the Greeks would say, the Alpha and the Omega. We, as we walk this earth, are the beginning and the end. But within is that which is immortal. It is neither born nor will it ever die. As with your atma. As with the divine presence."

"And just how can we benefit from this knowledge?"

"By identifying with that which is within us. Lord Krishna said as much. Read your Bhagavad-Gita."

I did. I had more than once. Before and since I'd first spoken to him. I suddenly realized that once more he appeared to have been reading my thoughts. No matter. It was long since I had any secrets from him. But many of Yeshûa's words, or concepts, still remained incomprehensible to me. Isn't Lord Krishna a God beyond human comprehension? Isn't He the Personality of God Himself? And then I remembered once more of Krishna's strange affirmation: '*I am the Self, O conqueror of sleep, seated in the hearts of all creatures. I am the beginning, the middle and the end of all beings.'* Could this be what Yeshûa has been talking about? Is Krishna really present within us to the exclusion of all other?

I glanced at my friend. He seemed to be counting the puffy clouds overhead. His eyes were shining with a strange light.

"You are beginning to get it, my friend." And his head nodded with added affirmation. "You are really beginning to get it...."

My mind returned to the Swami's sermon. It seemed that we all need purification. We all descend to the nether regions where we feel trapped and helpless. And the only way we can gain purification is by complete submersion in the river of life.

"I think you are beginning to get it...." I heard, as though from a great distance. Yet surely, he was right beside me.

* * * * *

10

The Awakened One

Most of the memories that had imposed themselves on my tortured mind have been embedded in a thick layer of emotions. I have been there; I saw, I heard, I felt, I witnessed and often shared in various events with my friend Yeshûa. My heart and my senses have been as involved in the fragments of our life together, or even more so, than my intellect. Then, there came a strange reversal. Almost an antithesis of my previous experience. Rather than having participated in the events myself, I seem to recall, just as distinctly, the newly found knowledge that Yeshûa recounted to me after the return from my last journey.

The day of my return was particularly glorious. The sun, the gentle breeze, even the cloud formations participated in the celebrations. In my hometown, Benares, my father and I were greeted by our extended family, as large as a small clan, *matteh*, as Yeshûa called it. He insisted that if things go right, then my great-grandfather will have sired a new race, a nation, which would gradually displace other nations from my immediate vicinity. I would then declare myself a king, better still an emperor, and extract homage from the faithful serfs.

"As for myself, " Yeshûa said with a perfectly straight face, "the least that I shall expect is to be appointed to the royal court as the chief magician, responsible for casting hexes on your enemies."

Even ignoring this last request, enunciating that which must have been considerably less than half-serious, the half that mattered manifested itself in some three hundred people, perhaps more, of all ages, lining the entrance to our estate. I should mention that on my previous trek to the west, I had wedded a young Persian woman who, though remaining behind in our home, has given me renewed energy to hurry back to meet my new son.

Guess what? I named him Yeshûa. What else?

Only we spelled it the Indian way. The wedding itself was an unusual occasion. Normally, as is customary in my country, one's parents arrange for their children to enter into mutually advantageous covenants. Marriages serve to consolidate the family wealth and thus gain advantage over one's neighbour. I had been long overdue for such a commitment. Along the way, I asked my father if he had lined up someone for me.

"What? And have her family fritter away our hard-earned money?" he asked.

I breathed easier. I'd met the Persian girl on the outward leg of our previous trip. She was not only beautiful beyond my wildest dreams, but her sense of humour exceeded that of most people I knew. It was then that we swore eternal love. We confirmed it on my return trip. That's when the wedding took place. It was now two years since we had seen each other. Hopefully, we would be together for the length of our days. Forever.

My father who, until recently, could not stay in one place longer than a few months, began to enjoy sitting on our broad verandah overlooking our estate, with two youngsters waving large, intricate fans to keep him cool, not to mention to keep away an assortment of gnats which infested our outdoors following each rainy season. At the time, it seemed, as likely as not, that I would lead the next caravan on my own. As it turned out, I didn't. But it came to be my father's last.

My wife, Almâs, served him his favourite teas and
tended to his every need in my absence. My mother seemed
too busy running up and down the estate, catering to the
needs of the younger generation. She was evidently deeply
in love with each and every grandchild of hers, to the detriment of my father. Not that we lacked servants. But, with
my mother's constant preoccupations, my wife looked after
dad out of love. When I met my Almâs, I wasn't sure if it
was her sweet nature or her name that I fell in love with first.
In Old Persian her name means a jewel, a diamond to be precise. I have seen and admired many riches in my travels
around the world. Yet never had I seen such a jewel before
she'd entered my heart. Even though my profession was
directed toward making money, I would not swap all the
wealth of Darius for one of her smiles. For me she was the
only jewel that mattered.

These snippets of memory prove to me that I did have a
life of my own. I needed this reassurance from the
moment I sat down here, alone, in this small, secluded
courtyard, with only my memories for company. So far, my
thoughts had only visited the days I'd spent in the company
of Yeshûa. And justly so. He was the motor that charged
my own growth as a man, a husband and later, a father. But
he was so much more than that. What I shared with my old
friend was the desire to be the very best that he or I could be.
It didn't matter that our paths seldom crossed on the turbulent waters of every day living. At least during the latter
years. What mattered was that whenever we met, even if by
accident, neither of us felt any distance formed between us.
It was as though the separation made us grow closer. Almost
from the start, Yeshûa had shared with me his most secret
thoughts. At least I think they were secret. Perhaps he
didn't trust others to take him seriously. Except for Sri
Singh, but Arum Singh was growing old. Very old.

"I visit him once in a while," Yeshûa said after the preliminary embraces and expressions of joy on meeting again. "It would give him great pleasure to see you, my friend," he whispered. He often whispered to me. His words seemed destined for my ears alone.

Since our first journey, my return to India with Yeshûa, Sri Singh lived on his own. Humbly, but lacking little of the creature comforts. Except for one thing. He lived completely alone. He said, he preferred it that way.

"I am too old to adapt to other people's idiosyncrasies," he said the last time I saw him. That was a good few months ago. As for living alone, it must have gone on for some twelve years, which is about as long as I have known Yeshûa. Before that first trip of mine, Arum Singh stayed with us. As my teacher and as father's right-hand man. They are right when they say that time flies. It really does seem like yesterday.

I went to see Sri Singh the very next morning. He lived on the outskirts of town – the far side. It felt that my elephant knew the way on his own. They really do remember. After some heavy arguments, I managed to persuade my old teacher to come back to our estate. In our mansion there was room enough for many more people – rooms built with future generations in mind. And the old man lived alone, with no one to wipe his brow on a hot summer's day. Nor even to bring him a drink of water.

"Thank you my friend," I said to Yeshûa the day after Sri Singh joined us. "How come you always know what is right?"

"It is not I who offered Arumji my own home to live in," he countered.

That was another thing about Yeshûa. He always placed everyone above himself. He had nothing yet remained a giver. He preferred to serve than to be served. To learn than to teach. To laugh, than to cry. And never had I heard him utter a harsh word to anyone. And he seemed to do it all quite effortlessly.

Time moved on....
I see him bending over my sleeping firstborn. The three-year-old awakens, probably under his gaze. He seems instantly intoxicated with joy. When I went to his side, Yeshûa withdrew, ceding to my paternal privilege.

"See Krishna in his eyes," he whispers, looking at Yêsh over my shoulder. "The little ones have the capacity to remember their place of origin."

I never stopped looking. Sometimes I think I did see the serenity that usually eludes this world. Yet it was there, present, in my own son's eyes. Yeshûa did say that Lord Krishna was omnipresent.

"The way of Buddha offers a way out from life's melodrama," Yeshûa said bending close to Sri Singh's ear. We were all relaxing on verandah. Sri Singh sat opposite. He didn't really participate in the discussion, but he liked to look at Yeshûa with fatherly eyes of both pleasure and approval. There were few things dealing with *atma* that the old man didn't already know, but he still liked to listen. He'd also become my son's favourite grandpa. So much so that my own father showed signs of jealously. Almâs sat on my right and Yêsh was playing with his nephews and nieces. There was always a crowd of kids gallivanting over the grounds. It gave the whole place a carefree atmosphere, if you didn't mind the noise. It was one of those evenings when one felt it was good to be alive.

I often had the feeling that Yeshûa's words had been mostly for my benefit. Almâs still confessed to Zarathustra's teaching, but since meeting Yeshûa, she'd never missed a chance to hear him talk. Not all people reacted to Yeshûa's presence in this fashion. I've seen men taking one look at him and walking away. I have no idea why, but I suspect they had something to hide. In Yeshûa's presence, one had the sensation of being stripped naked. That he could see right through you. There was no hiding your deepest secrets. I began to suspect he knew me better than I knew myself.

"And what have you been doing in my absence?" I asked after we finished discussing the family affairs and everyday events.

"I was looking for a way out of life's melodrama," he practically repeated his previous statement.

"Go on?" I encouraged. We all loved listening to him. It wasn't just the wisdom abundant in such a young man, but it was the way he put his thoughts to us that we all found entrancing.

"Almost five hundred years ago, a single man's eyes had been opened. He became the Awakened One. You all know his name. Siddhartha Gautama. For years he'd been confused. Even as we are. After the instant of enlightenment he continued to meditate in the shade of the Bodhi Tree, the tree of enlightenment. In time he wondered if he should be teaching his Dharma to others. 'It is too profound and too difficult to be taught,' he considered. 'It runs too much against the grain of stubborn and all-pervasive delusion. A world so totally caught up in attachment, so used to living in lust and aggression, has too much dust on its eyes ever to be able to perceive the truth that it hides from.' He decided that teaching would come to naught. And then once more he became inspired. 'If I teach, I might help countless beings to liberate themselves from the cycle of suffering.' His compassion prevailed. And thus, as you see, there was power, and light, and compassion in his awakening. But it was his compassion that changed the world."

Yeshûa was leading up to the first insights he'd gained at the feet of a venerable Tibetan monk, Ananda, a lama named after Buddha's close disciple. In my absence Yeshûa had travelled to Nepal at the footsteps of the Great Himalaya, somewhat north of Katmandu. I had been there but once. A thriving settlement formed on a trade route from India to Tibet, China and Mongolia. We picked up, I recall, some rice, sugar and jute – well-sought after further north. It was a fertile valley, but just a short distance north, breathing became an effort, and that only if you could stand the cold.

It struck me that trade opened borders more than any other human endeavour.

For some reason, we've learned in due course, Yeshûa had been instantly accepted into the congregation of monks. Usually, I have been told, the monks were virtually inaccessible to 'outsiders'. But not to Yeshûa. He'd already manifested a peculiar effect on people. I suspect it was his genuine love of man. All men. Men and women alike. It might have been truer to say that he loved humanity, yet he never forgot that humanity, or no matter what segment of it, always consisted of individuals. Even now, on the verandah, each one of us had the impression that he was addressing each one of us directly, specifically. Already before my last trip he'd told me that he saw Buddha in every man. Buddha waiting to be awakened. Waiting to rise above the clouds and experience the glory of the sun. Sometimes I thought he might have discovered Buddha's secret.

"There is no secret," he continued. Again I had an eerie feeling that he'd read my thoughts. "The truth is inscribed in every man. Until we discover it, it is as though we were dead. When the light comes...."

Yêsh ran up the verandah steps and continued toward Yeshûa. He sat on the floor, at my friend's feet, and seemed content just being there. A few seconds later, three more youngsters, and then another two joined them. They formed a semicircle facing Yeshûa. When the last boy came, Almâs thought it was just too much. She rose to her feet and remonstrated with the oldest of the children.

"Take them down there and play, as you always do...."

Yeshûa raised one hand. "Let the little ones come to me. They truly are where I long to enter."

As usual he'd lost me. A moment ago the kids were on the lawn. There was nothing to stop Yeshûa joining them on the grass. No matter. My friend liked to sound mysterious.

And then my eyes fell on old Singh. His face was awash with light. I thought it must have been the setting sun, until I realized that the sun was already around the corner of the house. And then I also realized that the same light seemed to emanate from the children's faces when they were close to Yeshûa. Was Sri Singh becoming a child again?

My friend held each child in turn to his chest, kissed each one and let him go. Without a word they all run down to the lawn again, immediately returning to their interrupted game. It all seemed like some kind of a ritual that had just taken place. Its purpose was beyond me. Only Yeshûa's smile went a long way to explain some of it. The children came to make my friend happy. Apparently, there really was no mystery to it. Their intent seemed clear. And just then, as fate would have it, I remembered Sri Singh introducing me to the name of Sri Krishna. "Krishna means pleasure, my friend," he'd said. "It means All Pleasure."

"They taught me to organize my mind," Yeshûa resumed recounting his trip to Nepal. It all seemed so simple. To attain *prajna* you must understand and think properly. For *shila*, you need to speak, and live right. But to achieve *samadhi*, you require the right effort, right mindfulness and concentration."

I leaned over to my wife. Her local Hindï vernaculars, which included Assamese and Bihari were reasonably fluent, but Almâs still lacked the more esoteric terms. "*Prajna* is wisdom, *shila* morality and *samadhi* is.... "

"Concentration. You might also call it single-mindedness," Yeshûa put in for my wife's sake. "You cannot serve two masters. You either serve your body or your soul. Or one of them will be shortchanged."

"You are saying that we have a choice?"

"Of course. We all have a choice. Otherwise life would be devoid of fun!" He laughed, his face was as filled with joy as the children's faces down on the lawn. But as you make your selection, some of your choices last, others dissipate into thin air."

He noticed my usual lost expression.

"Satya, Satya... my dear friend. When you feed your body, all too soon you are hungry again. But when you feed your *atma*, you never hunger again. Do you not see that?"

I would if only I'd met my atma and.... And the next minute he caught my eye, once again. It must have lasted only seconds, but in that instant of eternity I stood face to face with my atma. I met myself. My true Self. It was but a fleeting moment but I knew that something monumental had just taken place in my life. Only, for once, my friend had been wrong. My hunger had not been sated. If fact, it had just begun.

I convinced Yeshûa to stay with us for a whole week. One night, for some undefined reason I couldn't sleep. I got up quietly so as not to disturb my wife, and tiptoed to the verandah. It must have been close to sunrise, for the eastern sky was already losing its depth of darkness. The stars looked paler, as though they were withdrawing and saving their brilliance for another night.

And then I saw Yeshûa. He was sitting in his now usual *Padmasana*, completely motionless. I sat as quietly as I could, not wanting to interrupt his meditation. At least I presumed that was what he was doing. I was both, right and wrong. Right by my definition of the word, wrong by what he had in fact been doing, or had been attempting to achieve.

After a long while, Yeshûa took a deep breath and greeted me in half whisper.

"I'm sorry, I didn't mean to interrupt...."

"You didn't, my friend. And I wasn't meditating. Not in the usual sense of the word."

It was still too dark to see his face, or at least his expression, but I felt sure it was an expression of contentment. His tone was light-hearted. As if he was about to tell me something funny.

"I was attempting to become my breath," he said.

There was not much I could say about this declaration.

"When you meditate," he went on, "you concentrate on a minuscule portion of reality. Or on some abstract aspect. Whatever it is, it involves your intellect. I was attempting to rise above it, while remaining in full consciousness."

Now that made it perfectly clear.

I sighed. "Nothing confuses me so completely as do your explanations, Yeshûa. It might be better if I merely observed you...."

"And what would you see?"

"Why, yes, of course!" I caught my breath. The images were ephemeral, ethereal in their lightness. I saw a movement of air. A puff of wind. A breeze. A whirlwind resolving itself into absolute peace at its centre. Of course I didn't actually see it. I felt it. I experienced it. And then, with equal suddenness I could see his face. Quite clearly.

"But it is s-s-still d-dark," I stammered. "It is still dark...." The wind was smiling at me.

"You know what I mean?" Suddenly his tone turned serious. "When you look at the walls of a building, can you see what's inside? When you look at the outer cover of a scroll, can you say what is written in it? No, my friend. You do not see me. You see the outside sheath that protects me, a sheath which is forever changing."

"Of course we are changing. But the real self remains...."

"Precisely!"

The rest he told me without words. Apparently there was no need for daylight for his gaze to penetrate my inner being. It was only then, after years of knowing him, day after day, that I realized that whenever he spoke to me, he wasn't addressing that which other people were addressing. He was always communicating with that within me, which, in some strange way was unchanging, perhaps unchangeable.

He was a very strange man.

The next day my wife surprised me. She sat down opposite Yeshûa and studied his face. Then as though out of nowhere she asked: "And what of *nirvana*?"

"Why do you ask me, Almâs? Am I your teacher?"

There was a moment of uncomfortable silence. Yeshûa didn't want Almâs to feel badly.

"You confess your allegiance to the prophet Zarathustra. If so, I cannot help you." There was a suggestion of tears forming in her eyes. She turned her face away. "Your prophet teaches that there is good and evil. I do not accept such a premise."

At that she faced him again.

"Then tell me what must I do to know the truth?"

"Buddha already answered that question," and then Yeshûa took pity on her. "You see, if you accept the existence of evil, you give it reality. But you should never resist evil. Dismiss it from you mind. Expel it from your heart. It has no basis in your *atma*."

The teaching of Zarathustra was complex. It was based on the state of balance between the forces of good and evil. Both have been personified and raised to the level of divinity. Though ultimately the good was deemed to win, that was supposed to happen in the far distant future.

"Your prophet promised to return to earth in nine thousand years. Imagine that nine thousand years have passed. Zarathustra walks among us once more. The coming of the messiah who will provide an example of perfection, he said, shall follow his coming. Imagine that too has come to pass. What now? Now Ahura-Mazda can finally win his battle over the forces of evil. Over Ahriman. What would you believe in if you lived in such a time? Would not your beliefs then allow you to dismiss the existence of evil?"

Time dragged as Almâs studied Yeshûa's face.

"Believe me, my Jewel, there is no evil in you. Unless you chose to allow it into your house."

He used my favourite appellation for my wife. I liked the way he said it. He made it sound like a precious jewel, untouched by the forces of evil.

"When you realize that state, you will have attained *nir-vana..*"

Yeshûa, Sri Singh and I had been walking in the garden. Tomorrow my friend would be leaving. "So much to learn..." was his repetitive excuse. I knew I couldn't hold him, but I did want him to explain to me the problems of duality. He'd mentioned it before, but never expounded on the subject. When we sat down he put his hand on my shoulder.

"Are you sure I'm not boring you, Satya? You are doing so well on your path...."

I understood Lord Krishna's admonitions to Indra. But the thirst in me needed quenching. Yeshûa sighed and smiled rather sadly.

"It is my fault. I gave you wine to drink and now you are thirsty."

But he decided to tell me.

"There are as many paths as there are people in the world. If you don't listen to your atma, you will falter. They all faltered in the past, by trying to share beliefs. Yet, what is right for one man does not suit another. We are created, as my scriptures tell me, unto the image of god. How can anyone impose restrictions on a divine image?"

I glanced as Arumji. His eyes were half closed, contentment was etched on his ancient features. The old man was happy. Happy and, I rather suspect, proud of his favourite pupil.

"The Greeks had no Satan," Yeshûa continued, "no Ahriman nor any other personification of evil. On the other hand, all their gods had been capable of malevolence as well as good. It was a highly unsatisfying condition. Zarathustra preferred to set the two forces apart. Thus, he dispatched his people back into a congress of duality. Mithras later went one better. He refused to accept that evil could balance reality, but the price he paid was stoic indifference to suffering of earthly existence. Nor could Buddha escape it but by the withdrawal of all sensual and emotional desires. By such an action he rejected the efficacy of good as well as evil."

I wish I'd brought with me some paper to make notes.

"By rejecting Satan, the Greek rejected dualism. Yet in their lives, they did not practice what they preached. The only way you can really reject evil is by denying its existence. You, your atma, your life, are a state of consciousness. You alone can decide what factors contribute to your perception of reality. Whatever you believe in will, sooner or later, manifest in your house. Your house is your state of consciousness. It is where you live. It is your world. Be careful what you believe in."

My face must have registered a glimmer, but not full understanding.

"Why do we always look so far from our own village. You have Sri Krishna. You know his name means All Pleasure. Did you ever ask yourself how to become All Pleasure, how to unite yourself with Krishna."

This time I must have looked crestfallen.

"It is quite easy, really. When you align your will with that of your atma, you will have become All Pleasure. Because when all is said and done, there is only one Atma. All of us are but individualizations of that single Consciousness. When you align your self with your atma, you become one with the universe."

The rest I heard from him by some form of direct perception. The problem is, he conveyed to me, that people are always afraid of the unknown. The greatest unknown, to most, is their true self. Their atma. Hence suffering, which Buddha tried so hard to alleviate. The greater the separation, the greater the suffering. The opposite of All Pleasure. This is the true meaning of duality.

I sensed that Yeshûa chose to communicate these concepts to me subliminally because Sri Singh was there. Perhaps the old sage was so set in his ways that he also feared that final step of self-discovery. And he knew the price he was paying.

As for me...?

After this, I felt relieved that I had chosen my path. His was too dangerous. To reject the reality of evil, in some ways, one would have to suspend judgment. Surely, a difficult commitment in this day and age. On the other hand, I could imagine the rewards. I could see them sometimes in the eyes of my son. But only sometimes. He was already three years old.

* * * * *

11

The Way of Dharma

It is one thing to learn about the teachings of the Awakened One, quite another to live by His precepts. The next time I saw Yeshûa, some fourteen months later, he'd just completed a year in a Buddhist monastery. The other two months he'd spent travelling which, in itself, he said, was an experience like no other. To look at him, his face, his rusty curls, which by some means he'd managed to keep trimmed, his posture, his demeanour – nothing appeared to have changed. On the other hand, all things were different, as far as he was concerned.

It was a year ago that Almâs had asked him about nirvana. At the time, to the best of my recollection, Yeshûa described it from the point of view of the teachings he'd received in various monasteries he had visited. Although he'd visited them with total commitment to learning, he did not become a follower of Buddha. His commitment was total but only to learning. He maintained his detachment, he said, to develop an objective knowledge of the Gautama's way, of the method he'd employed to arrive at his personal enlightenment. The concepts he'd conveyed to me later, when he, Sri Singh and I strolled through our garden, did not really come from any particular religion he'd studied. What he'd shared with me, then, were the first seeds of his own personal perception of reality.

"Nirvana," he said on his return, "is not at all the extinction of all sensations one hears about. It is neither death nor a denial of life. It may be so in some respects, but it is also so much more. The life you deny is not the real life, not the life of atma, it is the duality of perception which keeps you from seeing the truth."

He glanced around to see if any one of us followed his words. Sri Singh seemed deep in thought, Almâs was staring at him as though seeing what others could not see, my father was dosing off. Poor father. He was a man of action. A few days of rest after two or three years of travel were all he could stand. Now... now he'd earned his peace. Sometimes he would call me to his side and give me instructions, as though we were in the middle of some desert crossing.

"Watch those camels on the back," he would mumble. "They stray...." And he would leave the sentence unfinished. Perhaps he'd already reached his nirvana. Perhaps he already lived in a reality to which the rest of us had no access.

And then there were, of course, the children. I often wondered if most of them understood more of what Yeshûa said than we did. We, the adults. The youngsters sat, this time a dozen of them, on the floor, cross-legged, two of the older ones attempting to enter the pose of *Padmasana*. I tried the Lotus Seat a hundred times, only to incur such pain as to take me hours to recover. Not the little ones. Yeshûa was their visiting teacher. He was also the beloved uncle. This last was strange. He was the only member of my family, for he was such, who had never given them any tangible presents. No trinkets, sweets nor even money to buy themselves some keepsakes. Yet they ran to him and surrounded him as if he bestowed magnificent gifts on them. Perhaps he did. Perhaps we just didn't know it. Yeshûa had a very peculiar effect on children.

"...it is beyond time." Yeshûa was still talking about nirvana. "You enter into an entirely different existence. You no longer have to overcome desire, or hatred or any of the usual human traits. You are freed from delusion. As for your previous attachments, the needs of your mundane character, you do not give them up. They fall off you like leaves from an oak tree on approaching winter. Effortlessly. Nirvana gives you serenity beyond words. It gives you oneness...."

As he talked, his words rose and fell, gently, as a surge and ebb of the ocean along a sandy shore. For some reason, discussing it later, even the children had the impression that he was both present and absent from our little gathering. His body, they sensed, his power of speech he shared with us. The rest he coalesced with that part of us of which we had not yet been fully aware. I asked my oldest nephew, a lad of eleven years, to explain to me his impression.

"Well, uncle, you do not see one flame when you put it exactly in front of another, do you?" he asked for confirmation. I nodded. "Well, uncle," he repeated, evidently unsure of himself, "so our own light seems obscured yet strangely alive within his. I mean, I know, really know it is there, I just don't see it...."

He wanted to run and play. I suspected I could have learned more from him, but I let him go. I probably wouldn't understand half of what he had to say.

As I'd noticed on some occasions before, Yeshûa appeared to have addressed our atma. That part of our being which can never forget, which really already knows, but must find a way to convey this knowledge to the rest of our awareness. He seemed to be the way, the bridge or the door, through which we could enter his inner world of wonder and enchantment.

"When you cross the bridge," his own eyes were filled with wonder as he continued to address our little gathering, "you come into a world of infinite possibilities. There are no barriers. No restrictions. Reality is at your disposal. It is your playground to do with as you choose."

We sat spellbound. No one stirred. Even my father was staring at Yeshûa as though seeing him for the first time. In a way he did, see him for the first time, I mean. Yeshûa's

path was so different from my father's that the two had never
really talked. Even now, I felt, my father had no idea why he
was so fascinated by my friend's words. As indeed I was,
and I've heard him a thousand times. Yeshûa radiated such
total commitment to the path he'd chosen that he was like an
expansive mountainous current sweeping all in its path,
wrenching and grasping and carrying all with him to some
unknown destination. It was this destination that he attempted to describe to us. If only we could really understand his words.

How many times have I already expressed this desire?
If only I could really understand his contention. For what
mattered, I felt sure, were not his words as such, but the substance behind them. Yet for that I, at least, had to wait.

The next day Yeshûa could not be coaxed into sharing
with us any of his insights. He gave an impression of being
carefree and acted likewise. He joined us in walks through
the garden, ate fresh fruit, drank wine, and played with children as though he was one of them. Later in the day, Almâs,
my precious jewel, two of my brothers with their wives and I
decided to take a stroll toward the town of Benares. Our estate was no more than a half-hour's walk to the river Ganga.
Usually there were wisps of fog hugging the meandering
course of the sacred current. Today we were lucky. Even
the dampness of the air was less obtrusive. As a rule, even
for such a short distance, we were accustomed to riding elephants. But Yeshûa loved walking.

"Lately I've spent so much time in *Padmasana* that
walking gives me sensual pleasure," he confessed.

There were always some people gathering at the banks
of the Holy River, hoping for purification, relief from stress,
from life's tribulations. Their faces invariably looked tired,
haggard, perhaps from a far journey, perhaps from what lay
heavily in their hearts.

I glanced at Yeshûa. His face, usually so filled with joy
and laughter, was obscured by an invisible cloud. His eyes
seemed to sweep over the mass of people, from left to right,

then back again, his hands following his eyes. He looked as though he was searching for someone. Then his arms dropped limply at his sides. His face grew even sadder.

"What is it, my friend?" I couldn't help asking.

He didn't answer at once. We continued walking until we passed the crowds who seemed lost in a desperate quest to quench their needs. They waded into the pensive waters, some just stood still – perhaps deep in thought, others floated or moved up and down, all ostensibly happy to have reached the Holy Ganga.

"They search for *el ixîr*," he pronounced it the Arabic way, "in the murky waters," and for the first time since getting to the river he smiled. "Indeed, they can find it. Is not Lord Krishna omnipresent?"

I wasn't sure if he was serious or joking.

"But if they only knew, they would find him within themselves, within their own hearts. There is no more Krishna nor Vishnu in the Ganga than anywhere else. All they need is Awakening."

So he does side with Buddha's way, I mused, seeing my friend's frown.

"I do not side with anyone, Satya. We are all one. How can I side with the particular when the universal is present? Does not my right hand know what my left hand is doing?"

He then turned as if to address all six of us.

"There is no right way or wrong way. All paths lead to fulfilment. It cannot be otherwise. You might travel one path in this life, another in the next. Only when you absorb them all have you a chance for success."

Almâs looked up sharply.

"Yes, Almâs," he said immediately. "Even the path of Zarathustra. You cannot travel a path you are not ready to absorb. It is not that one is better than another. It is what you are unable to get from it. To get all it has to offer. You never fail the path. It is the path that fails you, if you are not ready for it." She seemed satisfied with that. I wasn't.

"We all receive according to our ability to assimilate. According to our nature," he said looking at me.

That made sense. It sounded convincing.

We were now past the town centre. There were fewer people, not as many beggars and their counterparts – the aspiring gurus – attempting to sell their particular points of view. We all have to eat, I thought, but those who wish to teach others should have at least something or some consolation to offer. My friend Yeshûa refused to give public lectures. I had people asking me to ask him. By some means or another, during the last year or two, his name was being whispered on the streets of Benares. Lately the whispers grew into an intense murmur.

"That is why I must be constantly on the move," he smiled, "or hide in a monastery. Your estate is also like a castle to me. It is the only place where I am known yet allowed to just be. Other than among the followers of Buddha. Even in ashrams I am expected to talk rather than to listen. Somehow news of me has spread. We are reaching the time when I shall join you on a greater journey."

This caught me by surprise. In India we refer to the greater journey as transmigration, an incarnation into a new body. Before I said anything I noticed his broad grin. Instantly I knew why.

"You want to leave India?" I asked, still surprised but no longer in a state of panic.

For some reason the idea sounded preposterous. Yeshûa had lived here for, by far, the greater part of his life. He grew up here. We fished in the Ganga together. We swam in the ponds and climbed local hills and trees and then he ... he began leaving on his own. Yet I thought of him as my brother. It sounded absurd. I had four brothers and as many sisters. Yet it was Yeshûa without whom I could not imagine India. It would become empty. I know it sounds absurd but such thoughts welled in my mind.

"I shall always be with you, my friend. Are we not brothers?"

Was he reading my thoughts again, or did he feel the same way about me as I felt about him?

"You, Satya, are the only man I ever met with whom I feel at ease. Perhaps it is that you never asked me for anything. Other than what I expected of you. Friendship. You are the only man with whom I can share my innermost thoughts without fear that you'll create a religion around me and start calling me Swami or guru. Most people I love in spite of what they are, you I love for being just you."

It is embarrassing for a grown man to be seen crying. Yet Yeshûa had the capacity to melt me as butter melts in the midday sun. I felt inadequate, unable to reply. He put his arms around me. Held me as he would a child.

I felt like one. Perhaps that was why he loved me.

"The Way of Dharma is not a simple one," Yeshûa said when we were alone. "Different teachers have given me various definitions or different meanings. It concerns the law, the principle underlying rebirth as determined by one's karma. It also means the teaching of the Awakened One, yet the knowledge was there before he'd awakened. It also defines the norms of behaviour, particularly of the monks. And there is more, much more."

There were times, albeit rare of late, when Yeshûa liked to sit with me and just talk. He wasn't preaching, nor even teaching. It sounded more as though he was arranging thoughts in his own head. I was no more than a sounding board. My occasional questions, even facial grimaces never went unnoticed. Perhaps that's what I was there for. It seemed that he needed to be heard and to see what echoes, both verbal and emotional waves, he stirred in the psyche of another man. It could be that he was planning, ultimately, to share his findings with more than just one person. If that was so, than I felt proud and privileged to serve in whatever way possible.

On this occasion I did not interrupt him, but already the complexities of Dharma created a barrier for me. I found the teaching of Krishna, particularly as promulgated by the Bhagavad-Gita, much easier to absorb. It seemed more related to my heart than my mind. The Way of Dharma was beginning to sound too much like a mental exercise.

"You think so?" This was Yeshûa interrupting himself.

Lately he'd been reading my thoughts without so much as an apology. He knew I didn't mind, of course. I'd learned long ago that it would have been useless to try and hide my innermost feelings, let alone my thoughts. Not that Yeshûa did that with everybody. At least he didn't strike me as doing so. At no time had I seen any evidence, any noticeable reaction, directed at any members of my family.

There were advantages to it. On a number of occasions he'd let me know that a particular decision I was about to make would not work out the way I'd expected. At first I thought that he had the gift of prophecy. That over the years he'd spent studying the human potential, he'd uncovered the secret of knowing the future. He denied me instantly.

"Only God can do that," he assured me. He used the Hebrew word for god. He did this more often lately. "No one can know the future. It would be paramount to the denial of free will. What we can do, however, is to project the known factors forward, and be fairly accurate in whatever effect any one action could have within the fabric of space and time."

I'd never heard such an expression before. I said as much.

"Space is the matrix against which all things happen. Time is what stops all things happening at the same time."

"What?!" I recall exclaiming so loud that my wife who was playing on the lawn with our children looked up. "It's all right, dear!" I remember saying to her as I waved.

"Seriously," Yeshûa resumed. "Time is not an absolute. The way I see reality, and this is only my perception, is that all ideas already exist as patterns, ready for us to convert through our minds and emotions into material reality. I say material because if you think of yourself as sick, chances are that you soon will be. Thoughts are like little workers who combine elements suspended in a higher realm into tangible forms. You remember Socrates' concept of ideas? Well, it is something on those lines."

I sat up. Yeshûa was in the process of combining the sum total of what he's learned into...

"...into what exactly? I mean, what exactly are you...."

"...trying to do?" Once again his extraordinary smile lit up the space between us. "Why, discover the truth, of course. If we assume that that which is – is, that you are – what you seem, that the world really exists, then we must assume that we are born to understand it."

"But...?" I put in on the off chance of being right. There is always a but.

He didn't bat an eyelid. "The but is that we cannot use mind to know mind. We have to rise above the limitations of our intellect to know. To perceive fully. And then we are no longer that which we were."

"A sort of vicious circle?" I was beginning to feel sorry for my friend.

"I hope not...." He wouldn't say any more.

I waited a while for him to continue. Finally I got up to stretch my legs. He did likewise.

"Let's go and ask Arum," he said, his voice sounding perfectly serious.

He wasn't referring to our old teacher. Arum was also the name of my second son. He was just four months old. Judging by Yeshûa's expression, he was bound to know.

With the sun directly above me, an angel in a blue flowing robe descends from heaven to offer me a large jug of water. Actually, I expect water yet it turns out to be a most delicious and refreshing juice of pomegranates. My parched throat relishes its coolness. She must have kept it in some cellar, well underground, for it to be so cool. I take another deep gulp. Then as unexpectedly as she came, she sits down next to me. For some reason she waits for me to speak first.

"Thank you," I mutter, "how can I ever repay you?"

The word I used did not mean 'with money.' It referred to my having incurred a debt, which I wished to discharge. By service or in any other way. When the caravan finally gets here, I shall have an ample supply of silks, muslin and other merchandise that might please her. To please all of them. For some reason whenever I come to see Yeshûa, the thought of money never enters my mind. When I come to see him, for some equally strange reason, I am usually penniless.

"You knew the Master?" Her voice comes shyly from under her scarf. Her eyes are fixed firmly on her bare feet.

For a moment I am lost. Master?

"Yes," the shekel drops. "Yes, I know the mas... I mean I knew Yeshûa. He was a friend of mine."

She nods. "I know. That is why you are here."

She's right, of course. There is no other reason.

"Tell me about Him," she whispers.

I am a little taken aback. I thought that these were his people. The people he'd lived with. All the time. Well, at least the last three years. I must have mulled over that for a while because I hear her voice, again hardly above a whisper.

"Please...."

Whatever pain I thought I felt, hers seems deeper. Much deeper. Perhaps she was in love with him. Perhaps she loved him. We all did....

"I met him when he was just twelve.... A scruffy lad hiding from some men wielding sticks..." I start. And all the memories come flooding back like the current of a mighty river that won't be denied. The next moment we are both crying. Like little children.

Time passes slowly. The sun refuses to hurry its lazy journey across the pale blue sky. There was a little mist earlier but now it's gone. The sun took care of it. It will be hot today. Soon I'll walk to the other side of the yard and sit against the west wall. It will be cooler there. All is as it should be. The sun, the sky, the baked earth, the walls, the street... there is a bird chirping. I wish I had some crumbs to throw him. I don't. Disappointed, he flies off. Nothing has changed. I remember his words: till heaven and earth pass away, not one tittle shall pass from the law – till all be fulfilled.

"Did he really say that he was the king of the Jews?" I ask. It seems better to talk. The memories are kept at bay. For a little while.

"No. He said he was the Son of God." She lowers her head when she says that.

It doesn't sound like a direct answer, but after some thought, I find that it is. What better reason for an orthodox Jew to kill a man than to accuse him of sacrilege? What better man to kill than he who blasphemes? Surly, not knowing Yeshûa, they must have taken his statements as such. Had he spoken against the god they'd created in their own image? A vengeful god? Not even the god of Isaiah. How many times had he told me that we are all children of the Infinite Potential? I suppose that's as close to god as the Hebrews could get.

"Yes, he did say that," I agree. "Though he did put us all in the same playpen. Did you know that?"

She looks up and stares at me as though seeing me for the first time. Her face is still showing strain and deep sorrow. By some miracle she manages a smile.

"You really did know Him," she says.

And that's all she says. She seems content to sit next to one who not only met her Master, but really knew him.

"Didn't you all know him?" I ask quietly. I don't want to offend her. It is good not to be sitting alone for a change.

"No," she says, sadness returning to her voice. "No... most of us didn't know Him at all." A single tear rolls down her cheek. She remains silent but her import is obvious. At least to me. What her tear is saying: "And now it's too late."

Next week Yeshûa left our estate. I did not speak to him again for three months, at which time he'd asked me if, perchance, he might be able to join me on my next trip West. I couldn't believe my ears.

"You and I together....? Like in the old days!"

"Not quite Satya. Now you are Sahib Bihari," he said with a slight bow.

I reached out and embraced him. "And you are Sahib Yeshûa. My friend."

We stood locked in a bear hug – remembering. So many memories, so many bits and snippets of memories came to mind. The headlong dive into my tent, in Jerusalem. The apple he'd caught with one hand. The tree breaking under our weight. The....

"I think people are looking..." Yeshûa murmured.

"What? Ah, yes!" I released my embrace. "I j-j-just can't b-b-believe my good fortune," I stammered. I've never stammered before. And then a thought struck me that eliminated all happiness from my heart.

"You are coming back, aren't you?"

But I shouldn't have asked. I think I knew the answer to that question before it left my lips.

"Only He knows the future," Yeshûa pointed to the sky. And then he must have noticed the expression on my face. "Satya, we have a year together ahead of us. Day in and day out. Is that so hard for you to stomach?"

He made me laugh. Even now.

"Only you must find a worthy function for me," Yeshûa said, his voice insistent. "I am told that I am quite good at washing the beasts of burden. Particularly the elephants. I refuse to reincarnate myself just to pay you some rupees for my keep...."

* * * * *

12

Satyajit Sahib Bihari

For the next few months I was very busy. Extremely so. I had to organize my own caravan to Egypt. I had never taken the sea route, and the thrill of the unknown was almost more than I could contain while maintaining a degree of decorum expected of the leader. I recall when some of the men I'd first hired addressed me as Sahib Bihari. I looked over my shoulder expecting my father to be standing behind me. I found it hard to believe that, at the age of barely thirty, I would lead my own caravan, and by a route which my own father, a trader known across the civilized world, had never done himself. I have taken shorter trips, of course, a number of times. I've led men to destinations many weeks, even months, distant from our home. My father didn't make his fortune on international trade alone. He catered to his own vast country. And he made sure that I followed in his footsteps. But this? This was breaking new ground. New waters, to be more precise.

Some months ago, my father had decided that he would no longer take charge of any specific caravans. Since Rome had expanded its borders, trade followed, growing on such a scale that he'd spent all his time organizing, coordinating and expediting different groups of men and animals to diverse destinations. The rest of the time he spent in deep thought on our verandah. In fact, he seldom left his favourite porch. It became his office, his throne, his seat of power from which he would issue orders never doubting that they would be carried out. He kept busy. In addition to an abundance of local trading, there were the Silk and the Spice Routes and lately the Incense Route, which promised great rewards.

He organized armies of young and sturdy Bactarian camels at various points along the way to carry the wares across all sorts of varied terrain. The added advantage of the Bactarian camel was that the animals felt equally at home on sand as they did on snow. In addition, they required very little maintenance. For the established Trade Routes, they became indispensable. Where and when necessary, he had men who would take charge of the beasts of burden and transfer the wares onto other, fresh animals to save on delivery time. Time mattered. The trade across difficult terrain was of first come first serve profit basis. If you arrived a week after your competitor, you might have to wait two or three months before the market developed, once again, for the goods you had been carrying.

Further more, it was no longer practical to take very long 'personal' trips. It was easier to form alliances with other caravan leaders, and swap goods at shorter intervals. You had to trust your people, of course. And that is why, probably for the last time, when breaking into new markets, I would travel the whole distance to Egypt. It was a question of developing contacts we could trust. My father knew exactly what he was doing.

I didn't. Well, not really.

Although I would never admit such a weakness to my father, let alone to any other member of my family. Almâs must have known, of course, but her loyalty was beyond question. Anyway, she claimed that I was the smartest man in India. Probably the world. Dear Almâs. She so hated to be left behind. Yet she has never complained. As for her opinion of me, I did little to dissuade her sentiments. Dreams never hurt anybody.

Furthermore, only one of my brothers had attended two previous caravans, and thus I was rather short-handed in the choice of lieutenants. Of men in whom I had total trust – as dad had once in Sri Singh, and later, I dare say, in myself. In some ways, this may have been better. Had there been a number of candidates, there might have been jealousies coming to the surface. As it was, Dhanesh, only one year my junior, was the obvious choice. He didn't worry about his future, probably because his name, in my language, meant 'lord of wealth.' In India, we pay great attention to names. Or to their meanings. My own, Satya, is an abbreviation of Satyajit, meaning 'victory of truth.' In my country, total strangers would know that. My name could as easily have stood for Satyamurty – 'stature of truth,' Satyavrat – 'one who has taken vow of truth,' or even Satyendra – 'lord of truth.' But all guessed that one way or another I must be a trustworthy individual.

That's me!

By taking the trip with me, Dhanesh's portion of family wealth increased proportionately. There were dangers involved in travel. Sea or land. My other brothers made sure to remain busy assisting my father to avoid such risks. Frankly, my father needed considerable assistance. He still was the brain, but my siblings were his arms. And legs. And swords when necessary. Dhanesh was more of a free spirit. His company would be great to have. Even now that I knew Yeshûa was coming with us.

Originally we planned to go west as far as the Indus River, and then descend toward the port Barbarcon. It wasn't the best route over land, but I was hoping to renew a contact we developed some years ago. From there we would take sail to Kana on the north shore of the Arabian Sea and then, with a bit of luck, sail on to Muza before deciding by which route to continue. On the way we would pick up and dispose of goods, as per market demands.

We had to leave in time to catch the prevailing off-shore winds. While I expected to have a minimum of twenty oarsmen, plus steersmen, the sail was a much-preferred means of propulsion. With favourable winds, the oarsmen needed less food and drink, and the atmosphere on the whole trip would be one of camaraderie. So I've been told. I have also been told that the prevailing monsoons would get me to my destination faster than any land route.

A week before our departure, all was ready. Yeshûa had spent the last four days in our house, a celebration enjoyed equally by all. He asked me not to tell them that he might not be coming back. He wanted to leave on a joyful note. Weather permitting, we spent the last evenings on the verandah, chatting and joking. Once or twice, Yeshûa had been coaxed into sharing with us some of his thoughts.

I wanted him to tell us what he thought of India. After so many years, I tended to forget that he came here from a far and very different country. Indeed, we had all forgotten. He spoke our language without a trace of an accent. In fact he could hold his own in Assamese, Bengali, Bihari, Marathi, Punjabi, Hindustani, Lahnda, and one or two other Hindï dialects which I had considerable problems understanding myself. And I was the linguist in our family! I knew from Sri Singh that he also had a thorough command of Vedic, Sanskrit and Prakrits, including their older Pali versions. He must have been well versed in Pali Literature to gain his intimate knowledge and understanding of Buddhism. I rather hoped he still retained his command of Hebrew and Aramaic.

He also ate our food and knew our customs, both social and religious, by heart. Outwardly, he was as Hindû as anyone of us. To us he was Bihari. A member of our family. Clan, perhaps. Well, except for that curly reddish hair and the blue eyes, of course. But it has been a long time since anyone of us associated those traits which anything foreign. I noticed a number of maidens who, over the years, gazed at him, unabashedly, probably having children with a reddish halo of natural curls in mind.

"Just how would you sum up your first visit to India," I asked, trying to sound as flippant as possible. Whatever my misgivings, I decided to keep them to myself.

"India is a vast and mysterious country. It is also beautiful, full of contrast, rich beyond my wildest dreams. But the greatest treasures you have are your people."

I wasn't the only one who looked up at this.

"You are very kind," Arumji smiled, speaking for all of us. He seldom took part in any discussions these days. Yeshûa's presence was the exception. I suspect that he was also the only one who sensed that Yeshûa was not alluding to material wealth.

"Their riches lay in areas other than gold and precious stones. Their wealth is born of necessity. People are often so poor that they have to substitute an act of faith for the so-called reality, in order to survive. I've witnessed men and women survive on next to no sustenance, for extended periods of time. Buddhist monks are a good example of this. Often not even a single bowl of rice keeps their body and soul together. They survive on literally nothing."

He looked at me making sure that I believed his words. Also, I felt, knowing my friend better than the others knew him, he wanted to make sure that no one would take it as a criticism of our family fortune, which was very extensive indeed. He firmly believed that everyone must walk a different path. Those lumbered with material wealth, he'd once told me, are travelling a much harder road. They have greater temptations, and particularly greater distractions. From what? From the journey which ultimately we all must take.

"By my old scriptural definition, these people perform miracles. Only... in reverse. They do not manifest new reality, they survive on sustaining the process itself."

He lost me again. Only Arumji nodded, the others looked at Yeshûa doing their best to absorb his words. My father's face was skewed up as though he'd just eaten a lemon. 'Why can't he talk like other people,' he seemed to be saying. 'I really do want to understand him. He doesn't make it any easier by speaking in riddles.'

"Can you say that..." I was searching for the right word, "in layman's terms?"

He looked at me for a while. Then his face lit up.

"You are a swordsman," he said as though remembering the old days. I don't know how he knew because when we travelled together we were boys. Swordsmanship had been left to men. Later I did fend off many a marauder, but he wasn't there with me. He remained in India studying his... whatever he was studying.

"I am now," I confirmed.

"Didn't you ever ask yourself why you always win, even against, often, absurd odds against you?

I did survive. "I must have been better at my craft." I asserted, with not a little pride.

"You sure that was all? Just better at your craft?"

"Well," I had no idea what my friend was driving at, " I assume it was. It never crossed my mind that I might loose...."

Yeshûa continued looking at me without another word. Slowly, as though emerging from a deep sleep the truth was beginning to dawn on me. I'd won because I believed I would. Not even the slightest shadow of doubt ever entered my mind. There was no alternate solution. It was the way it should be. I had to win and therefore I did. I was protecting not just my goods but the wares of others. Sometimes people's life savings.

"Are you telling me that I couldn't lose?"

"Oh, you could, and would, my friend. If even for one second you'd lost your faith." He then looked across the verandah. "In *yourself*," he added accentuating the pronoun.

"So it was not my skill...."

"Of course it was. A man cannot act without skills. You learn walking as a baby. That is a skill. The learning process never stops. But your consciousness, your life force cannot use skills you do not possess. At least, not all at once, and certainly not to the same degree."

"Which explains why some people with lesser skills still survive..." My father put in. His voice sounded reserved, but his eyes showed that he was drawn into the discussion. And then, as though on command, we all looked down on the lawn. The children were playing with the usual total commitment to their game. Nothing mattered, but the game itself.

"And that's what you discovered about India?" My father spoke after some minutes.

"I've learned a great deal from you, Sir, and from your grandchildren."

At this dad's head shot up, his chin jutted forward, his cheeks took on a pinkish hue. Father was undeniably delighted. Could it be that he too yearned for Yeshûa's approval? My dad, the hard-nosed businessman? Yeshûa was either kind, or a shrewd politician.

"Both you and the children always put all you've got into the game. You all manifest total commitment to whatever the cause. This, Sir, is a prerequisite of any success."

"Aah, yes," my dad muttered. "I suppose I did do that..." And his cheeks turned even redder with satisfaction. "I dare say I did..." he added, as though to himself.

There was one game only that Yeshûa had played for as long as I've known him. He'd spent years searching for the meaning of life. He'd examined his game from so many different points of view that sooner or later he would find his way into its heart. And then into our hearts. Then minds. Or the other way round. I lost track of which came first.

"They are really the same thing," Yeshûa smiled his old, boyish smile, as if he was playing a joke. "We tend to dissect ourselves into so many parts that we forget who we really are."

We all rose at dawn. Not just the men I was taking with me, but the whole clan. For some reason the occasion seemed more festive that the usual departures. I strongly suspected it may have had something to do with Yeshûa's going home. As for my friend, he was sitting on a knoll to the left of the house with a dozen or more children looking up at him as he was performing some tricks. He'd done that sort of thing before. From somewhere he kept producing small coins, and then made them appear in some of the children's hands. They were of very small denomination, but the fun was in guessing which child held the silver piece.

When I got closer I realized that on this occasion, something a bit different was going on. The children had been told to keep their little fists closed and try very hard to imagine a coin inside their closed hand. The scream of joy at each successful discovery was ear splitting.

"I hope you don't mind," Yeshûa said when I got closer. "I came into a little good fortune and I thought the little ones might enjoy sharing it with me." He said that with an oversized wink.

There was one other thing that I recall about that game. While to me Yeshûa's game looked and sounded like some sort of magic, the children behaved as though it was perfectly natural. They really did expect to find a coin in their little closed fists if they managed to imagine it hard enough. It is amazing what flights of fancy children are capable of, I thought at the time. Some months later I learned that the good fortune Yeshûa had acquired was another piece of the puzzle. A puzzle he called reality.

It was a small caravan. Its purpose being not so much to acquire wealth as to develop new contacts. This left me with less responsibility for the material aspects of the venture. I expected that by the time we reached the Barbarcon, on the Arabian Sea, we would have exchanged a number of items for other goods, ever mindful of the variety, which the local and the next market had to offer.

A day before our departure, there was a change of plans. When Yeshûa heard that there was an alternative way to arrive at our destination, the seacoast, by going through the city of Mathura, he contrived to look so miserable that I burst out laughing. Missing the opportunity to visit the famed shrine must have been painful to contemplate.

"There is a change of plans," I announced. When Sahib Bihari announces a change of plans everyone listens. Everyone under my command, that is.

"We shall proceed by way of Mathura, and then make for the harbour of Barygaza."

What followed was veritable pandemonium. There were shouts of joy, loud cheers and a general feeling of festivity. It transpired that everyone preferred to go by way of Mathura, and not only for its religious blessings. Although the route through Mathura meant veering east-north-east in the direction of Pruyag, and cutting through the Kushan Empire before turning south, the route was well-travelled, frequented more often, easier, and thus safer. Travelling on elephants would also offer additional safety against the Kushan horsemen. Not that my men shirked danger. But only a fool chooses the more dangerous route without hope of reasonable rewards. Thanks to Yeshûa's acting ability I would not be taken for a fool.

It so happened, that father knew a man in Barygaza with whom we could leave the elephants. He was a local dealer, local on the sea shore, who, by his emissary late last year, had already expressed interest in such cooperation. Thus, we would follow the main route to Mathura in the district of Brajbhoomi, where, according to a legend, Sri Krishna had been born and spent his youth. Although Mathura, a town on the river Yamuna, was lying on the main trading route, it was better known for its religious tradition than as a trading centre. Some years ago it had been an important metropolis and the capital of the Surasena Kingdom. It had passed its golden age some three hundred years ago, under the Kushanas, and before that under the enlightened rule of Emperor Ashoka.

There are many places in India saturated with history, but Yeshûa's interest lay in the myth of Lord Krishna. I was glad I could offer this last gift to my friend. Who knows what the future might bring? From Mathura, once Yeshûa had his fill of history, we would bear south to Barygaza, the harbour on the river Narmada, known for its richness of trade. It was a city on the newly opened routes of both the Silk and the Spice trade. Ships from here sailed to and from Arabia and Africa, and even from as far as Europe. In addition the Romans brought there their onyx stones, while we, the local people, supplied them with murrhine.

The *haudah*, a litter carried on top of my elephant, was protected by a colourful canopy against the overhead sun. It was large enough to accommodate two passengers in relative comfort. This would give Yeshûa and me ample opportunity to catch up on the last few months.

We first travelled together in one of these contraptions while on our first trip together, some sixteen or seventeen years ago. I recalled that the Arab traders who had come with us called it *haudaj*. I remember this detail, because the trader's haudah had been filled to the brim with merchandize. The traders walked beside their beasts. That first litter, which Yeshûa and I shared, was less ornate, but the basic structure was the same. Of course then, the elephant was much smaller though it looked much bigger. Funny how age changed one's perception of scale.

"It changes our perception of reality, my friend," Yeshûa nodded peaking into my thoughts.

On the third day out Yeshûa started fidgeting with a hopeful expression on his face. Not that you have that much room to fidget atop an elephant.

"I don't suppose you know much about the myths of Sri Krishna?" he started.

I knew it was coming. Although every Hindû knows the legends, I took the precaution of polishing up my knowledge with Sri Singh some weeks before departure. I had been weighing the pros and cons of taking the Mathura road for some time. The only reason I'd originally ruled against it was that it did not really break any new ground. Originally I'd heard the story of Sri Krishna and Mathura before my very first caravan. I couldn't have been more than ten years old. What kept me abreast were my children. Usually it is the wife's prerogative to teach the children of myth and religion, but she still adhered to the teaching of Zarathustra. It fell upon me to bring our children up on our fundamental history. And the story of the birth of Krishna was very much a part of it. Once we decided to take the Mathura route, it wasn't hard to figure out what was coming. And this time, Sri Singh wasn't there to satisfy Yeshûa's insatiable curiosity.

As we moved at a leisurely pace toward Lord Krishna's birthplace, I told Yeshûa, as best I could, about the ancient legend. His face reminded me of the boy's rapt attention, the boy I'd seen so many times sitting motionless, when Arumji was recounting, for us both, various historical anecdotes.

"They say that Sri Krishna was born in Dvapura-yuga. Traditionally, the present Kali-yuga is said to have begun some three thousand years ago. Scholars like Arum Singh will tell you that it must have been much further back, in the mists of time so ancient that we can't even imagine. Whatever you choose to believe, Sri Krishna was born in the yuga preceding the present one. It was also known as the...."

"Sir Singh told me about those," Yeshûa interrupted. "According to the Vedic system, 'time' is a manifestation of the Supreme Being. The units of time occur in multiples of 432,000 years in the Golden, Silver, Bronze and the present Iron ages. Only there are four such multiples in the first, three in the second, two in the third and, luckily for us, only one in the present."

"Shouldn't you be teaching me?" I asked in all seriousness.

"I much prefer to listen. One learns so much more that way," he gave me a mischievous grin. "But the part I like," he added nevertheless, "is the duration of our lives in the various sections. Apparently, in the Satya-yuga our life span was one hundred thousand years. It shrunk to ten thousand years in the Treta, and a mere one thousand years in the Dvapura-yuga."

"And now we are limited to one hundred years, if we are only so lucky!" I knew of no one who lived that long. "Anyway, all the yugas together add up to 4,320,000 years. And that my friend, is but one day of Brahma! Nevertheless, the last incarnation of Lord Vishnu, namely Sri Krishna, may have lived a really long time, but we have no records confirming or denying his life-span."

"It's strange, you know," Yeshûa said pensively, "that in the Torah a number of ancients are reputed to have lived around a thousand years. That would place them in Dvapura-yuga."

"You're kidding," I really thought he was just showing off.

"Well, for what it's worth, Abraham died at a mere one hundred and seventy-five, which would put him somewhat later by your reckoning. But Adam was said to have lived nine hundred and thirty years, Seth nine hundred and twelve, Enos nine-oh-five, Cainan nine-ten, Mahalalleel eight-ninety-five...."

"All right!" I couldn't help exclaiming. "All right," I added in a more normal tone. "You really do know your Torah."

My friend said nothing. But it became obvious that the almost seventeen years he'd spent without the near constant supervision of the Essenes did little to dampen his memory.

"Yes," he said after a brief pause. "Nothing happened to dampen my memory. But it took a great deal to put it into a different perspective. What I wanted to tell you was that by your reckoning, the men I've mentioned must have lived at the tail end of the Bronze Age. The Age in which Sri Krishna is said to have been born. Some scholars put Adam's birth, creation they call it, at around four thousand years ago. But the others came later... "

All this in response to my friend reading my mind again? I sometimes wondered if it was worthwhile talking to him at all, if he already knew my thoughts.

"I am not a scholar, Yeshûa, you know that."

"Believe me, Satya, reading your thoughts will never take priority over hearing your voice. The two are miles apart," he said ignoring my last assurance. "Firstly, I don't really control the hearing part. It happens when it should, not when I want it to. I cannot decide that now I shall decipher your innermost secrets. But if I am supposed to know them, then I shall. I am still trying to figure it all out."

I practically expected him to look far away and repeat his favourite maxim: 'There is so much to learn.'

"There is," he said, and we both laughed. "But tell me more about Krishna's youth. I studied his teaching, not his life."

We took a drink of water and ate some dry fruit before I resumed my story.

"Well, they say that Sri Krishna was the eighth son of a Yadava Prince Vasudev and his wife Devaki. What was more important, he was also the reincarnation of Lord Vishnu." I didn't dwell on that, as I was sure that Yeshûa knew more about Lord Vishnu than I.

He nodded.

"They also say," I resumed, "that the avatar was born in a prison cell. In Mathura. Some time later, his father aided by several celestial forces managed to get him out of prison and across the raging river Yamuna to safety. History is mute as to why he was in the prison to start with. At least Sri Singh didn't know. At any rate, once there, in safety I mean, young Krishna stayed at the house of Nand in Gokul. It was there that Krishna spent his childhood and there that the first signs of his divinity became manifested.

"How old was he then?"

"I really don't know. Sorry." When Yeshûa didn't pursue I continued. "New trouble started when his uncle Kansa attempted to murder him. I'm not sure why, but it must have had to do with his expected heritage. After all, he was a prince's son. Anyway, Kansa's murderous attempts forced Krishna to move once again, this time to Nandgaon, a more secure dwelling in the hills. It probably turned out for the best. The adolescent Krishna stayed with the *gopas*, the cowherds. He spent his days wandering around the village Vrindavan, which abounded in fragrant groves and forests. He played with his many friends and it was there that he'd met his first love. She was the beautiful Radha."

"It's a lovely story..." Yeshûa murmured.

"There are people who claim that the forests around Vrindavan are still imbued with echoes of their erotic love. It was there that Krishna played and instilled a deep connection with nature. Each tree, each bush speaks of the divine couple's love for each other...."

"You are a romantic people," Yeshûa said in a far away tone. Then he added a lot louder: "The size of your family alone attests to that!"

What could I say. He was seldom wrong in his observations.

Toward the evening of the next day, we arrived in Mathura. My brother was to arrange for camping while I took Yeshûa for a stroll. We walked in silence over the same knolls and valleys that once enjoyed the presence of Sri Krishna. I am not a religious man. But walking in silence over the grassy slopes, among the fragrant groves, I felt Lord Krishna's closeness like never before. I wondered how Yeshûa felt, but somehow it seemed inappropriate to break the silence. We might have missed the silent echoes of young Krishna and Radha rejoicing in their carefree youth.

* * * * *

Part Three

Gnosis
The Evening of the Second Day
and the Night

13

Farewell to India

When I first saw the ship that was to take us across the sea known for it turbulent monsoons, I thought it would be best to cancel our trip and take the long coastal road all the way. It was only after I'd heard that this very ship had taken no fewer then twenty-eight trips to the destination we sought that I relented. But only slightly. I thought it would be best to spend a few days resting after our journey so far. People who'd never ridden atop an elephant might presume that we travelled in great comfort. They would be wrong. In spite of a two-day stop at Mathura I felt stiff and tired. Perhaps I was just getting old. If I was to live to be a hundred, I'd better do something about my shape, which was beginning to show preliminary signs of rotundity. Not as much as my father's, but not nearly as little as Yeshûa's. In fact, my friend looked and moved like an athlete. He must have studied some Greek methods for maintaining his posture, whereas I, when not journeying, had spent ninety percent of my time sitting or reclining on our verandah. As for Yeshûa, whatever the subject matter he was pursuing, and as far as I knew he never stopped studying, was constantly on the move. And his favourite mode of transportation was his own feet.

On the morning of the third day in Barygaza, Dhanesh reported to me that most of what little goods we had been carrying with us had been loaded aboard, distributed strate-

gically across the ship's deck and tied down in case of rough
weather. We didn't carry that much. Mostly muslin, gems
and ivory. The rest of the goods we brought with us, we'd
already traded at very good prices. We also picked up some
new wares, which were said to be highly sought after in
Southern Arabia.

It had been ages since I took time to pray, but now I
thought it best to invoke all the gods whose job it was to
protect sailors and traders, as well as those who controlled
waters, winds and generally the idiosyncrasies of weather.
Afterward, I felt a lot better. Only I was still a little perplexed
as to why Yeshûa showed absolutely no sign of any nerves.
As far as I knew, the biggest waters he'd ever crossed had
been rivers, of which the Ganga was the broadest. Well, the
Ganga and the Indus river, ah... and the Tiger and Euphrates. So he'd crossed some rivers. But this? This one should
make anybody and everybody nervous. Why, you couldn't
see the other side. There was no horizon. Not even an is-
land. Nothing! Not even a precise line where the sky and
the water met. The horizon was protected by a layer of mist.
I wasn't sure men were meant to venture into such an envi-
ronment. It was like embarking on the river Styx. You
didn't know what to expect on the other side.

I was glad I took the precaution of promising our gods
a goodly offering on our safe return. Assuming we ever got
to our destination in the first place....

As for the port in Barygaza, there is little to remember it
by. People were too preoccupied with making a profit.
They looked at us with hungry eyes, as though trying to strip
us of our entire domain. Even the clothing we wore. As I'd
noticed only once or twice before, most of them seemed to
keep a good distance from Yeshûa. I suspected that my
friend was affecting them at some deeper level in a manner
with which they couldn't quite cope. So they moved away,
their heads turned, as though they hadn't noticed him at all.
For some reason they looked angry. Yet not one of them
had uttered a single word. It was only later that I'd learned

that the inhabitants and regular visitors of various harbours seldom display high levels of ethical standards.

By any definition.

I expected the town to be trade oriented. That is was. After all, that's why we were there. The only thing that really surprised me was the number of ships. There must have been twenty or more of them, all along the river, which made for a natural harbour. They all looked similar. I also learned, though only some weeks later, that most, if not all of them, were of Roman design. Similar in length, each sporting a single mast for hoisting a large, rectangular sail. At the prow of the ship, another, much smaller sail, was rigged between a horizontal boom atop a spar inclined at some forty-five degrees, and a single point at the end of an impressive bowsprit. On large ships, the twin sails were supported, during infrequent doldrums, by up to sixty or even eighty oars.

I also learned later, that, should the occasion arise, the ships could and would easily revert to their original purpose. They had all been designed as warships. The proof was in the sturdy post protruding at the bow, just below the water line, evidently used as a battering-ram. Ramming one's enemy broadside must have been a preferred form of marine combat.

Again, I found the Romans to be sneaky, underhanded people. At least in warfare.

Most other vessels in the harbour were considerably larger than ours. *Iburnias,* as they were called, in times of war carried up to fifty or even eighty *remiges*, or oarsmen, and were used throughout the Roman Empire including on the Nile, Rhine and the Danube rivers.

Our particular ship had been subleased by a country-man of ours, the same man who took over the care of our elephants. The beasts would return to Benares with appropriate goods. Our ship had been leased together with the crew. The moment I came aboard, I noticed a most amazing thing. The officers on deck were all purebred Romans. I can't say that this discovery inspired me with new confidence. I wouldn't be at all surprised if they didn't come

from the ranks of deserters, or some other defunct faction of
the Roman legions. I'd never heard of Romans working for
'lesser' genres of man.

    By then we were already aboard.

    It came as no surprise that two other groups of mer-
chants had already been installed on the ship. They sat in
various places, probably keen to reserve seats best protected
from the wind. They didn't even bat an eye as my party
boarded the vessel.

    We were welcomed, instead, with polite aloofness by a
man clad in a short tunic, a slightly rusty breastplate and an
equally worse for wear helmet. Two other men stood behind
him sporting even older regalia, nevertheless with hands
resting on the hilts of short Roman swords. I saw two more
men similarly attired and armed, keeping guard at the stern
of the ship. They too were looking us over with suspicious
eyes.

    I imagine that their misgivings may have been directed
at the eight men who accompanied me, each armed with a
sword, curved and lethal looking, and somewhat longer than
its Roman counterpart. The 'officers' as I was deemed to
call them, seemed to be measuring us with their eyes, weighing our ability to inflict trouble on them. Evidently they
preferred their opposition to be shackled. I never liked Romans. They were cruel, murderous or conniving. Perhaps
the genteel members of the Empire remained in Rome.
Where they belonged.

    The floor of the ship, the deck they called it, felt amaz-
ingly solid. I even tried stomping my feet a bit, to the great
amusement of some sailors below. They were all sitting in
rows, facing the stern. I could see them through a number of
hatches left open. Probably to give the men air. I counted
eighteen of them; all but one were black as ebony. I didn't
ask, but they must have been slaves. When I bent down on
the pretext of adjusting my sandal, I could see their ankles

were shackled to the wooden benches upon which they were
sitting. I was told that since we relied on the monsoon winds,
we didn't need as many *remiges*, as ships used on rivers or in
unpredictable marine conditions. The winds blew first one
way, and then another. I was to learn more about that later.
One man of a slightly paler skin was leaning against the rudder, which consisted of two ores roped together. At the prow,
a youth no more than twelve, stood leaning against a raised
platform, a stick poised, ready to beat the rhythm for the
oarsmen to follow.

And then the *remiges* dipped their blades.

The ship did not seem to be moving until the third or
fourth stroke of the oars. Then, suddenly, the shore began
receding from us. India, my India, was left behind.

I saw Yeshûa at the stern looking towards the shore. I
truly got the impression that he was saying his last good-
byes. For reasons I cannot explain I knew that this was his
last gaze at the country in which he'd attempted to fathom
the mystery of life. Of life and living. Perhaps he'd become
the Enlightened One, like Gautama whom he said he loved so
much. Like Krishna whose fragrant groves we'd strolled but
a few days ago.

This was his final good-bye.

The moment we'd cleared the harbour, the men, officers
assisted by some traders, hoisted the sails and the ship began
to make good headway. Within an hour there was but a thin
line separating the sea and the sky. This thin, irregular line,
barely rising above the horizon, was the mighty land of my
fathers. Would I ever see it again?

I remember reading that, in the months of October, when
the monsoons blow from the northeast, the cyclones only
attack sailors fairly close to the shore of the Indian sub-
continent. Further west, or east for that matter, they are seldom seen unless one travelled much further south.

It was just our luck.

The cyclone was supposed to have missed us by a couple of days. Regrettably, weather forecasting was not an exact science. By the evening of the third day, the waves agitated by the circular motion of the wind, yet still augmented by the directional monsoon, began tossing our ship like a cork on a mountain river. My recollections of what followed are hazy at best. Not only had I been scared out of my wits, but my eyes had been virtually blinded by the driven rain. I can face any enemy, face to face, without fear. There and then, the enemy remained invisible, untenable, refusing to present a target I could face. It was all around me. Its power making itself known by repeated assaults across the deck. Portside and starboard alike.

In spite of the unremitting onslaught that Mother Nature imposed upon us, the Roman officers found strength to open two hatches at the raised stern of the vessel, and pull out two huge drums of thick warp. They proceeded to feed the rope out into the boiling sea, through two openings in the freeboard above the deck. After unwinding most of the rope, they attached the ends to oversized cleats next to the openings. During all this, the ship's deck was performing a whirling and howling dance of unremitting madness. It forced me to assume most impossible angles to sustain my balance. The Romans persisted, seemingly unperturbed.

Likewise the man at the helm, just as the mariners who were previously working the oars, gave the appearance of relative indifference. The oars had long been lifted and tied securely below the deck. The men, wet though they were, seemed happy to be sitting around doing nothing much, if anything at all. Even the deck washing had been delegated to the rain, which appeared to be doing a fine job of it.

The same cannot be said of Sahib Bihari or of Dhanesh, his able and brave brother. It was my job to make sure that at least my own men did not fall overboard. With such limited responsibilities there was nothing for me to do. I suffered from an acute attack of helplessness.

And that was precisely the trouble.

When I'm busy, my mind functions on higher revolu-
tions. Blood seems to flow faster. I am, and have been
proven to be, capable of fast and good decisions. Perhaps it
was a question of an equitable balance between imagination
and intellect. Now, I could use neither. The same energy
that I usually channelled into the decision making process
now ran amok imagining all sorts of things that could go
wrong. I pictured the mast braking and sweeping most of us
overboard. Then I imagined the shrouds and the stays tan-
gling around the men's ankles. The two rudder oars could
snap, making us sail in circles until we had run out of food
and water....

I suffered from an over-fertile imagination.

"And how do you like Neptune's realm?" I heard the
voice over the roar of the sea.

"Man was born to walk on solid ground," I answered
slipping again on the wet deck.

"Not if you make your living as a fisherman..." he
countered. I could just see a little smug smile playing about
his lips. For the first time since I'd met Yeshûa I found his
smile profoundly irritating.

"What is it that you find to smile about?" I had a habit
of speaking my mind.

"I love the sea. When I was little, my father took me
out, a couple of times, on the Sea of Tiberias. The fishermen
were as fine sailors as any men I've ever met. They seemed
unperturbed by the dangers. At least, most of the time."

"What dangers might those be?" I was being facetious.

"I don't know. Drowning? What else could happen?"

He was right. That was the very worst thing that could
happen at sea. And for some inexplicable reason this absurd
assurance restored my peace of mind. Over the years I had
to face danger so often that it become commonplace for me.
What I feared at sea was not the danger, nor death, but the
unknown. What is it in human nature that makes us fear the
unfamiliar, I wondered?

"You are a complex character, my friend," Yeshûa
shouted over the wind. "Most people's fears originate in

death, which they regard as the greatest unknown. You are the reverse. You do not fear death, but little things seem to upset your balance."

I always thought that the greatest fear lay in the termination of all. Of all that is known. Of the familiar. He could be right. But right now, I really didn't feel like indulging in an extensive discussion on the relative merits of my character. But there was a grain of truth in what he said. "You are a man who cannot be idle," he added.

This time he scored dead centre. Give me a problem to solve and I'm happy. Maybe it's true that idleness is Satan's playground. I felt sure we talked about this once before. Only I could dismiss the iniquities of Satan's playground by diverting my attention. Maybe that's what it was all about. One's attention.

"You are where your attention is..." I heard over the wailing of the wind.

"Thank you, my friend," was all I needed to say. And simultaneously I looked around to see how I could make myself useful. The moment my interest was diverted from my own fate, I found plenty to do. There were some loose ropes which needed tightening. One man was sick and staggering. He needed help. The barrels of water seemed to be working loose. There was a great deal to do if you put your mind to it. I found it embarrassing that my brother had reached this same conclusion before me. Together we worked hand in hand. I never saw my brother in this light. Not that there was much light. The sun, well hidden by a thick layer of clouds, must have been nearing the western horizon. Soon it would be night. No matter. The skipper, I felt sure, would know what to do.

And then I stopped in mid-step, my mouth hanging open.

Yeshûa was standing at the prow, without any support, his arms spread out loosely on each side, as though inviting the waves to sweep him overboard. Somehow he maintained his balance. And even as I watched him in this ludicrous pose, the waves broke and dispersed before reaching him.

Then the wind took a long gasp as though too tired to continue howling. The waters remained angry but not to any degree which endangered the safety of the ship. Then, just before the sun retired over the far horizon, the clouds parted and a long, lateral beam washed over the ship. Yeshûa's slim body balanced precariously at the bow had been backlit, from the front, detaching it from all that was dark and forbidding.

I couldn't believe my eyes.

When I recovered my wits, my friend was sitting on the deck, seemingly lost in thought.

"Did you do that?" I asked.

The innocence in his eyes was a thing to behold. "I can do nothing of myself," he said.

For the rest of the journey, leaning over the rail, time and again I pondered upon his response.

The next day I learned that the Romans had fed the warp out into the deep to slow the ship down. With the wind at our stern, we had been running before the wind. Without the rope, the ship would have turned and twisted to present the broadside to the wind, and thus would be in danger of capsizing. Also, even with the sails down and stashed safely away, we had been rising and falling atop the swell like a small riverboat. The drag of the sea anchor slowed us down sufficiently to stabilize the mad tossing and turning of our vessel. It also served to present only the relatively narrow stern to the wind.

There was one other thing.

While I had not revised my opinion of the Romans in general, I was forced to acknowledge a degree of respect for the stoic detachment that the Roman officers presented to danger. Fancy that.... Romans who had long rejected the teaching of Zeno. Arumji would be amused!

A strange metamorphosis takes place in you when you're sailing the ocean. For the first two or three days, my eyes drifted towards the stern, seemingly of their own accord, on the dwindling hope that there may still be a snippet, a distant contour of a mountain, a hazy crest, to behold. The fourth day marks a new beginning. You start facing forward. The past has left your mind. The future is there to be won. To be conquered.

There is one other reason that may be a contributing factor to this shift of interest. At first one sees, then one hopes to see, a bird crossing a familiar sky. Some of the seafaring birds drift a goodly distance into the open seas. For some reason they always know when to stop, before they reach the point of no return. It could be that those intrepid flyers convey the message to the human mariner. It had been they who carried my final farewell to India.

We were now within a day's journey off the coast of Arabia. The *remiges*, under the supervision of the Roman officers, checked the oars and their housing, in case they would have to navigate close to shore without the benefit of a friendly wind. All was progressing automatically, with unhurried precision as must have been done many times in the past.

After the storm, I had befriended a trader, who wanted to find out what we had to offer. After exchanging pleasantries and establishing a business relationship I had asked him about the monsoons. Ashore there were also prevailing winds, but they were much more variable than their counterparts on the open waters. Even assuming the occasional cyclone, such as had caught up with us the week of our departure from Barygaza. The merchant was definitely keen to please.

"Changing monsoon winds," he said, "are blowing the sailing boats steadily to Barygaza, and other Indian ports, and back. They change direction according to season."

"So the monopoly of trade routes with India and Africa is about to be broken..." I mused.

"Precisely," he smiled displaying two rows of equally despicable brown teeth. I wished he would keep his distance

when addressing me. Or at the very least, have the decency
to sit down wind. "The Roman ships," he continued, "can
now leave Egypt in early June for the port of Muza, or even
Kene harbour with the well-sheltered port of Qana, to which
some charts referred to as Kana. Once there, they have a
clear sail for Barygaza, Barbarikon or even Muziris."

I'd heard of Muziris. It was a harbour near the southern tip of our continent. I'd heard talk of people sailing
ships along the east shore of India and even further to the
Far East. It all seemed too good to be true. Perhaps my father had been blessed with the gift of prophecy. He must
have heard stories from the tradesmen who'd never failed to
pay him their respects when passing through Benares.

"There are two basic directions," my foul-mouthed
friend concluded. "The Southwest monsoon takes us to India in September. After trading for two months, the wind
changes and the Northeast monsoon takes us back toward
Africa. By February you can do business in Alexandria."

Gold, myrrh and frankincense could flow in abundance
providing great profits. And the ancient Silk Road through
the Fertile Crescent and Persia, which we used so many times,
was no longer the only option, no longer the only channel
for the luxurious and exotic goods. There was a new connection between India and the Near East.

As for my toothy friend, he was almost right. Actually,
wet or rainy monsoons blew from the south/west in summer
while dry monsoons blew from the north/east during the
winter months. Only the north/east monsoons sometimes
blew from north/west. I assumed that was just to make sea
travel more interesting.

But from wherever they blew, my father knew exactly
what was in the air. In the wind, to be exact. The monsoons.
Dear father, I thought. I wondered how Almâs was. And
Yêsh. And Arum. And dear old Arumji. I looked out over
the vast ocean. A dark cloud drifted across the face of the
sun.

The scorching sun is no longer baking my eyes even through my closed lids. The shimmering brightness of the waves dissolves into a pale grayness. I open my eyes.

"I thought you were sleeping, my friend." It was his shadow that had dulled the sun from my eyelids. I had forgotten to change over to the other side of the courtyard.

"Just memories," I say. "Just memories...."

"I won't invite you inside, though you are always welcome there." Yôna speaks with his usual friendliness. "I've been watching your face – for a little while. I rather think that your memories bring you more joy than ours..." he nods his head in the direction of the doorway.

I am still trying to find my bearings. The images of the sea and the ship were still particularly vivid. So was the bad breath of my interlocutor. I'm all right now.

"Shall we move to the other side?" He points to the shadow cast by the western wall.

I get up, stiff as usual, and wobble after Yôna. He seems as bright as a newborn babe. I wonder from where he gets his energy. Surely not from sitting around and moping.

"That's better," he sighs, lowering himself to the ground beside me. "You won't believe this, but it's a lot cooler here than inside."

It strikes me that his normal, everyday conversation sounds strangely out of place. For some reason we are supposed to be mourning. Be sad and miserable. Suffering.

"He always smiled," says Yôna. "Even when they led Him away, He smiled."

My young friend seemed to answer my qualms. He is right, of course. I can't recall Yeshûa not smiling. When I picture his face I see the steely blue eyes, the curly hair and the smile. That's about all. The three make up Yeshûa. We have a strange way of remembering faces. With my father the image is always of a man pensive, calculating, and most of all, in command. Yeshûa seemed able to control every situation he was in, but he was never commanding. If I looked for a metaphor, I would think of water. Or a blade of grass. Bending easily with the wind, but always returning to its original posture. Position? He changed every day. Every day he'd acquired new knowledge, yet, in some strange, inexplicable way, he was unchangeable. Probably the only truly unchangeable man I'd ever come across.

"Yes," I agree. "He always does."

Yôna looks sharply at me. "Always did," I correct myself. He nods. He's not as happy as he looks. He just tries harder.

I suddenly realize that I am experiencing Yeshûa in the present. They are memories, but I relive them. Though re counting, I am still there with him, reliving each moment with all of my senses. It seems that this is yet another gift from a man who had nothing.

"I suppose all my memories are pleasant ones," I say, for some unknown reason feeling guilty. That's something he never made me feel. He made me feel happy. Always.

"I will bring you some water," Yôna says and rises to his feet. "I'll be back," he says. But I feel that he needs to rebuild his happiness within himself. Why do people complicate their lives so? It sounds like something he would have said.

"And what will you do with all that money?"

This time it was Yeshûa's face that obscured the sun. I was back aboard the ship, the gentle rolling motion making me sleepy. My eyes were burning again from staring toward the horizon. The sun flirting with the waves was putting a great strain on my irises. I suppose I shouldn't have been looking constantly towards the west. Towards our destination.

"Money?" I asked lamely.

"The money from the fleet of ships?"

So he'd been reading my thoughts again. He was right. Since I realized that Romans had all these 'toys' and were making money from them, I was racking my brain about how to convince my father that we should develop a fleet of our own. It seemed to be the modern way to run a business. One had to move with the times or be left behind. And that would never do. Not to the Biharis.

"It's not a question of money. It is a question of doing something as well as you possibly can." I was on the defensive but I felt I was holding my own.

"And what will you do with all that money?" He repeated as though I hadn't spoken.

So it wasn't a question of making it. Of making money. It was a question of what to do with it. I never thought in those terms. The act itself, the outwitting of the opposition had given me all the satisfaction I needed. It suddenly struck me that I had no interest in money, as such. Once won, it seemed to lose its value. Perhaps there were noble ways of spending it. The poor? The Untouchables? The sick? There were priests and monks for that. But who gave them the money? Even my own share of the family fortune was already more than I could possibly spend in a single lifetime. What should I do with all that money? I would hate for it to go to waste.

"I don't know, Yeshûa," I said waving my head from side to side. "I really don't know."

He looked at me for some time. Silently. Then he got up and stared into the ocean.

"Think about it," he said. "Consider the options, lest you grow attached to it."

I recall Arum Singh once telling me that money is said to be the root of all evil. For the first time I thought I'd learned something Singh didn't know. It is not the money that is at the root. It is the attachment to it. It is the attachment that limits your freedom.

* * * * *

14

Landfall

The first landfall I ever experienced in my life was un-
eventful. We'd dropped sails at the very last moment,
with only three sets of oars on either side plus the
double rudder being used to bring us to anchor. I believe
the oars served only to reduce the vessel's speed. Evidently
the whole procedure was an established routine.

With the aid of two tenders we put ashore one group of
traders and picked up another. My men went ashore, but
remained in and around the harbour. Except for taking an
occasional stroll up and down the pier to stretch our legs, we
all remained aboard. All, except for Yeshûa. Within minutes
of casting anchor, he'd disappeared.

Back on board, my men moved our goods below the
main deck, to protect them from the salt water and the pun-
ishing rays of the subtropical sun. In Barygaza we had been
the last to board and thus had to secure our wares on deck.
Now, finally, with more than half of our journey and all of
the open waters behind us, we'd earned priority. Like in all
business dealings, first come, first served was the rule. Providing the price was right, of course.

Yeshûa went ashore with the first dinghy. He had said he
wanted to find someone. He was like that. I could as well
have asked him what he would do with all of the knowledge

he was amassing. Somehow I didn't have the courage. He was my closest friend and yet I felt shy about prodding him with such a question.

"What will you do with all of your money?" he'd asked me.

"What will you do with all of your knowledge?" I could well ask.

Or perhaps I was apprehensive of what the answer might be. With the irrepressible serenity that Yeshûa radiated, there was also an intensifying aura of the unknown that clung to him, and thus, to whatever he said or did. There was also the mystery hidden in his words. With his mind, his acquired knowledge, he could have made a fortune. As a teacher to the very rich, as an orator in any public forum, as an adviser to kings and emperors. Over the years, he'd given me some words of advice which vastly increased my profits. He did it for free, and categorically refused any compensation.

"And what would I do with all that money?" he'd asked in all innocence. "I would have to carry it with me in a big bag, wherever I went. If I left it behind, it would probably get stolen and I would be back where I'd been before. And surely, you see that I cannot carry it with me."

He'd often offered me such impregnable reasoning. On any subject. Indeed, it would be peculiar, not to say embarrassing, for a man to walk into a Hindû ashram or a Buddhist monastery, totting a large bag of money. I could picture the situation.

"Where can I put my bag?" he would ask.

"That depends on what's in it," would be a reasonable inquiry.

"Money," would be the answer.

"Money?" I suspect disbelief colouring the monk's voice.

"Money," he would confirm.

It would be a rather stupid conversation. They didn't let people into ashrams or monasteries who wanted to study stupidity. In fact, a fair degree of poverty was taken as evidence of good faith. Was it really impossible to combine the two? Money and the pursuit of spiritual knowledge?

"Your heart is where your riches are," he'd once told me. I've never asked him again.

The 'real' landfall came two days later.

We all went ashore in Muza. After we had rounded the strait between Africa and the southwestern tip of Arabia, our ship entered the waters of the Red Sea. Muza was still on the Arabian peninsula, and the trade there offered more interest and variety. To my eyes many items were new and exotic. The Himyarites of the Hymar Kingdom, who maintained a trade route in the mountains along the Eastern Shore, made Muza their main port. Here goods from India, Alexandria and East Africa, were traded at very interesting prices. At least to us merchants used to the land routes. I have even seen ships here all the way from China. So much for the Persian attempts of maintaining the Crescent of Fertility linked with the rest of the Far East and the Silk Route. The wind was free, beasts of burden cost money. A new era was growing in the business. And here I was, probably just in time. Yet in spite of the variety of goods offered, they said that the most money was made by levying taxes on ships themselves. Of course there was smuggling. But the penalties for such were of the most unpleasant and painful variety. Not many dared, in spite of the heavy burden the taxes imposed. And of those who dared, not many had succeeded.

The harbour was ten times busier than our native Barygaza. The number of ships running after the same trade was enormous. Yet the trade was also ample. In addition, the harbour was overrun with hirers, crews, and men offering an array of services and of course, mountains of merchandise.

Whatever we purchased or traded here had to be marketable as far as Alexandria. I needed to learn as much as I possibly could. Regrettably I did not speak the local vernacular. I made do with a dozen languages, as best as I could. Frankly, most people spoke an amalgam of a number of tongues. A sort of bastardized form of Latin was quickly

becoming the universal lingua franca. It was in the merchants' interest to understand. We all made an effort. It is
amazing how much you can comprehend when a few people
are really trying hard to understand you.

Money, or rather potential profit, is a great stimulus.

In three days we were reloaded onto a different ship.
The one that had brought us here was coming about and,
after some minor repairs, returning whence it came. The
moment the winds turned, of course. The owners specialized
in the India – Muza segment of the sea trade route. It
seemed to have worked for them. I was told that after a mere
ten years, the slaves could buy themselves out. After com-
paring prices of myrrh in Muza and further up north, I understood how they did it. The same was true of pepper and
ivory. Apparently many ex-slaves stayed on as oarsmen. I
wondered what would happen to their shackles.

Once aboard, I could finally relax. It was pure joy to sit
back with Yeshûa and once again enter his world so very
much apart from my own. I always found it fascinating that
across the mental and emotional isthmus we found so much
in common. It was as though we were examining the same
jewel from a different angle, being aware of only one facet at
a time. At least that was true of me. Yeshûa had a vastly
broader view of reality.

It was hardly surprising that having entered the sea
sandwiched between Arabia and Africa, our thoughts would
drift towards Egypt. A land as old as time itself. It seemed
that Yeshûa had already met someone, back home, who had
imparted to him some basics about the history of this ancient
country. I found that my friend practically equated history
with the development of religion. In the case of Egypt, at
least, he was definitely close to the mark.

"The Egyptians had many gods. You might say that
they were the progenitors of the age of divine specialization.
A god for any and every occasion, every cause, and any purpose. Since their gods had very limited powers, this frag-
mentation of responsibility seemed appropriate. But the in-

teresting part was that all the gods existed exclusively to cater
to the needs of man. You see where I am going with this?"

I had to translate my attention from the mundane to the
celestial, so to speak. Apart from the evening meals, I hadn't
spoken to Yeshûa for three days. There is a great deal to
think of, to see to, when traversing an unknown terrain. My
brother has been of tremendous help, but he refused to make
the final decisions. Which was, after all, as it should be.

"At the last count I got to about sixty gods," Yeshûa
continued, as though he was just getting down to something
interesting. "Now the Greeks have shown us that all gods
are created unto the image of man. Anthropomorphic they
called them. With appropriately and proportionally enlarged
powers, and egos to match."

I studied his face. His eyes shone as they always did
when he spoke on his favourite subject. As always, his enthusiasm was contagious. I smiled at the thought that within
minutes he would have me completely absorbed in his tirade.
I nodded noncommittally.

"Now the same Greeks also produced a man named
Democritus."

Now this sounded better. Sri Singh had given me a
thorough grounding in Greek scientific thought. If Yeshûa
enjoyed dissecting religious beliefs, I liked to delve into
physics. And Greeks, ancient or contemporary, were leaders
in this field.

"He lived in Abdera some 400 years ago," I put in,
with a tinge of pride. "He was a very smart man."

Yeshûa smiled at my haughty interruption.

"Quite right," he agreed. "What made him so smart
was that he managed to distinguish between things as they
really were and as they seemed to be. Arumji told me about
this when you went asserting your masculinity in Babylon. I
would have gone with you if it hadn't been for the old man
being free that day."

Now that was, frankly still is, embarrassing. How on
earth did Yeshûa know that on that particular night I'd lost
my virginity? I most certainly remember that night. Every

boy, man, always does. But Yeshûa had been asleep by the time I got back. And I'd gone on an errand the next day before he got up. That's how well I remember that time. At least I think I do....

Yeshûa gave me a vague look, smiled his understanding, then continued. I was sorry I'd just indulged in those thoughts. I bet he'd read them unerringly.

"You see," he nevertheless continued unabashed, "it seems to me that Democritus succeeded where I am still groping: to distinguish between the real, and the perception of real. He made one statement that stayed with me to this day. Later they created whole philosophies on his assumptions, but I kept only the very essence of that single statement of his. He'd said, and mark this well, this was a good four hundred years ago, that, and I quote, 'nothing exists except a-toms and empty space – everything else is opinion.' A-tom being the smallest indivisible particle or constituent of tangible nature. It is embarrassing to realize that at the time of Democritus, my own people lived in a vassal state of Persia."

In spite of this admission, Yeshûa didn't look in the least embarrassed. Instead, he continued.

"Now, this went against the grain of the Sophists who, less than a century earlier, began an intellectual revolution which directed philosophical attention toward man, toward individualism. At least they thought so. In my eyes, Democritus enabled man to look at himself in an entirely new light. What, to my knowledge, Democritus did not answer was whether opinion can influence the interrelationship of a-toms."

"The what?"

"A-toms. He did not answer how the constituent parts are put together."

Now this made it perfectly clear!

"It is truly amazing," he continued, seemingly in a world of his own," how differently various cultures develop. And I always include religions in the cultures. After all, religion is the fuel which fires the furnaces in which cultures are cured."

I was at sea in more ways than one. Just what do a-toms, the smallest supposed constituents of matter, have to do with religion?

"You are losing me, Yeshûa..." I admitted. I was no longer self-conscious about admitting my mental limitations to my friend. Providing we were alone, of course.

"It has to do with the division between what is real and what isn't," he continued as though uninterrupted. "But what really got to me was his statement about 'the opinion.' I've spent a lot of days, nights, well years frankly, trying to figure this out. And then, sitting, no, not under a bodhi tree, merely on the river bank, I realized that opinion is virtually all that matters!"

There had to be more to it than that. We all have opinions about virtually everything. Usually the less we know about anything, the more adamant our opinion. I'd never rated opinion high on my list of preferred human traits.

"Nor would I, in your sense of the word," he interrupted my thoughts.

By all that's holy! By then he'd not only read my thoughts but interpreted them also.

"Sorry," he smiled. "A force of habit." And then his face got very serious again. "Do you realize that if you substitute the word faith for opinion, then you can actually manipulate matter?"

And Yeshûa never lacked faith.

About three days later it began to dawn on me what my friend was trying to tell me. Actually, he wasn't trying. He'd said it as clearly as it was possible to express an axiom that can change the world. My new understanding of his words was that if we firmly believe in anything, anything at all, we cause it to become reality. It was a matter of faith. I wondered what kind of faith it would take to acquire a fleet of ships. Or to double my profits from all transactions. Somehow I doubted that he was referring to such mundane things. And yet? And yet I remembered the game he'd played with the rupees in our garden, delighting the kids. Was that it? Was he actually manifesting those coins out of nothing? Out of thin air? Or was he expressing an opinion about the configuration of free-floating a-toms as omnipresent as the air we breathe.

My head was starting to ache. I had to ask him about miracles.

"You cannot change that which is," he told me later that evening.

Somehow we always discussed such matters after sunset. The daylight reality called for too much attention. It was too absorbing, distracting, to free oneself, or at least to free myself of the established attachments. No matter whether the attachments were to things good or bad. They were part of an ingrained, established reality. A reality that my mind accepted as real.

"Thank heaven for that," I put in inconsequentially.

"Whatever *is* remains subject to indomitable laws which sustain this reality," Yeshûa ignored me as he continued. "Heaven and earth shall pass, yet one tittle of the law shall not be changed till all is fulfilled. Until the whole of the creative force which sustains this reality returns to its source."

"Tittle?"

"It is an ornamental horn on Hebrew letters," he enlightened me once more. "It is a thing of virtually no consequence, yet necessary for understanding...."

"I get the message," I interrupted. I am not a complete moron.

"Sorry," he smiled his apology and went on. "You can only breathe life into undifferentiated atoms. You can imbue them with creative force...."

One would have thought that by now I fully understood what he was saying. One would be wrong. I wondered if it would take me as long as it took him. After all, I'd never met a boy, or a man, smarter than he was. Yet, it took him all of fifteen years to get a handle on reality, as he'd once called it. He didn't really believe in any miracles. He told me that once we understood how the world worked, we would all manipulate matter at will.

"It is natural for man to create reality. It is as natural as thinking and loving, and walking and...."

Even as he was talking, a coin appeared on his flat, extended palm. He did not move his hand at all, yet the coin appeared seemingly out of nowhere. He flicked it over to me. It was a perfectly good coin. Only... only it showed on its face a meticulous imprint of the emperor Octavian, later known as Augustus. The coin looked brand new. The only Roman coins I'd ever seen bore the face of Octavian's granduncle, Julius Caesar. There were no other coins in India. I certainly hadn't seen any.

"You might find it useful when we get to the Roman Empire." And seeing my discomfort he added, "Octavian too is dead now. But he did great things for Rome."

"I thought he'd murdered all his opposition," I countered. The traders kept me well-informed. "Are we supposed to respect such men?"

"Remember what Krishna told Indra about his duty as a warrior. We all have a function to fulfil. You must give Caesar what is Caesar's."

That is all he'd said at the time. But in my head I heard his voice as clearly as though he'd spoken the words out loud: "And give God what is God's."

I was too stunned to speak. Out of habit I mumbled a weak 'thank you' and blinked hard. The coin was still resting flat in my palm, as real as my palm itself. Lying there as though it belonged to me. Was life that easy, I wondered? Or did it simply take fifteen years of hard work, total commitment, unwavering faith, an excellent brain, and a lot of skill? "Anyone can do it," he'd said. Well, ha, ha, ha. I still have to work for a living.

"And so do I," my friend. "We are here to fulfil the law, not to break it."

The moon over the open sea is like any other moon, until you look down. Then you see a long line of sparkling ripples, following the contours of the waves, shimmering towards you. No matter from where the wind blows, or in which direction your ship takes you, the glittering line follows you, follows your ship, making its way into otherwise impenetrable darkness. The moon was so bright that the stars paled, paying it obeisance. No wonder there had been people who saw god in the face of the moon. Selena, Hecate, Diana, Diktynna, Artemis, Juno.... In Rome they had *dies Lunae* in honour of the moon. The earliest myths of India speak of the dynasty of kings, of the 'race of the moon,' who reigned in Pruyag, not far from my own home.

Yeshûa's hand touched me on the shoulder. He must have been standing behind me for some time, perhaps sharing some of my thoughts.

"The moon also symbolized what the Greeks called the psyche, your inner self, maybe even the atma. People always needed symbols. Problems had started when they began to worship the symbol and not what it stood for."

For some reason my mind drifted to the last time we spoke of atma and psyche and reality.

"The world you see is the effect," he'd said then. "Within you, knowingly or not, lies the cause. You sustain that which is, for as long as you can. But all the time, the world passes on. It is in a constant condition of decadence. Only the process goes on."

I recall him saying that when I asked what he'd been doing the last three months before our departure from Benares.

"I was identifying with the cause," he'd told me.

And then he'd explained the previous assertion. When he didn't detect understanding in my eyes, he continued.

"At the moment of creation, the universal becomes contained, you might say encapsulated, within the particular. Until it returns to its source it cannot contradict its own laws. People grasp onto that which is dying. All that you see, hear, touch or smell is in the constant process of decay. Dis-

carded, relegated to this world. It is dead. Let the dead walk
with the dead. I offer you life. The process of eternal becoming."

Even just remembering those words raised goose bumps
at the back of my neck. I felt that I was the first man to have
heard something monumental. There was incredible authority in his voice. In his tone, even in his eyes. Again I had
the feeling that he'd looked deep into my heart. I felt
stripped, quartered and reassembled. I would never be the
same again. How much have I understood there and then?
Little. But the seed had been planted. From that moment on
I could recall every word he'd ever said to me. Every syllable he'd uttered. I felt joined with him by ties greater and
more mysterious than any bonds created by man. And yet,
was he not as we all are? Why did he speak like a god
trapped in a human form?

And then, sitting here, washed by the silvery rays of the
silent moon he heard and answered my thoughts again.

"We are all gods," he said, "but we all die like men."

*"Thank you," I say as Yôna brings me a cup of cool, deli-
cious water. "Surely, my friend, I can get it myself?"*

*"The women bring it from a deep well. That's what
makes it so cool."*

*They must have crossed the yard while I'd been dream-
ing.*

*Yôna lowers himself onto his hunches next to me,
against the western wall. It is much cooler now. Perhaps
because of the shade. Then my mind wonders about what
he'd just said.*

"Thank heaven for women," I say in all earnestness.

*I also think of my own Almâs. I left my children in her
care, without the slightest qualms that she might not cope.
For some reason I entrusted her with that which was, is, by
far the most precious to me. Apart from herself. All the
riches of Nebuchadnezzar could not equal the single jewel*

that became mine to hold and to love. We, men, think we run the world but without a thoughtful woman we would surely die in no time at all. As would our nation, our race. Humanity. We philosophize, puff out our chests with high effusive notions, with dreams of fortunes and empires, and they bring us water.

"I never really understood women," I murmur.

"He did," Yôna says in a tone as quiet as my own. "Do you know," he continues sounding as though sharing with me a wondrous secret, "that Mary and her sister Martha, and Maipa and His mother, of course, travel ahead of us, from place to place, and establish places of refuge for us to rest, or hide, or just to spend a night? They've done this for some time now. Even here, this house, has been arranged by them for us to stay together." The tone of his voice speaks volumes of his gratitude and admiration.

We sit together, our minds taking their own paths through history. Through history which is limited to events in which Yeshûa had been involved. And then Yôna catches my eye.

"He said something I couldn't understand," he starts. "We had been sitting together trying to understand the Kingdom, that the Master kept talking about. Simon Peter, always a bit of a hot head, once said that the Master should send Mary away when we were talking about some lofty subjects. Simon said something about women not being worthy, or something like that. The Master refused. And then He said something strange. He said that he will make her male, so that she too might become a living spirit. And then he said that every woman who makes herself male will enter the Kingdom of Heaven. Can you explain any of this?"

Yôna said all this in a quiet voice, as if not wanting anyone in the house to hear. Perhaps there are still arguments amongst them as to the rightful place for womenfolk. And anyway, somehow it seems inappropriate to talk, here and now, in a loud voice. As it would in a temple or ashram. One speaks in a normal tone, but only loud enough to be heard by whomever one was addressing. You wouldn't shout

to your friend over the heads of others in a temple. This
courtyard is like that. Or perhaps it's just his absence. Or
could it be his enigmatic presence? We speak on subjects as
far from his person as everyday chatter. We talk about wa-
ter, and women.... But, somewhere, at the depth of our souls,
we are all thinking: 'what would he have said?' His absence
fills this yard, this house, the air we breathe, the silence we
share. Could he really be dead? And then for the third time
since I arrived I recall his mysterious promise.

"I'll be with you always...."

I was looking at Yôna's face but my mind drifted, again,
to the Roman ship sailing the open waters of the Red Sea.
For some hours each day, the skipper assigned his oarsmen to work. A steady breeze took us along the gently un-
dulating mirror. Ever northward. With hardly any sensation
of movement. Also, there was no term of reference. We
were too far from shore, and not a single cloud offered a
point of referral. Nothing against which we could measure
our progress. We were at peace with the world. Time slowed
down, and then came to a halt. Yeshûa and I were standing
at the bow, our elbows resting on the high wooden rail. A
pulpit they called it. Ahead, a single ibis was gracefully
crossing our line of vision. A minute later, he too was gone.

I glanced at my friend. His eyes were as blue as the
cloudless sky stretching to the horizon far ahead. His face
was smiling. As usual.

We were together once more.

"What is life?" I asked. The outer stillness seemed
conducive to directing my attention inwards.

"Consciousness," he replied immediately. "Have you
seen a corps showing signs of being conscious? Breathe life
into a corpse, and he lives. Remove it, and he dies. The
same is true of a man as of a tree. Consciousness is life. At
whatever stage of evolution. Life is life. It is the process of

becoming. None is superior, none is inferior. Some people call it the spirit. But it is all the same. It is Life."

"Surely, we don't all manifest it to the same degree...." He had me half-convinced.

"Ahhh, there is also self awareness. Better still, awareness of Self. How many men do you know who manifest the awareness of atma? And if they do not, does it mean that atma does not reside within their being?

"Krishna is omnipresent," I said. "You taught me that."

"Precisely. Life is omnipresent and Krishna symbolizes life. As does your god Vishnu, the Preserver. Preserver or the Sustainer. In this form he manifests the Process itself. Life itself."

"And this is true of all men and women?" I was thinking of men who steal and murder, of women who never seem to take time to sit and just think. I must have been thinking that women I knew were always too busy catering to us men, to our every whim.

"Of course. What differs is only our realization of this fact. Men tend to analyze what they know and reach some conscious conclusions. Women possess the same knowledge intuitively. Their soul dwells nearer to their hearts...."

"...ours closer to our heads?"

"Yes."

"Does it really matter?" I wondered aloud.

"You can only enter the Kingdom in full consciousness," his voice was as gentle as the smooth wavelets lapping the boards of our ship.

"Kingdom?"

"Kingdom of Heaven. A state of consciousness without limitations."

"How could that be?"

"For us it is impossible. But for atma, for the Vishnu within you, all things are possible."

I supposed. Vishnu is god. He can have no limitations. And then I remembered my previous dilemma.

"And what of women?"   But I knew the answer already.   "They too must do so in full consciousness...."

He said nothing.

"When your heart and your mind become one...."

So that was it.   We had to become whole.   I knew I was right.   He only smiled.   Perhaps a little broader than usual.   But I knew he was pleased.   Maybe I was beginning to understand what he was after.   Or at least, what he was taking about.   For the last fifteen years.   Or longer.

* * * * *

15

Yam Suph

"Our minds are like the Yam Suph," Yeshûa said looking into the distance. "Not here, but further north, the sea is like the Sea Of Weeds. That is what Yam Suph means. The Sea of Weeds. They also call it the Red Sea."

"It doesn't look red to me," I put in looking over the side.

"The colour red always symbolizes emotions. When my people crossed the Red Sea they turned over a new leaf. They were supposed to have freed themselves from false beliefs and start believing in themselves. Instead they got entangled in a Sea of Weeds." His voice took on a tone of distress. "They never changed, really...."

What could I have said? I didn't even know much about his people. Not that I know so much about my own. Yet I felt sorry for my friend. In such rare moments, he looked and sounded as though he was taking upon himself the errors of all his countrymen, of all his people, seemingly at a loss as to how to help them. At the same time, particularly recently, I sensed that he was racking his brains trying to solve the problem.

"I have a head start..." he seemed to be thinking aloud in response to my own thoughts. "Do you know that the Essenes raised me to be the messiah?"

I looked at him with, what must have been, horror in my eyes. He started laughing. Out loud.

"I know. Little me – the messiah. That is funny, isn't it."

"You mean like Mithras? In Persia?"

"That sort of thing. They must have thought that if the Persians can have one, then why not us?"

There was an awkward silence. I wasn't quite sure if I should take him seriously. It was one thing to spin myths, quite another to give them body and soul.

"And I have body and soul...." He reiterated my thoughts word for word.

My mind was in turmoil. Surely, my friend, my dear friend Yeshûa, was not going to take on the job of a messiah? It sounded preposterous.

Suddenly snippets of our conversation, years ago – on the outskirts of Babylon, flashed across my mind. It had been even before we'd reached India. Yeshûa, a boy with energy to spare, had been uncharacteristically depressed. He'd told me about Judith, about the Essenes and his near-prison on Mount Carmel. I recalled the plans others had for him. Surely, he didn't intend to sate their selfish needs?

And then I found a ray of hope.

"Your people do not worship two gods, of good and of evil – like the followers of Zarathustra. So there is no need to save them from the evils of Ahriman." I still remembered the lecture Sri Singh had given us about the struggle between Ahura-Mazda and his evil counterpart.

"Sufficient unto the day is the evil thereof," Yeshûa assured me. It sounded like a quotation. "Remember, we only personify and then raise to godhood our own traits. It cannot be otherwise."

He was staring at me again, questioningly. Was he expecting confirmation from me? It was I who looked toward him to hear an explanation of his words. He said nothing more. I was probably expected to have understood. Or, he may have been just thinking aloud.

"So what would a Hebrew messiah save, so to speak?"
I didn't know how else to put it.

For a while he didn't answer. This time not just his eyes
drifted away, but his whole being seemed carried to some
distant land. I pictured him in Jerusalem as a little boy.
Then I tried to visualize him, also in Jerusalem, preaching in
the Temple. I couldn't. Yeshûa didn't preach. As forward
as he was with a helping hand, with sharing his ideas when
the two of us got together, I never saw him preach to people.
He didn't even preach to me. He suggested, implied, planted
the seed. But it was always up to me to allow the seed to take
root and eventually see the light of day. He never pushed,
never threatened. No. For the life of me I could not picture
Yeshûa as a saviour.

"Nor can I, my friend. Nor can I," he repeated. But
there was nervousness in his voice. As though he was trying
his best to escape a storm that was gathering with indomitable
certainty. And he had no idea where or how to hide from it.

"You are a good friend," he said at last. "I know you
wish me well."

And then he lowered himself into *Padmasana* and
closed his eyes. He meditated like this for hours on end. I
never invaded his privacy when he did that. Not that he'd
ever asked me to refrain from interrupting. There are certain
things one just knows. Especially when concerning a friend.

*"They must become whole," I say. Yôna is still sitting next to
me.*

"He also said that. But what does it mean?"

*"It is not for me to interpret your Master's words," I say
a little defensively. "I believe he thought that the mind and
the heart must become one. That you can only enter the
Kingdom, as he called it, in full consciousness."*

"After we die?"

*At this I couldn't help smiling. I imagined Yeshûa's re-
action to such a question.*

"I met Yeshûa more than twenty years ago. In all that time he never once spoke of death. Nor of any 'hereafter.' To my knowledge, he only concerned himself with life. He was quite clear about that."

"So we must enter the Kingdom right here...?" Yôna's voice was hesitant but there was light in his eyes.

"That Kingdom of his is, I think he said, a state of consciousness. He said the dead were not conscious." And then a thought struck me. "I think he would allow that should we achieve this Kingdom here and now, it could well be that we would remain in it in the, ah.. the hereafter." I hated talking like a second rate guru.

"Whosoever believeth in me, shall never die..." Yôna's eyes were getting wider.

"By 'me', I think he meant in 'life'." I try again feeling that I am loosing the ground I sit on.

"I am Life," this time my young friend stands up and grabs his head in his hands. "You do understand!" His voice is considerably louder than before. And then he starts walking up and down the yard as though trying to rid himself of excessive energy. Finally he joins me again at the west wall, drops down on his knees and kisses my hand.

"Thank you Satya," there is joy in his eyes. "You brought Him back to me. Thank you."

I need all my resolve to pull my hand back before he chews off my fingertips. I've made one man happy. Considering the atmosphere surrounding the yard and the house, it is no mean achievement. And then I wonder who will make me happy. Yôna seems to be very close to bringing his mind and heart together. I still suffer from the excess of mind.

"Help me, my friend," I whisper for no one to hear. I wasn't thinking of Yôna. I could only think of Yeshûa's blue eyes. And the next instant, once again, his voice rings clear in my ears. "I am always with you."

Perhaps I am learning to listen with my heart. Like Yôna. My little new friend.

" **A**nd then there was, or is I suppose, Hor-Pa-kred – pictured as a naked child with one finger in his mouth; Harsiesis – the 'son of Isis'; Hathor – seen as a cow, or cow-headed woman; and also Hata-mehit – the fish-goddess of Mendes in the Delta; Heqet – the frog-goddess who helped women in childbirth; Re-Harakhty who once was a sky-god while a son of Osiris and Isis; Imhotep who earned divinity by constructing the step pyramid yet later specialized in learning and medicine; and we also have Isis...."

"I heard about Isis!" I broke in the moment I could. I was certainly impressed with Yeshûa's knowledge of the Egyptian deities, but hearing them recited alphabetically was more than I cared to reflect on.

"Indeed, there are many others," Yeshûa said quite unperturbed by my interruption. And then he looked at me with a plea in his eyes. "Tell me, dear Satya, how on earth can I make heads or tails of all this celestial menagerie?"

"Try Ra and Anubis," I suggested with some exasperation. It was my feeble attempt at humour. Ra aspired to the fatherhood of all gods, while Anubis, as the jackal-god, must have sported a good tail.

"The point well taken," my friend's smile didn't really widen, "but surely you see that I am facing a major problem. I am here to learn...."

"You are everywhere to learn," I put in. He ignored me.

"...and attempting to find the real meaning hidden under the mass of symbolic meanings, metaphors and paraboles, requires more energy than I can muster."

He looked genuinely crestfallen. I was hardly the right man to help him. Whatever I was able to suggest must have been mulled over and already rejected. And then an idea struck me.

"What if you discard all gods whose specialty is too narrow. Their function must only be attendant to their higher counterparts?"

"I thought about it, but I am afraid of missing an important god."

"Why such punctilious pedantry?" I asked. "Surely it is not your intention to offer your people Egyptian myths as an alternative to Yahweh?"

This time I did elicit a grin. A broad one. "Thank you my friend. I was getting bogged down in the Yam Suph. No wonder my forefathers preferred to run than to dissect Egyptian religion. Yet for some reason, I detect, I can almost smell in their myths, a mystery greater than meets the eye. Yet I can't quite put my finger on it."

I could commiserate with my friend, but this wouldn't do much good. As far as I could see, Yeshûa's distress was more intellectual than emotional. I didn't believe that there was anything between heaven and earth that could upset his balance. He was the rock upon which philosophers could safely stack their stones. But all his theories did have a cumulative effect on me. What bothered me a lot more lately, was the question of my own future – in terms of my own, Hindû philosophy. Not that I've ever been a religious man. But... there was always a nagging 'but' playing at the back of one's mind.

But what if others were right?

And that brought me to vague misgivings about my own past, and thus the karmic consequences that would result from it. As the leader of a number of caravans, I had been called upon to defend that which belonged to the people I led, and also served, as well as that which was mine. I had been called upon to defend my charges with my sword in hand. If necessary, without mercy. I knew that Yeshûa held life to be unconditionally sacred. That was what bothered me the most. How can I reconcile my responsibilities with his views? His views were becoming increasingly important to me. Awaiting a propitious moment, I asked him point-blank.

"What if you kill a man?" I had meant to ask him that for a while. When it finally did come out, it shocked even

me with its apparent brutality. I had no choice. I have had
occasion to kill a man. More than once. I'd do so again, if
my people or even my goods were threatened.

"Remember Lord Krishna's words. The words he'd
spoken to Indra: 'By your nature, you will have to be engaged in warfare.' We all have a destiny to fulfil. As for
killing? We all die. Sooner of later. Who can tell what that
man's destiny might have been? You temporarily suspended
his process of becoming. You released his life force. It returns to its source. Remember, life force manifests in relation to the mode available to it. You cannot make a stone
bleed. Nor can a man fly."

My facial expression must have registered confusion.

I recall those words even as he spoke them. My mind
was racing forward. "So we are no more after death?" I
nearly added "after all?" So many religions had promised
us heaven and hell, immortality, or at least some form of existence hereafter.

"Lord Krishna also said that that which pervades your
entire body cannot be destroyed. For the soul there is neither birth nor death. Your immortality, as you call it, depends on whether you identify with that which is life, or that
which is dead. After all, what is life but a state of consciousness?"

"Why did you use the phrase 'as you call it'?" I was
still groping in the dark.

"As I just told you, you are a state of consciousness,"
he spoke gently. Thank god for his patience. "Fragments
of your personality, your personal traits, can survive by becoming part of the individualized consciousness that you call
atma."

"Fragments?"

"The creative aspects of your stint on earth, if you like,
which enrich the fabric of the universe. In other words, the
universal traits survive, the others...."

He left that hanging. Are cast into hell? Burnt in eternal fires?

"Hell, like heaven, are both states of consciousness. You alone can create those states. No one can create them for you. But if you must think of hell's fire at all, think of it as a process of cleansing."

I let that sink in. Somehow the hunger remained.

"How can I do all this? How can I put it into practice?"

"You already have. You are honest, kind, hardworking, and fair to your charges. You are even kind to your animals. I've watched you."

"Is that enough?" I knew the answer even before I'd asked it. I knew what I had to do. I could leave the charge of the caravan to my brother and... well, and just follow Yeshûa wherever he went. In time, I would learn. I would understand. I felt that faith had given me guidance and energy, but knowledge would raise me to another level.

"Your time will come," Yeshûa said, probably trying to restore peace to my turbulent mind. And then he said something very strange.

"There is no hurry, my friend. Whoever believes in what I say, shall never die. And though he were dead, he shall live. We shall meet again. Trust me."

If I needed reassurance it was then. Whatever were my shortcomings, I did trust him. I trusted him with my life. My atma.

There was yet another thing I found so amazing about Yeshûa. He never attempted to explain to me anything in terms of his own religion. He met me on my ground. He always gave expecting nothing in return. He once told me that to give and expect nothing in return was the beginning of immortality. He must have achieved this condition long ago.

Our ship docked in a number of ports. Some traders parted company, others took their place. There was never any deck space going to waste. My business-

man's mind couldn't help admiring the organization of the
sea captains. They often sent men ahead along the shore on
fast horses, to advise others of their coming. On arrival, the
tradesmen had their wares ready, and in no time at all, the
ship would be on its way again. There was a lot to learn here,
as Yeshûa would say. Only this learning was strictly for me.
And particularly my brother. Watching Dhanesh I was becoming convinced that he was more than ready to take
charge of the whole marine operation. For our family. For
father. And taking care of business for our father meant
looking after all the local merchants in the valley leading to
and from Benares. My father had many friends, and even
more business associates. He would have made a good chief
administrator. A king, perhaps. Only he'd never agree.
Business, for him, was duty, passion and love. Helping his
friends came a close second. He might cut off the heads of a
dozen robbers on one trip, but he would do so regardless of
whether he was protecting his own life or the lives, or even
goods, of others. I know. I've been there. By his side.

     In moments free of business, my thoughts invariably
drifted to Yeshûa. What was he doing? Did he manage to
find a new source of knowledge? Was he progressing along
the path he'd chosen according to plan? I noticed that lately
he was preoccupied with, what he invariably called, 'his people'. I had asked him about that.

     "Why do you always call them 'my people'. Why not
just Hebrews or Jews?"

     "Because they are neither," he replied with a slight
shrug.

     "Do you mind explaining?"

     "Well, it's not easy. Do you know what Hebrew
means?"

     I shook my head. "It's a language?"

     "Hebrew means 'belonging to Eber'. It is a patro-
nymic of Abraham. It also means a nomad. Well, we are no
longer nomads, and a great many of us are not of Abraham's issue. My people intermarried more than probably
any other nation. On the other hand there are many Semitic

people who claim lineage from Abraham, who are not 'my people'. Not in the sense that they are Jews."

"So, why not call them Jews?"

"With me it is a question of honesty. The words in the Hebrew language carry great history behind them. They are imbued with power, with meaning often lost in the worship of symbols. The true meaning has been lost somewhere along our previous nomadic existence."

"You mean 'a Jew' also has a special meaning?"

"Everything among my people has a special meaning. We are a complex group who seem to cherish our little secrets. 'Jew', or in Hebrew Yehûdi, means a descendant of Juda. In later times some also called them Israelites, which is equally as erroneous. It should be well understood that in the Torah's sense Jews, Israelites and Hebrew are not synonymous. Juda, or Judah, by the way, also means praise, or praised – meaning let God be praised."

"And they taught you all that?"

"Who, the Essenes? Not really. They wanted the facts. Precise facts. They were the most orthodox people you could imagine."

With that, he looked away. I sensed that the Essenes were not something he wanted to discuss or share knowledge about. But then he sighed and looked back at me. There was a suggestion of tiredness in his eyes. A rare thing for Yeshûa.

"Satya. I was twelve years old...."

I guessed the rest. Those who escape from prison seldom wish to discuss time spent behind bars. Any bars. Even the bars of orthodoxy. But there was something else. Yeshûa preferred to say nothing rather than criticize. Yet, I was his only listener and unburdening one's soul might do him a lot of good.

"I suppose you're right," he said once more reading my thoughts. He did it so often I stopped taking notice. Yet he found it easier to admit that it might help him, than to actually do so. This time there was a longer silence. I thought he'd forgotten about it all, when he spoke again.

There was more than just the Essenes who prayed on his mind. It was priesthood generally.

"The Sadducees speak with authority of life after death. They mete out punishments and rewards in an afterlife. Yet which of them has come back to confirm their ravings? Let one man return having left his body, and he alone will speak with authority."

This came like a flood of waters restrained for too long. It reminded me of when we spoke about the priesthood in Egypt. He was equally as annoyed, as though he took the transgressions of the Egyptians personally. Almost as if they were his own people. In the middle of our discussion about Egypt I'd asked him some inconsequential question about the Pharisees. At least I thought it had been inconsequential.

"As for the priesthood throughout the Egyptian history," he'd said, his voice, at least at the beginning, unaccustomedly raised, "the moment they rose to power, they turned religion into a commercial enterprise. They prayed upon the fears of their people for their own gratification. To gain the advantage. They prayed on superstition, spread trinkets and amulets, growing fat on the ignorance of the masses. They were the serpents, the vipers of every generation...."

As he spoke, his voice trailed towards silence. Perhaps he'd found the subject too painful to consider any further. I'd only learned later that his mind had drifted to his own scribes and Pharisees. Probably precipitated by my seemingly innocuous question. When he'd finally admitted this to me, he said it was his moment of weakness. He also admitted that he had little respect for the priesthood of any ages. He never raised the subject again.

The last time we spoke on this subject, his voice was barely above a whisper. "They persecuted the prophets who tried to show them the truth. Is there no god whom the priesthood will not destroy? I must show my people a god that is only, yes *only* in the depth of their hearts. No one but they will have access to him."

And then he squared his shoulders as though emerging from some acrimonious pit dragging him persistently down into its dark quagmire.

"My job is neither to criticize nor to condemn, but to find a way," he said. "I shall not do Satan's work. He is the hater, the accuser. I shall not allow him to speak again."

I have never seen Yeshûa wrathful. Before or since. The sins of priesthood must have weighted heavily on his mind. I didn't know what to say. In my country he never criticized anyone or anything. Particularly not the monks or the swamis. If anything, he seemed to admire them. He certainly loved Sri Singh. I know he loved the monks who had given him shelter in the monastery north of Katmandu. He said so many a time. "They are the chosen ones," he'd said at the time. "They have already found their way. My people are still wandering in the desert."

The desert, I also learned later, was a symbol of spiritual starvation. Those last memories reached back several years into the past. How fresh they flourished in my mind. How true. I shook my head. Yeshûa was still standing at the rail, his eyes afar as always when a commitment became firmly established in his heart. His jaws were set.

"I must find a way," he said with firmness that defied contradiction. "I must become a way. The way," he added. I've known Yeshûa practically all my life. He always did what he set out to do.

* * * * *

16

The Land of the Pharaohs

The monsoons expended less energy within the Inland Sea of Weeds than along the open waters of the southern Arabian shores. Actually, there was little sign of weeds as we sailed along, except for those clinging to the shore waters and between the various islands. I expected to find more of them further north, where the Red Sea split into two branches. One leg continued due north by northwest, the other followed an equal inclination due east. It is the first branch, the one stretching northwest, that Yeshûa's forefathers crossed to escape the wiles of the Pharaohs.

Or so they said.

I took my men as far as the great port of Berenike on the west coast, where they traded the remaining goods at prices vastly exceeding those we negotiated in Muza. While the whole of the Egyptian shoreline was sprinkled with small harbours, all doing a brisk trade with the wealthy Romans, there was one other major port which, being considerably further north, promised to offer even better prices. This assumption had later proven false. It was true that being further north, it was more accessible to the illustrious members of the Roman Empire. On the other hand, it meant sailing

into the difficult northerly winds which favoured these waters. As empires go, the Romans were ready enough to part
with their money for good quality, exotic goods. But they
were also good businessmen. It proved later on that
Berenike became a gold mine designed for trade with India,
while Myos Hormos, further north, lost some trade. On our
first journey into these waters, we couldn't have known that.
This is what this trip was all about. Research. As for business even further south, the Romans relegated it to their subordinates, thus paying for the middleman's profit.

My father had long taught me to avoid middlemen like
the plague.

After some discussion my brother Dhanesh, my very
able lieutenant, had joined Yeshûa and me on the sail to
Myos Hormos, while men awaited our return in Berenice.
They had been instructed to negotiate the best prices for
goods that we were to take back to India.

And then, it was I who changed our plans once again.
In Myos Hormos Yeshûa and I bid an emotional good-bye
to my brother, as he boarded a ship for the return sail to his
men. Under the pretext that there was little more to learn
further north, and that I could easily travel to Memphis and
if necessary even to Alexandria on my own, we parted company.

There was a touch of selfishness, on my part. Strictly
from a business point of view, I could have returned with
Dhanesh. Theoretically, my job was done. But by the same
token, I was free to do as I chose. Assuming Dhanesh could
handle the return trip himself. I knew he could. Who
knows? Perhaps better than I could. But the true reason for
my staying behind, I hardly admitted even to myself.

I was growing quite sure that Yeshûa would not be returning with me to India. Whatever his plans – I am not sure
his future was fully crystallized in his own head – they would
not deter me from trying to linger on in his company for as
long as I could.

It was then, at this realization, that I made my seemingly demented decision.

Inasmuch as I missed my wife and children terribly, the thought of parting with Yeshûa put an even greater strain on me. For reasons I could not explain, I became convinced that once he and I parted company, I'd never see him again. It was a feeling I found very difficult to deal with. Over the years, many years, Yeshûa had grown to have a tremendous effect on me. Even as I made my business decisions, even when in theory it seemed most inappropriate, I couldn't help asking myself how *he* would handle this or that situation if *he* were in my shoes. Not that he ever would be, of course. But the thought, the nagging thought was there.

Now, the dice had been cast. For as long as I could, I would stay with Yeshûa, and return to India at the latest time the turning southwesterly monsoons permitted. It seemed that nature would decide the exact duration.

Already in Muza Yeshûa had spent two days meandering within districts associated with learning. He had a talent for it. He could ferret out the local sages with the unerring ability of a man who'd spent his life doing just that. He'd learned a little of the Arabian history, but his heart, or perhaps his nose, drew him toward Egypt. Now, finally, we were both free. Free to sail further north, free to take the shore road, or even travel inland across the mountains to the Nile and from there sail down to Memphis, or Alexandria or, for that matter, to Rome.

The dice had been cast but they haven't stopped rolling.

If Yeshûa suspected the true reason behind my decision, he gave nothing away. Instead he jumped with joy, as he had so many years ago, when the two of us played on the banks of the Euphrates. Frankly, to my mind, we both felt like boys who had pulled a fast one, like missing classes in school and getting away with it. Yeshûa was, of course, quite incapable of such a devious and premeditated action, but there was nothing to stop me from acting like a schoolboy.

Yeshûa played along. The resulting fun and atmosphere akin to a vacation was quite palpable.

The two days that Dhanesh and I had been making new contacts in Myos Hormos, and preparing lists of goods we might bring back with us on the next trip west, Yeshûa was busy in his own right. That very first evening, after my brother's departure, he shared some of his findings with me.

"There was a time," he began the moment we'd settled down in our inn, "when I had to make a decision. I could dismiss the Torah and all the prophets altogether as a collection of fables designed mostly to scare people. Or I could search for meaning, which would make sense to me. Which wouldn't insult my intellect."

He studied my face as if searching for approval.

"Of course," I said dutifully, wondering what was coming. After innumerable hours of discussions with him, over so many years, he never failed to surprise me with an original way of looking at the world.

"You must realize," he went on, "that under my tutors, most of my time had been spent copying the sacred texts. On and on and on. As though that function alone would raise me to some sublime level of understanding. They must have believed that by copying the scriptures we would metabolize them, absorb them into our consciousness. Judith herself, our leader if you remember, had done that herself for hours on end. She loved keeping records. In a way she'd been right. I can quote to you whole passages, as the Romans call it, *verbatim*. But this kind of knowledge has not made me any wiser. If knowledge of the Hebrew scriptures alone was enough, I wouldn't have spent the last seventeen years studying."

How well I understood him. Before Sri Singh took over my tuition, for the most part together with Yeshûa's, I had been also told that by memorizing the text of the Vedas I would gain wisdom. Their understanding was, apparently, of little consequence. Obedience to the law was what mattered.

"Yes Yeshûa," I could honestly agree. "The understanding is what matters, not the bare facts. This applies to all types of knowledge." I was thinking of business. "Un-less, I suppose, your ambition is to become a scribe."

We both laughed. The very idea of becoming a scribe, endlessly copying other people's conclusions, sounded like a fate worse than death.

"Can you imagine anything more boring?" I asked when we quieted down.

"Yes," he replied. "Watching someone else becoming one!"

We went for a walk.

Since Mathura, in the enchanting groves of Sri Krishna's youth, it was the first time that we actually walked together. We'd lent a lot of weight to the rails on the ships we had sailed, but walking has a rhythm to it that loosens the tongue, frees one of inhibitions, and helps to think clearly.

"I wonder what Egypt will bring. Somehow, I've built up great expectations. I think the ancient kingdoms will contribute to my understanding in a way in which neither the Greeks nor the Romans did."

I pictured petrified mummies exuding knowledge at Yeshûa from behind their bandages. I must have been tired. I shook my head.

We were strolling along a lane overlooking the sea. On our left, the crescent moon was just rising above the waters. The air was so calm that we could see smoke rising from the fires burning along the shore in straight vertical lines. I hoped my dear brother had enough wind to fill his sails. I cheered myself with the thought that, in open waters, the wind often died down at sunset, but picked up later. Though it certainly did not pick up on shore.

"The Greeks and the Romans worship Psyche, the nymph personifying the soul," Yeshûa's thoughts drifted far from mine. His tone was as dreamy as the atmosphere over-looking the ancient sea. "They weave stories about her mythical attributes. But they do not worship the real soul. The *atma*. Our true and only Self. They worship Zeus or

Jupiter, the gods wielding power of life and death over their subjects."

"Surely, both these gods are no more than symbols," I put in.

"True," he said. He sounded pleased with my comment. "They do not worship Life itself. We all choose to live in the twilight of the gods, forgetting that it was us who had created those gods and their twilight in the first place. Forgetting that real life, that limitless reality, the real Light, is ours to behold. Do you understand my words, Satya? The words I use are also but symbols of the truth. When I cast away symbols, I am atma. I am the truth. And there is none other."

Whether I understood him or not, I felt privileged to hear him speak. I felt that his words were filling some sort of void in me. Sating my thirst that was growing of late.

The fires along the shore were nearer now. They spouted no more smoke – just gleaming embers stretching into the distance. It was cooler now. The warm glow looked inviting. Passers-by could buy fresh fish and bake them wrapped in a number of layers of dark green seaweed. We decided to sup at one of the fires. The fish were delicious. I bought four of them for a single Roman coin. The fisherman looked surprised at my generosity. I decided, first thing tomorrow, to check on the currency exchange. Things like that changed without any official notice. There were so few officials. So far from Rome things were left to find their own momentum.

As we licked our fingers, a group of urchins stood by, silent, seemingly deriving vicarious pleasure from our meal. Now and then one of the men tending to the fires would chase them away. They always came back. Whether it was the fire or the smell of baked fish that attracted them was hard to tell. Then, with a causal movement, Yeshûa stirred the smouldering remains of a fire with a stick, and raked out another fish, all wrapped up in a charred leaf. He let it cool a little, then picked it up and held it out at arm's length to the nearest boy. For a moment the lad seemed lost or suspicious. He edged a little closer, then with a quick lunge he run up to Yeshûa, grabbed the fish and retreated into the darkness. A moment later another fish found its way from the embers, and another urchin found courage to reach for it. I was so taken by the seek and hide game that I completely lost awareness of time. The kids came and went, the fire remained glowing, and continued to provide ready-baked fish. After what must have been a good half-hour, probably much longer, I asked Yeshûa just how many fish I had bought. In the same instant I remembered the number. Something was terribly wrong with the fire. Or with my eyes. Or with my mathematics.

"How on earth do you do that?" I asked, not quite sure what it was that I was asking. "Where are you getting all those fish, Yeshûa?" I was more precise this time.

"From the same place I sate all my needs," he said smiling.

And when I looked at his face, he wasn't merely grinning. His face was aglow with much more than just the reflected glimmer of the fire. I could swear I saw an Inner Light radiant in his eyes. Perhaps in all his face. I've seen such radiance twice before. Once at night, when we'd been alone. The other time was when he'd been playing tricks with the children in our garden. But this was different. For some reason I could not explain, I felt sure that what my friend was doing was testing his knowledge. Or his theories. Or maybe, just maybe, testing his power. Although I had no idea why.

"Isn't it sad how empires come and go? Like the seasons that govern human greed." Yeshûa asked and answered his own question during breakfast the next morning. We bought fruit and milk. It was safe to drink milk early in the morning, before the sun turned it into yoghurt.

"And what empires might you be speaking of?"   I
asked. Yeshûa could jump millennia with a single example.
He did.

"Think of the Old Kingdom, and of Darius of the Persian Empire."

Even as far as India there were few men of any stature
or education who haven't heard about the Old Kingdom.
Let alone about Darius. The Old Kingdom lasted for centuries....

"...a millennium," Yeshûa corrected peeking into my
thoughts. "Over three thousand years ago Egypt had been
united into a single kingdom. The Old Kingdom. There
had been six dynasties of Pharaohs, Egyptian 'per-o'
meaning 'royal' or 'great house'. Their secret was that the
Pharaoh was not above the law. His power was limited.
Darius wielded absolute power. The difference of the efficacy of the ruling systems can be measured in time. The six
dynasties of the Old Kingdom – one thousand years, Darius
– thirty-five years. While the power of Persia obviously
lasted longer, it never matched the glory of this briefest blink
in the eye of Brahma."

I loved it when Yeshûa used Hindû metaphors. I sometimes wondered if he did it for my sake, or if the years he'd
spent in my country did in fact rub off on him.

"Both," he replied, before going on. I began to wonder if there is any point to my opening my mouth at all.
This elicited a bashful smile from my friend. "I know, I am
overdoing it," he looked down at the ground. "But you are
the only friend I have... you are so close to me, your
thoughts are as though I was thinking them myself...." His
tone was truly apologetic.

"Let me know when I think of something you
shouldn't listen to," I said in all seriousness.

This time he laughed out loud. I joined him. We were
happy together. I knew I was and surely he must have been.
It was becoming evident that even a man of his unique abilities needed someone with whom he could share his inner-

most thoughts and feelings. I realized that my decision to
delay my departure for India was a wise one.

"Thanks," was all he said. Then, after a pause he
added: "It may or may not have been wise, but I appreciate
it very much. You are truly a friend." There was love in his
voice but there was also sadness. Perhaps he knew something
I didn't.

*Mary bringing us food and water interrupts my reminis-
cences. Yôna decided to share his evening meal with me.
We both rise to thank her and sip greedily some of the delicious water. To my throat, it tastes better than wine.*

*"You know, Yôna," I say still standing, "Yeshûa knew
he and I would soon part company some three and a half
years ago. In Egypt." My eyes follow my thoughts toward
the setting sun. The fiery disc already began dipping behind
the mud-brick wall surrounding the yard. "I realize it only
now, but he'd known it even then. What a strange man he
was...."*

"Yes, Satya. He was a most unusual man...."

*With some difficulty I bring my mind to function in the
present. Judging by the length of the shadow the wall casts
over the yard, the sun will set within an hour. Evenings are
short here. Soon the stars will claim their rightful place in
the sky. Round and round and round. The wheel of Awagawan. Everything comes and goes. In circles. Only love
seems to last. Forever. You cannot love in the past or the
future. You can love only in the present. Now. The eternal
now. Even when your brother, your friend is gone.*

*"He knew the future," Yôna says. And then he corrects
himself. "At least his own future. He would not say when
other things would happen."*

"What other things?"

*"The end of the world?" He answers with a question as
though he isn't sure.*

It sounds like an example. Thank heaven for little mercies, I think. Imagine how we would live if we all knew that it was all for nothing. "He told me that we should always live in the present. That, and that we should not worry about the future," I add. *It sounds like wise advice.*

"Take no thought for your life, what you shall eat, or drink," Yôna recites from memory. And then he looks up at me. "How can we not worry about food when we never really have enough?"

My mind's eye pictures the urchins at the shore of the Red Sea stuffing themselves with fish appearing out of the ashes.

"We wouldn't have to worry if we lived as he did," I murmur under my nose.

Which of us could live as he did? It takes eighteen years of continuous study with total, uncompromising, absolute, dedication. And even then there are no guaranties. Some people work night and day and they remain poor. Could success or failure also be written for us in the stars? I am sure Yeshûa didn't think so. He wouldn't have endured the hardships he had to put up with had he any doubts that he wouldn't eventually be able to obtain the knowledge he yearned. He wouldn't have been able to commit his life to his search with such loyalty.

"Behold the fowls of the air. They sow not neither do they reap, nor gather into barns, yet your heavenly Father feeds them...." *Yôna again drifts far, far away. His plate rests on his lap, untouched. His eyes wonder about without aim or purpose.*

"He spoke in parables?"

"What?" *He looks at me.* "Oh, I am sorry. I could see Him standing, his arms hanging loosely at his sides, with palms open towards us, talking. Just talking. He never lost hope that we would understand Him. At least some of us... He never lost hope...."

He cannot continue. Tears weld in his eyes. He lets them run down his cheeks, without shame.

"Eat, Yôna," I say. "Your food will get cold."

"Yes, Mas..." he catches his breath. "Yes, thank you Satya."

He wipes his cheeks with his long sleeve and digs in with a wooden spoon. Once he starts, the food disappears in no time at all. He must have been speaking the truth. They seldom had enough to eat. The youngster was hungry. Youngsters always are. When he is halfway through, I gently repeat my previous question.

"Did he speak in parables often?"

"To us almost never," he answers between bites. "To others almost solely."

"So he treated his closest disciples differently?"

"Yes and no. All men were equal in his eyes, had equal access to Him. Only He picked us individually, as though He thought that we had a greater chance of understanding."

"And did you...?" It was rather a rude question but he didn't seem offended.

"How I wish we did. You seem to understand His words better than any of us!"

"I've know him for eighteen years..." I say in a way of an excuse.

"And I three..." he whispers, and tears again seem to well in his eyes but this time he manages to blink them away. "I'm just a big baby, aren't I," he says, a weak smile raising the corners of his full lips.

"No, my friend. You've just learned to love too much too early."

I let him eat, after that. He really does look very young. So very young. Too young to carry such a burden....

"Another fascinating thing about the Old Kingdom," Yeshûa spoke slowly evidently preparing to make an important point, "it was founded on a policy of peace and non-aggression. While the Pharaoh had been designated the Son of the Sun, and while his chief subordinates had been priests, neither the chief priest nor any of them, nor even he were above the law. The citizens, as the Greeks would call them, although very few resided in cities, had been left, for the most part, to fend for themselves. And hear this! The Pharaohs had no standing army!"

"That is indeed rare these days," I agreed.

"Satya," Yeshûa was really excited. "These people, without a central government, without a standing army, without a god, human or heavenly, wielding absolute power over life or death, lasted one thousand years!"

He had my attention. There was something absolutely unique about the Old Kingdom. No kingdom, empire nor any other political organization for that matter ever lasted that long. What did the ancient Egyptians know that we didn't?

"And just why did it come to an end?" I asked as if a millennium of peace and prosperity were not enough.

"Well, from what I have read, there may have been several causes," Yeshûa's tone still carried a hint of fascination at the Old Pharaohs' millennial achievement. "I wasn't there. It is easier to cast stones than to find the truth. But what followed was an era riddled with periods of anarchy and invasions by various barbarian tribes of the desert. Whatever other contributing factors, this sad time lasted for some one hundred and fifty years."

"And then followed the Middle Kingdom?" Arumji had done a good job on me.

"And then came the Middle Kingdom. During this period the masses had fought for and attained greater access to power. Nice though it may sound, the masses are seldom disposed to be wise and benevolent 'monarchs', Disorder resulted in the nobles regaining their influence."

"I never knew they ever had power."

"Some. During the strife at the beginning of the Middle Kingdom. Anyway, the various invaders helped the now fragmented people to consolidate themselves under one ruler, the founder of the Eighteenth Dynasty. He was Ahmose I, a man who'd also learned the dubious but apparently indispensable value of a regular army. We now enter the

third period in Egyptian history that the scribes refer to as
the Empire. The Empire is marked by extensive military
ventures into Egypt's neighbours, including, my friend, your
own country, Palestine. By the time they settled down, they
eventually controlled lands from Euphrates to the upper
cataracts of the Nile. And then history repeated itself. The
influx of plundered goods undermined the national fibre.
Corruption followed. The conquered provinces began to
regain their freedom."

"It seems that the good life in not as good as it seems,"
I quipped. Yeshûa sounded terribly serious.

"Excessive luxury always precedes decadence. You can
learn it from history, or you can just listen to Buddha. But it
is gratifying to see that the Old Kingdom might be considered the closest to a Buddha ideal. They really did walk the
middle path."

"For one thousand years!"

"Precisely. And it is not just a question of the loss of
land. The same factors, which undermine the strength of the
empire, also debase cultural standards. This can be seen...."

"In all of Sri Singh's lectures. I remember." And
then I had to ask him. "Yeshûa, why are you so preoccupied with the social and military history?"

"Am I? What good is a prophet, not to mention messiah, whose teaching cannot survive the test of time? How
else can I learn?"

I was taken aback. "You really intend to take on the
establishment in your own country?"

For a long time Yeshûa said nothing. We sat side by
side, looking at the ships moving in and out of the harbour.
Finally he got up and picked up a flat stone. As he threw it,
the pebble bounced many times before submerging. Just
like it did so many years ago.

"It has been almost eighteen years. Today, I suppose,
the Essenes would be taken to be a bunch of freaks. The
thing is, though, or at least was when I was there, that the
higher echelons among my people suffer from an extreme
predisposition towards superstition. The higher, the better

established, the more they have to lose, the more nervous
they are. My tutors carried orthodoxy to the extreme. But
they also let it be known that they dabbled in the arcane.
The mysterious. It had to do with creating conditions for
the... ah, the coming of the messiah, but they kept this
knowledge secret. Anyway, as such, they assumed to be in
possession of some esoteric powers. And as such the upper
crust of priesthood left them alone. It seemed wiser...."

"That goes for the Essenes, but can they offer *you*
enough protection?"

"I might sow some knowledge before I go under," he
said, his eyes still on the spot where the stone sank. "Who
knows, maybe I'll succeed where others have failed."

"Aren't you afraid?"

"Terrified. Most of the time. But less and less every
day. All we can do is our best." He picked up another
stone. It followed a similar path as the first. "And you
know, Satya, going under is not so bad, if you don't value
material life. All that I truly love is not of this world. Who
knows? Perhaps there is a life hereafter."

And in that instant I realized that Yeshûa was never
afraid of the establishment, or the Romans, or anything made
of flesh and blood. He was terrified of failure.

* * * * *

17

The Nile

Crossing over the mountains was an experience in it-self. To ordinary mortals they seemed inaccessible. Not because of the difficulties of crossing the terrain. They didn't match even the foothills of my Himalaya. What made them inaccessible was their abject desolation. No life at all. Not even a viper seeking shelter from the unrelenting sun. Reddish, mostly smooth rock formations; no variety of colour, like an ocean with gigantic waves. Only there were no crests to define the ending of one surge and the start of another.

If it were not for the merciless sun, we would have been lost. It alone provided us with an approximate bearing. There were no roads linking the Nile with the Red Sea. There were but a few meandering paths.

Perhaps, in time, the Romans will improve the crossings. They would, if they deem such good for business. It takes money to run an empire. I thought of all the garrisons they had to maintain in all the conquered countries. The Old Kingdom didn't have this problem, yet, even though the

Pharaohs squeezed their people just a little too much. Especially, toward the end.

"Have you studied the geography of Egypt?" Yeshûa asked me, I suspect, out of politeness. He knew I had, but I was keen to hear his version. "You first," I said. He took a deep breath.

"The great river nestles between two deserts. The stark mountains to the east, and sand, endless sand, on the west side. On the East you are lucky if you find a scorpion. On the West you are lucky if you find anyone. If you do, they are probably roaming marauders, nomadic tribes plundering the land, which offers nothing to plunder. Between these two seas of red sand and rock there is the black land of the valley. The richest land eternally renewed for its people. The valley of fertility."

I knew that much.

"And each year, nature performs her annual balancing trick with amazing precision," he continued. "With too little flooding, there is not enough irrigation. With too much, the seeding season is delayed by the slowly retreating waters." Yeshûa wagged his head from side to side. "Isn't nature clever? And all this thanks to Osiris!"

"The god?"

"None other. Before Osiris became the god of the underworld, he served as the god of inundation and vegetation generally. I suppose later he was too busy judging the dead to have much time for controlling the Nile. Yet somehow nature managed all by herself."

"Lucky for the Egyptians," I put in. I regarded my friend with renewed admiration. I wondered if there was a single god in Egypt, in the world for that matter, that he hadn't studied. Studied, dissected and put together again. He was a very thorough man.

"You have prophetic thoughts, my friend," Yeshûa laughed, but I would not be deterred.

"I understand that Osiris was also busy lavishing his marital love on his divine wife, Isis, not to mention fatherly love on Horus."

"The very same...." It was Yeshûa's turn to look impressed.

His usual smile got broader. This, by itself, wasn't anything special, but when his smile broadened his eyes sparkled. They literally sparkled like rays of the sun do when they hit ruffled waters. Yeshûa was the most joyful man I'd ever met. He seemed exhilarated by the simple act of living.

"Thank you Satya," he interrupted himself. "I fail to see what there is not to be joyful about. Look around you. Have you ever seen such beauty?" He was gazing towards the scorched and barren mountains.

I pictured the Hymalaya in the winter when the peaks wore deep cowls of glittering snow. In summer when verdant nature climbed a great deal higher.... Then, the intricate riches of the southern jungle, and even the flowers in my garden flashed before my eyes. They were all beautiful. Sometimes breathtaking. Yet he was right. I've never seen *such* beauty. Yeshûa saw beauty even in desolation. Beauty does not compete with itself. It just is.

"Anyway, you can't really blame Osiris for dropping out of the inundation business. Set, the god of storms, violence and general mayhem, was also Osiris' brother, and rather jealous of his sibling's position. To raise his own stature, Set not only murdered his brother but scattered his body in fourteen different places around the world. Isis, undeterred, managed to locate the pieces and stick them all together. Evidently pleased by her extraordinary act of restoration, Osiris promptly impregnated dear Isis with the previously mentioned Horus. However the glue Isis used must have been of inferior quality, because after a single night of delights, Osiris fell apart once more. It was then that he became, very appropriately, the god of the dead."

"The very dead, I presume. And what of Set?"

"Oh, Horus took care of him."

"And Isis?"

"Dear Isis henceforth lives on as the divine mourner both in heaven as well as on earth."

"Sounds like an equitable resolution."

We both laughed for quite a while. Yeshûa was becoming a great storyteller. He could be as serious or as light-hearted as he chose, on a moment's notice. I never got bored listening to him. Well, just once. That time when he started enumerating all the Egyptian gods in alphabetical order. Now that I think about it, I am sure he'd been doing that on purpose. He most probably wanted to see how long I would last without screaming out loud in protest.

Next morning we set out with a guide and four other men for the mountain pass. As we had no goods to carry with us, we rode small and swift Arabian horses. We'd both done a fair amount of riding from my father's stables, so we felt comfortable enough in the saddle. After four hours, however, the comfort wore thin. My back hurt, my legs felt like iron and my head started bobbing up and down with each horse's step. Mercifully, the guide called a stop. We dismounted but remained standing, not daring to sit on the hard, hot rock. Nevertheless, after four hours in the saddle, standing and walking felt a vastly preferable mode of transportation. And this was only the first morning....

Thus, after a short rest, we continued on foot. It wasn't a difficult route. Boring, if anything. An hour later we mounted our steeds, which took us and our aching behinds past the summit. We began the long descent into the river valley. There were moments when the wide blue ribbon of the Nile shimmered in the midday sun. Then it hid behind some outcropping only to reappear wider, more powerful, to our eyes. By three in the afternoon the terrain was almost flat. We changed our horses at the trading post, and continued on fresh mounts all the way to Thebes.

Yeshûa's eyes were shining.

"Did you know," he asked knowing full well that I didn't, "there was a time, in Egypt, when each locality had their own, private god-protector? Over generations the various local gods consolidated their influence into a single deity, the Amon or Ammon-Re, after the chief god of Thebes.

From simple polytheism their religion evolved into philoso-
phic monotheism."

Was there nothing my friend didn't know about gods?

He smiled saying nothing.

"Do you mind if I peek into their temples? They are
usually storehouses of all sorts of interesting titbits," his eyes
pleaded like those of a boy hoping for a favourite toy.

"While I attempt to organize the next leg of our journey. I presume you want to go north?"

"You presume rightly, my friend. And thank you.
Thank you very much."

I was certainly more qualified to organize the journey
than he was, although he'd travelled extensively in India, lo
and behold, without any assistance from me. I swallowed the
temporary influx of my pride and we parted company.

"See you at Karnak," he threw over his shoulder.
"When you're ready."

Ready for what, I forgot to ask.

"To eat!" he shouted already way down the hill.

Thebes is situated on the east bank of the Nile. Just as
well, I thought. I'd hate to have to swim to the other side just
to rent a boat for the next leg of our journey. Yeshûa was
not there to laugh at my thoughts. My eyes followed his
back as with a determined step he made his way toward the
nearest temple. I wondered how many he'd visit before he
would be ready to make our way down the river.

After examining my tender posterior, the river seemed
the only option. Slow, but less painful. Both elephants and
camels were definitely much kinder on one's hindquarters
than were horses. Over a long haul, that is. Of course, we
always asked for the very best *houdahs*, with soft seats and an
abundance of pillows. No matter. At the trading post they'd
already given me some information about the boats heading
down the Nile. Apparently there wasn't that much trade this
time of the year, and it should be easy enough to hitch a ride
for two men on any number of relatively small sailing vessels, provided that we didn't mind changing boats fairly often.

There was a catch I hadn't thought about. The Nile is a *really* slow moving river. The current does not promise to sweep one to the Mediterranean Sea in one easy motion. In fact, the constant northern wind made it easier to travel up the river on sail, while doing little more than drifting when going north. Unless you had money to pay for oarsmen. And the Nile is a mighty long river....

It was a strange feeling.

Two hours later, Yeshûa and I were strolling, relaxed, as though nothing had happened, between two long rows of sphinxes leading us toward the temple of Karnak. In a way, nothing had happened. We were two men, free, taking some time off. No meetings scheduled, no negotiations pending, no constant questions from my men.... It was like being on a holiday. It really was a strange feeling.

On both sides of the approaching courtyard, lions with their enormous ears, rested their chins upon human figures, probably Pharaohs' heads, daring anyone to come closer to the statues they were protecting. Yet the noble beasts no longer threatened visitors with their feral, if stoically controlled, power. They were no more than relics of an era gone by, of the days when a visitor, perhaps a pilgrim, cringed at their sight.

We walked unperturbed, carefree, feeling a touch of superiority over those who had once walked these same steps cowering in fear. At least I did. I felt superior. I wondered when it was that I rose above the gods contrived by other men, perhaps by priesthood, gods who would attempt to impose their will over my own. Yet it wasn't really a question of superiority. It was a question of freedom. Freedom from superstitions, from the burden that one man inflicts on another. Freedom which allows me to meet and talk to any man I choose, to talk to a man like Yeshûa, who dares to look all the gods in the face and remain steadfast, confident in the responsibility that he feels is his to discharge.

For that is what he did.

Yeshûa did not hold himself higher than any man let alone a god. He merely lived up to the prophecy of his own ancient scriptures, which proclaimed that ye are gods, and all of you are children of the most High. Yes. I've read 'his' Psalms. And the Torah. And all the Prophets. When I saw the attention he'd paid to Bhagavad-Gita, could I have done otherwise?

Yeshûa was waiting for me at the entrance to the Karnak temples. There were three main buildings, some smaller ones, and several outer temples probably for the lesser among the faithful. Lesser gods for the lesser men. No wonder. The temple, or temples, had been built over a period of some thirteen hundred years. They grew as the population multiplied. Enormous brick walls had enclosed the Mut, Monthu and Amun temples. The outer ones remained more accessible. Now, at this day and age, one could enter them all. Hardly a priest guarded their glorious history. The temples were still there, the gods had long departed.

Yeshûa had already visited three of the temples in the inner sanctum. He'd talked to some men, learned whatever he wanted to learn, and came out to meet me.

"Come with me," he called waving to me from afar.

I followed him inside and then past the main courtyard. Beyond the rear wall, now partially crumbling, there stood a number of great obelisks. After passing through the Second Pylon, we entered the Hypostyle Hall. Having travelled more than any man I know (with the possible exception of my father), I can safely say that it was the greatest architectural masterpiece I'd even seen. The lofty ceiling was supported by two rows of six papyrus columns. No mud brick here. They were all carved from blocks of solid sandstone. Each row was flanked by seven to nine more rows of columns. All tall, the outer half as high as those in the centre. Yeshûa led me toward the outer walls. There, in deep relief, he pointed to battle scenes of yesteryear.

"Here Seti battles with people of Palestine and Syria," he said. I suspect that it must have been for him a quiet yet emotional discovery to have come across this treasure.

He next pulled me, literally by the sleeve, outside, through the Third Pylon, to a narrow court, which had several obelisks. He pointed to one of them.

"If historians are right, then this one was erected about the time when Moses was leading my people out of slavery toward the Promised Land..." his voice sounded dreamy, as though he'd been there. With Moses. Or maybe with the Pharaoh overseeing the construction. "...some fifteen hundred years ago," he added.

He examined it, evidently for the second time; his eyes still wide open like a child's at having been given a new toy. "Tuthmosis the First must have built them...."

The name was unfamiliar to me. I was surprised at how strong Yeshûa's attraction was to things even vaguely related to the Jews or Hebrews. His homesickness must have been growing in direct proportion to our nearing his homeland.

There was a great deal more that he'd selected to show me. Walls and columns covered with relief, paintings alive with still vivid colour, all depicting scenes from a far distant history. I looked and wondered if anyone would bother to record our own period with such diligence and commitment. Are we worth recording for perpetuity? Have we, as a people, achieved anything worth while?

"Have they?" Yeshûa shared in my meandering thoughts. "I'm not sure it is ours to judge. The Romans will claim a scroll of history. Not for their contribution to culture, at least not so far. But all conquerors enter the scrolls, perhaps as a warning to posterity. We must just live and let live. And let history judge us."

His hand swept all the temples before us. And then for the first time Yeshûa took his eyes away from the countless artefacts.

"We can build temples not just of brick and mortar, nor columns and walls made of sandstone, marble, or granite," he said looking into the distance. "We can raise altars that will remain untarnished for millennia... for eternity...."

His voice trailed off into the distant future. It was time to go. I felt hungry and tired. I had no idea from where Yeshûa drew on such a storehouse of energy. He seemed fresh, ready to go for hours. I was not Yeshûa. No one was.

"I'm hungry..." I said.

"...and tired," he finished for me. But there was nothing tired about his smile.

After a long drink of water, I ordered wine. I felt like celebrating. It worked. Yeshûa, who appeared to have spent the last few hours in the hoary past, was finally returning to the present. For some reason it was the past that repeatedly preyed on his mind. Perhaps he was afraid of history repeating itself. I knew that everything he did, everything he'd ever learned was carefully steered to the fulfilment of a single objective.

"I must find a way..." he said leaving the sentence unfinished.

We had just both swallowed the last morsels of fish. We had lived on fish lately. Only today our meal had come from sweet water.

"Gods and religions are both transient," he started again. "At least the ones we create in our dubious image. How can I create a god that will outlast my generation? Amenhotep tried and failed. Yet he'd spoken of a heavenly father who watches with benevolence over all his creatures. Why did such a religion not sate mankind's needs? Must gods forever remain good *and* evil? Must they subject us to rewards and punishment? Forever? I tell you, Satya, resist not evil. There is no evil other than that which resides in a man's heart. Rid it from there and it has no reality."

"Perhaps we were not ready then. You said that Amenhotep ruled Egypt over thirteen hundred years ago. Perhaps we've matured since?"

Yeshûa looked at me with unmistakable admiration. "You always know how to cheer me, my friend." He reached over the table and embraced me like a long lost brother.

"Watch the wine!" I cautioned. I breathed easier when the jug tottered but remained standing.

A minute later, his face unaccustomedly darkened.

"Your own religion teaches that we live in the Kali-yuga. The age in which evil prevails over that which is good...."

"I never believed that part of our scriptures," I confessed. "And surely, it is not evil over good but rather matter over spirit," I offered.

"You are quite right, my friend. Thank you, Satya. I seem to be gravitating to my old beliefs. Nevertheless, the ancients had their reason for proposing such a philosophy. What I am afraid of is that what they postulated might not apply to individuals, but the currents of devolution might sweep the helpless, ignorant masses. Look at the Old Kingdom and what followed after. Knowledge is power, my friend. Yet people tend to neglect it."

"You're speaking of just one country," I insisted. " I see no evidence that my forefathers had been so superior to our present generation." Actually I'd learned more about other people's pasts than about my own. I prayed that Yeshûa wouldn't contradict me.

"You are a good man, Satya. In my heart that is all that matters."

I believed he meant that. But it made me feel uneasy about my ancestors. Have 'my people', to use Yeshûa's expression, also regressed from a more brilliant past? I felt I'd rather not find out. Not now. Now I rejoiced in Yeshûa's company. The man who'd chosen to worry for me. And for my ancestors. And for his own people. That's a lot of worry for just one man.

Although, on second thought, it wasn't really so much worry as concern. It was an extraordinary, unreserved compassion that flowed from my friend, seemingly toward all men. Past and present. Equally. Like the Nile.

Like an inexhaustible river....

The next day we spent most of the day in the Valley of the Kings, the Thebean Necropolis. There were tombs galore and an equal number of gods guarding them. It had been established fifteen hundred years ago and abandoned a mere four hundred years later. The Pharaohs had been buried in chambers cut out of solid limestone. Only some were accessible. Some had already been robbed. So much for the guardian gods.

"Why did people create so many gods?" I hardly expected a serious answer.

"One could say that there are as many gods as there are men. It is the action of Atma. Others in your country call it the Perceiver. Few realize that the Perceiver and the perceived in you are one." He stressed the words Atma and Perceiver as though capitalizing them.

"I do not follow...." After so many years he still spoke of things I couldn't fathom.

"The Perceiver is your Atma. Yet the only mode in which Atma can manifest itself is through you. Thus you are Atma. Thus you are searching for who you truly are. It is like a dog chasing its tale."

"Than why is it so hard...?"

"It isn't. We make it hard. Each time we are near the truth, we divert our attention. We escape lest that which we find will kill that which we have created. It is like a parent not wanting to release the hold they have on their children, that they might develop in their own right. We are afraid to lose the fruit of our labour."

Light was beginning to glimmer.

"Look at history," Yeshûa continued. "Whenever people found something that worked, they began looking further. Life is change. If we stop changing, we die. Not

just physically. We lose the purpose for which we have created the mode in which we can experience life. In which we
can experience the process of becoming."

I must have looked dumb.

"Look around you," he tried again, a lopsided smile of
concern playing about his lips. "Can you see anything that
is static? Look at the trees, plants, the animal kingdom, the
sun and the moon, the stars, the wind.... Nothing in our reality is static. Life manifests through movement, through
change. Constant change. When I admire the Old Kingdom
it is not because they maintained a political system for a
millennium. It is because they got closer to the eye of the
storm."

"So that within us which causes the change is itself unchangeable?"

"Precisely. That peace within is our true nature. If we
bring it forth from within ourselves, that which we bring
forth will save us. If we do not have that within ourselves,
that which we do not have within us will kill us. Why? Because that which is outside only exists for that which is
within."

"And yet that which is within needs us...."

"...as much as we need it. At the ground of being, the
two are one."

I was beginning to get the message. It really did make
sense. One has to be aware. To embrace it with our consciousness. To bring out our inner, our higher or true consciousness, is the object of our lives. It alone can save us.
Likewise, should we fail to do so, that which we do not have,
which we do not bring forth, will surely kill us. Discard us.
We would be of no use to it.

"But surely, that which is within, the atma, can always
create a new mode of becoming."

"It does. Only atma can manifest in the tangible reality
to the degree to which the mode allows it."

I must have looked slow again. "I thought you implied
that atma is divine, didn't you?"

"In every sense that matters. But no man can play a musical instrument unless he has one in his hands. Atma needs the means through which it can manifest. And even then it can only play the tune that the musician is capable of playing."

"So the more we learn the greater use we become to the Atma." I suddenly realized that I was not endowed with Atma. It is Atma that is endowed with me.

He said nothing. But when I looked at him his grin was accompanied by the most pleased expression I've ever seen on his face. I think I just graduated to class one.

After dinner I ordered a small jug of wine. I still felt like a student on holidays. We walked together, we ate together and most of the time we talked. Actually he talked, I listened. Tomorrow we were boarding a barge half filled with sugar cane which would take us down the river. I refused to board yet another Roman ship. I was looking forward to anything remotely more comfortable then a camel, an elephant or a horse. And after the amount of walking we'd done, these last few days, I was ready to remain sitting on something very soft, or even lying down, preferably on my stomach, for as long as I could.

And the idea of lying down and doing nothing brought me to the idea of heaven. I'd raised the subject a few times, but I still wasn't satisfied. I tried again.

"We all return to our place of origin," Yeshûa replied to my probing. "We, as all that is perceptible to our senses, are no more than illusion. Arumji taught me that. Our true Kingdom, our true place, our home, is in heaven. Only your true self does not *go* to heaven. It never leaves it. It resides there in an eternal state of being. To experience the mode of becoming it creates you and me. All of us. Atma remains in a constant state of grace."

"Just what is this heaven, then?" I had to ask. Most if not all religions promulgated some sort of heaven. As a place in the hereafter. Designed as reward. For the righteous.

"Righteous simply means – right thinking. That is why ultimately faith, hope and charity are the means. Knowledge is the point of arrival."

"To acquire knowledge takes an effort..." I mused.

"And total commitment. You cannot serve two realities. Unless you have a single eye, you miss both. You fail in this world and the next."

"Next?"

"Not in the temporal sense. Next in the sense that it is the next step you take on the evolutionary scale. Evolution simply means new or deeper understanding. It is the travel of consciousness through time. The physical manifestation of evolution is only a result."

"Surely, the results matter?"

"Anaximander of Miletus was a practical man. Some six hundred years ago he made some observations of fossil remains as well as of how sharks feed their young. Based on these, he concluded that man originated in the sea. That in fact we derive from the fish."

"So...?"

"Based on his observations he declared that man should not eat fish. He assumed, I presume, that it would be a sort of protracted cannibalism. He confused the cause with the result."

I remembered vague echoes of Sri Singh's lessons.

"So what of heaven?" I persisted.

"Heaven is the true reality. It is also a state of con-sciousness. All things exist there except for time. Unless you encapsulate time into eternity. Whatever you desire in heaven – it is yours. Whatever you wish for – is yours also. Whatever you dream of – it is already there. There is no be-coming. No beginning – no end. Everything is already there, here, everywhere. Heaven is. Atma is. Even as you are, as I am. I am that I am, not the I am you see with your physical eyes. Yet the two are one. Do you understand my words?"

I am sure he did not expect me to answer. He read my thoughts much faster than I could possibly formulate them

into words and sentences. Even as I watched his face, I was
still seeking understanding, and waiting for my conscious
mind to accept and absorb all he'd told me, his words were
transposing me. Their essence was becoming metabolized
by my mind at the rate faster than I'd been able to absorb
anything in the past. Later, even if I still had no ability to
repeat his words in the same, exact order, I knew, without a
shadow of doubt, that those words were mine. Mine to keep.

Finally Yeshûa seemed satisfied. With my rate of absorption, I suppose. He put his hand on my shoulder.

"Don't worry Satya. Heaven, even as the truth, needs to
be continuously rediscovered. And it is. Atma speaks
through different men throughout history to keep us on an
even course. Just think. In India, Buddha taught us the
middle way. He advocated a proper balance. That was some
five hundred years ago. About the same time, in Greece,
Empedocles, regardless of his other theories, said that health
is a proper balance between the opposite components. He
didn't invent this theory, but he gave it distinction." Then
Yeshûa's face lit up in one of his disarming grins. "You
know, Satya, this definition is very close to my concept of
god. God is what the opposites have in common."

And then we both went to sleep.

* * * * *

18

Memphis

At first light we climbed aboard. It transpired that the barge carried not only sugar cane but also two enormous blocks of granite. The Egyptians never tired of building monuments. Or the blocks could have been for the Romans. I'd been told that in Alexandria, where the Ptolemic 'Pharaohs' were no more than Roman puppets for some time, the invaders began raising monuments to their own glory. Or to the glory of their divine Caesar. The last Ptolemaic to truly rule her country was Cleopatra the Seventh, who died some sixty years ago. Her defeat was mostly due to her navy loosing to the Romans at Actium. Now, a garrison of soldiers is stationed in Alexandria to keep the peace. A sad end to a great history.

Frankly, I didn't care. Four thousand years of recorded history should suffice for anyone. I would place odds that the Romans wouldn't last half that long. And rightly so.

On board, our own 'quarters', turned out to be more comfortable than I'd imagined possible. We were placed at the bow, offering us a magnificent panorama of the river and surrounding shores. The land on both sides of the Nile was exuberant in lush vegetation. There was not even a suggestion of any desert on our left, on the west shore. On the east, behind the plantations, groves and fields of rich vegetation,

we could admire the stark oblong contours of the red
mountains. They looked a lot less forbidding from our
comfortable seats.

A straw roof protected our heads. It didn't cut out all
the sun, but enough to let us appreciate the breeze from the
North.

"This beats any beast I've ever mounted!" I nodded in
appreciation.

"That goes double," Yeshûa agreed.

The barge had been loaded yesterday and within minutes of our arrival, a dozen men had pushed us away from
the shore. Four men with long poles directed our bow towards the speediest current. We began the last leg of our
journey. Together. The lazy river sauntered northward, indifferent to our fate. The old lady was in no hurry. We
floated, seemingly through time more so than through space,
which resolved itself into images of calm and serenity. Here
and there, forgotten echoes of yesterday came into our view.
We acknowledged the gift that the river offered us. We were
both grateful.

This was the laziest, the most comfortable, the most
luxurious journey of my, and surely of Yeshûa's, life. Later
I thought of it as the calm before the storm. The storm
Yeshûa brought about and had no idea how to stop. Perhaps
it was meant to be. Knowing him as I do, I have certain
doubts. But, as he would say, history will be the judge.

We dallied for so long, we sailed so slowly, that I was
forced to bid Yeshûa good-bye in Memphis. The westerly
monsoons refused to wait for me. And we each had our mission to fulfil. How I wish he'd returned with me.

"Why are you going back? Home I mean?"

I meant to ask him if he'd been unhappy living in India,
or even travelling with me, the world over. I'd made enough
money for the two of us to continue like this for years.
Travelling. We would visit my wife and children, visit my
father, the elderly Arum Singh, and then return. We could

go on to Rome, visit Gaul, continue to the far-west Iberian Province.... We could do so much together. So much.... See so many places. It could all be so easy. For the first time, ever, I was hoping he was reading my thoughts.

"I've spent almost thirty years taking. Filling my chalice to the brim. It is time I gave some of it back." His voice was very matter-of-fact. As though it was obvious.

"Some of it?"

"As much as it is mine to give."

"Forgive me Yeshûa, but if it took you more than seventeen years to awaken my understanding, to convey to me just some of your ideas, how do you propose to teach them to your people? Over the next seventeen years? Will they understand you so much better than I?"

"No Satya. They will not understand me any better than you. I shall sow what I can, where I can. If my words fall on fertile ground, the seed will take root and in time will blossom. If not, I will have done my best."

"And this will give them a new religion?"

"What? The last thing I want to do is to create yet another religion. The world is already replete with religions. And anyway, my people already have one. All I really want to do is to show them where and how they strayed from the path. I am the door, but they must walk through on their own. Not under some priestly whip. At best, I hope to free them, at least some of them, from the burden of tradition. To set them free."

That made much more sense. In this he might succeed. He has the knowledge, the talent and certainly the charm. Oodles of charm.

"Isn't this roughly what Moses tried?"

"He'd succeeded in his own way. In his time. But we've moved on."

Joy and sadness seemed to have mixed into a strange amalgam that set his features into an expression of desperate hope.

"The most I might hope for is to gather a small group, ten or twelve people around me who might understand at least some of the truth." He closed his eyes, as though visualizing a small gathering. "They would have to have minds uncluttered by previous maxims, previous postulates which had already set them in a rut. Minds fresh to receive without having to forget a great deal of any previous teaching. Yet who would have been raised in Hebrew tradition."

I knew that whatever I said would not dissuade him from his plan. It seemed such a pity. I knew how hard it was to explain anything to anyone who is not willing to put in the effort to understand. Especially if the new concepts are at odds with the established, traditional ways. People, simple people, cling to traditions. They seem to protect them from the new, from the unknown.

"So your mind is made up?" It was a rhetorical question. He knew that I knew the answer.

"Like I've said, Satya. It is time to pay my debts."

If the occasion hadn't been so sad for me, I would have laughed outright. I couldn't think of any man alive who had fewer debts to pay than Yeshûa. Yeshûa's debts? The world owed him a debt. A debt for spending his life reaching for the truth, only to give it away for free. Debts?

"You make me laugh, Yeshûa. You make me laugh..." I murmured.

But neither he nor I was in a laughing mood.

They served us a lunch of fresh fruit, water and for dessert, a pie baked by the captain's wife. It was the first dessert we had eaten in months. It tasted magnificent. We then had a visit. The captain was almost doubled over. Though he looked as if he suffered from a bad back, he came around to ask us if all was to our liking. Yeshûa got up and took the captain to one side. He must have done something to the man's spine. When they turned back, the captain stood as straight as a needle. There was awe in his eyes. He reached for Yeshûa's hand in an attempt to kiss it in gratitude. Yeshûa withdrew it quickly, evidently embarrassed.

"It is nothing, my friend," he assured the rejuvenated skipper. "It was nothing really...."

"But sir, for years I couldn't...."

"It is nothing. It is I who must thank *you* for the delicious food you sent us."

"More? You will have more?"

"Later, my friend. Later."

The captain bowed deeply, this time with no difficulty, and went about his business. "He is a good man. But he must stop...."

"What, is he beating his wife?"

Yeshûa laughed, a little awkwardly. "Never mind. You said earlier that you were going to ask me something."

The question I had still concerned Yeshûa's plans.

"Just how do you intend to teach them?" I was thinking of a school, a lecture tour, whatever. I might be in position to finance such a venture. I knew I could easily afford it.

"No my friend," he was reading me like a scroll, " I shall not start a school. Frankly, I don't know what will happen."

"You haven't a real plan?" In any successful venture a plan is a must.

"This is not a business venture, Satya. It is more like playing a musical instrument. You practice and practice and practice to become proficient, to acquire the very best technique you possibly can, and then, when you finally perform, you forget about the technique. You just play."

"You are the instrument. Your knowledge is the technique. And the performer?" I asked suspecting the answer.

"That's right, my friend. That's all. Just Atma."

The same stars, shimmering over the Nile, just a short distance away, are now over my head. Again. I'd ridden day and night to get here. I'd changed horses many a time, just so that I might hear him talk. No matter what he had told me, I knew, somehow, that this would be different. That I would hear not my old pal, my brother, but a man confident in fulfilling his mission. The mission he'd chosen to deliver to his people.

Would he have recognized me?

It can only be a little after midnight but my bones hurt already. It could have been those weeks in the saddle. And now on a stone bench. Yôna must have gone back inside. He needs the company of his people. I have no one. Isn't that what Yeshûa had said? He said he had no one, and nowhere to lay his head. And then he'd realized that he'd hurt me.

"Except for you, Satya. Except for you. You are always there when I need you."

Only I wasn't. Hadn't been. I had my business to run. My family, children. And now, even now, I arrived too late.

I try again to get some sleep. The rough stone is just too hard. I am not a boy any more. It's not true that people live to be a hundred in the Kali Yuga. Some do. Most won't make it past fifty. Sixty at best. As boys, he and I, we'd slept on anything. Once on a branch of a tree. Just for fun.

I move from side to side, then give up. Again, I look at the stars. My mind is too full, too busy recalling each detail of his life. Not in any particular order, but still, determined not to lose a single word he'd ever spoken to me. The words I would never, never hear again.

Once again my mind drifts to the Nile, even as our barge drifts along the sluggish river. There too the stars littered the ceiling above us....

What a magnificent ceiling. We both slept well that night, but I woke up, now and then, thinking of his words to me. Thinking of the time he'd compared his mission to playing a musical instrument. Was this then – or right now? Memories are like that. You don't control them, you just relax and let the mysterious workings of the mind do its wonders.

Memories....

Sometimes it is beautiful music, sometimes a masterful painting or an exquisite sculpture. Or it could even be a mountain with a particularly beautiful contour. Sometimes the memory of such a thing, or event, lingers on, ready to reveal itself to you again and again, to defy time, and once again join you in the present. In such moments you become one with that memory, you are absorbed into its realm, to the exclusion of all others. They, the memories, have the power to infect you for life.

Yeshûa was like that. He infused himself into my consciousness. I feel that a part of him will forever survive within me. That in a way I could neither explain nor even imagine, he and I, at some level of being, had become one.

"We are all one," he'd said once. "I am within you even as you are within me."

It was so real, when he said it. So very real. And now? Is he still here? He is as surely in my heart as he ever was. Ever. Yeshûa, the deliverer.

Neither a work of art, nor an event, yet a universe unto himself. The words he'd spoken, even his gaze or the touch of his hand, became indelibly engraved within my memory. They are etched on the essence of my soul with such power that, now and again, they fight and win the battle for the present. My present. My mode of being. Time doesn't retreat. I don't go back to remember. The past comes forth to meet me. Now. In the eternal now. And here he is, alive, larger than life, immortal. And the wondrous thing is that in such instants of eternity he pulls me with him into his kingdom where all things seem, no, where all things *are* possible. A kingdom where there is no fear, no hunger or thirst. Where my heart and mind and all my senses are sated. Where peace rules supreme. At least it feels so. Perhaps that is the greatest gift he'd bestowed on me. In my heart and mind, he never died. He never will. Is this immortality?

As we neared the parting of our ways, the places became less distinct, even as he became more real. The west bank moved slowly, lazily. Settlements abounded, some reaching back into antiquity. Contrary to what they'd told me at the trading post in Thebes, our barge did not come ashore till many days later in Memphis. On the way I saw Yeshûa's hungry eyes staring. He looked at the pyramids, I looked at Yeshûa. I could always see the pyramids later...

And then we arrived in Memphis. It had been Hor-Aka, also known as Menes, who'd made Memphis Egypt's capital. Hor-Aka means 'Horus of the reeds,' from the time when Isis had hidden him among the papyri to live, to survive, and become the first Pharaoh of the first dynasty. It had been Horus who fought the battle with Set, who ruled Upper Egypt. Eventually Horus had won and unified Egypt into a single kingdom.

"Even as Mosheh had been hidden in the reeds by...." Yeshûa seemed to have been thinking aloud. I couldn't quite hear him.

"Mosheh?" I asked.

"You know him as Moses. Even as the Egyptian legend of Horus, so too a Pharaoh's daughter, one of many I suspect, had hidden Mosheh among the papyrus reeds. He too grew up to lead his people."

"Although he experienced problems uniting them," I added.

"Indeed. Mosheh had many problems. My people are not easy...."

I knew the story. Since meeting Yeshûa that fateful day in Jerusalem, Arumji had made sure that I would not remain ignorant of the Hebrew history. As much as was known. Unfortunately there had only been quasi-religious sources, which invariably chose spiritual truth over physical accuracy.

The story said that already toward the end of the Old Kingdom some thirty thousand people lived there. Originally it was founded over three thousand years ago.... There were so many stories. But my time was coming. I had to go back to join 'my people'. To join my brother and sail back home, to India. Would he have waited for me?

Yeshûa continued to pursue his passion for learning. My own mind, or perhaps just my emotions, became preoccupied with the impending farewells. I tried, a few times, to suggest that he change his mind and come back with me. Each time he diverted the subject to some unimportant item. He avoided the subject. Finally I asked him point blank.

"Yeshûa," I said as earnestly as I knew how, "you know that we are brothers. In my father's mansion there are many rooms. You can stay with us, in Benares, for the length of your days...."

He raised his arm to silence me. I stared at my feet. I knew I was beaten.

"I must stay in Egypt and study the works of Ikhnaton."

I looked up. When his words dawned on me, I expected him to add: 'I have so much to learn.' I was spared his modesty. The ridiculous thing was that I am sure he would have meant it. He really believed he still had a great deal to learn. The name he mentioned, Ikhnaton, was strange to me. So many things my friend said sounded strange to my ears. Then, with luck and some perseverance, some of them appeared to ripen. Regrettably, not all of them.

"Ikhnaton means 'Aton is satisfied'," Yeshûa offered. "It was the name Amenhotep assumed after he drove the priesthood from the temples. Amenhotep means 'Amen rests'."

I was still lost at sea. He smiled his usual, understanding smile.

"After Amenhotep, whose name had been derived from Amon or Amen, the great god of Thebes, freed his people, he commanded them to worship a new god he called Aton, or Aten, an ancient designation of the sun-disk. Aton was to be worshipped as the great god-creator. I suspect his intent was to separate the imagery of man, as Amon had been portrayed."

I wondered if all this was necessary. Necessary to live a good life. An inoffensive life. A life filled with beauty and comfort, surrounded by people whom you loved and who loved you. Back home.... But Yeshûa still had different plans. Leading him into the great unknown. Possibly into danger that he couldn't control. Once more he'd read my thoughts.

"Do not worry about me, Satya," he sounded relaxed, confident of his purpose, "No matter what I achieve, all has its transience that enters the wheel of becoming."

I tried to picture Yeshûa preaching to masses, to learned doctors, to priests and priestesses. I tried to see him attired in princely, imposing regalia, standing on a high podium, admiring multitudes hanging on his every word....

I tried hard, but I just couldn't picture it.

Things of which Yeshûa spoke did not belong in their mundane reality. They didn't even belong to the masses. They were for the few, the chosen ones. His words seemed to trickle, cautiously, through tiny cracks in the foundations of heaven. Now that I knew him, I could detect a joyful innocence flowing from his communion. He never preached to me, nor have I ever witnessed him preaching to any man, woman or child. The most I could sense was him sharing his mind, his heart, but mostly his soul with whoever cared to give ear. He cast the seeds and let karma decide their ascendancy.

"Material things... the bigger they are the sooner they crumble into dust...."

I recalled the countless empires he'd studied, as he sat, cross-legged, later in *Padmasana*, at Sri Singh's feet. Hour after hour, day after day, as the old master shared with us, so eloquently, his prodigious phenomenal knowledge.

"The less ostentatious works last a little longer." Yeshûa's voice was dreamy. He too must have reached back to the many works of art he and I had admired the world over.

"Next come those currents which stir our emotions," he continued. "Great love and great hatred linger for generations without dissolution. Then, finally, we come to ideas. These blossom slowly, take even longer to mature, but then last for millennia. We recall them with deference, often admiration, and even try to resurrect them in our own time of becoming. Yet even pure concepts run their prescribed course. Not due to their inferiority, but simply because after we pay them homage, as we once had to images of gods and goddesses, we must return to our lasting residence. To the abode of our true self. Into the house of Atma. We must return, always, into the timeless, eternal present."

There was neither pleasure nor emotion in his words. Certainly no animosity. He was reciting the law. It was indifferent, precise, like mathematical equations. It had nothing to do with pain or with pleasure. It was defining the matrix within which those who understood could achieve their highest awards.

After that discussion, my memory became jumbled. I recall snippets, detached phrases, fragments from Yeshûa's words. From his life with me. Or close to me.

"...ultimately Ahura-Mazda would win...." I saw his face, clearly, as when Arum Singh had said these words. So many years ago. *"...but only after the coming of messiah, who would be born miraculously, and bring about the resurrection of the dead... and, ultimately, the last judgment."*

As Arumji spoke then, Yeshûa's face had remained cast in stone, just as the Sphinx, frozen in time, just as the Sphinx we saw on our way to Memphis. *"The good would be rewarded with immediate bliss, the wicked would be cast into the fires of hell...."*

The words reverberated in my head like an echo of something very important. Yeshûa sat down, drew his legs beneath him. He remained silent. This happened more and more often. He would suddenly leave my company, only his body would stay behind. I was left to my own thoughts. And then I heard that voice again still echoing in my head.

"...Mithras had suffered greatly in his earthly form... he performed miracles... saved lives by feeding men...."

Yeshûa was equally motionless – then as now. Then, even as now, he sat next to me.

"...the poor people identified with Mithras, not just in Persia, but his worship reached out as far as Rome...."

Why did memories of Mirthras fill my mind? Was it he who'd been feeding those ideas to me?

I looked away.

The moon hanged still, indifferent to his, as to my, fate. Tomorrow I would go back. He wouldn't. And then more fragments filled my mind. Different thoughts, ideas, whole sentences... Where did they come from...?

...I am he who is within me... I am the honoured one and the scorned one... I am the silence that is incomprehensible...

Yeshûa remained quite still. I didn't take my eyes from him. His lips didn't move.

I am the one before whom you have been ashamed... I am strength and I am fear... I am war and peace... I am the one who has been hated everywhere....

I could hear his words quite distinctly yet his lips still didn't move.

I am the process of becoming... I am the one whom they call Life. I am the one whom they call Law... I am the one whom you have hidden from... I am sinless... I am the one who alone exists....

Fear and peace washed over me. Simultaneously. I felt fear yet I wasn't afraid. I felt troubled yet I remained at peace. Does that make sense?

I am the first-born son who was begotten.

After a time impossible to determine, Yeshûa opened his eyes. He looked relaxed. At peace with the world.

"Who are you, Yeshûa?" I asked. My head was still reverberating from the fragments of thoughts, esoteric ideas, mysteries, I've been given to hear. "Who are you, my friend? In spite of his preoccupation with 'his people' he didn't seem to belong anywhere. Anywhere on earth. Anywhere....

"Have I not just told you?"

He looked up at me with his usual friendly and slightly mischievous little smile. Like in the old days. Yet it took all my will power to smile back.

"I am your brother, Satya. You know that?" There was a question hanging at the end of that answer. I think I knew the rest of it. What he meant was that he was brother to all men.

And then I remembered no more.

* * * * *

Epilogue
The Morning of the Third Day

One more time I pull myself to my feet. I am stiff, dejected, sad. Sadder than I've ever been in my entire life. I try to stretch. I hurt all over. I feel stiffer than after a week on the back of an elephant. This bleak courtyard is my home. The stone bench is my bedroom.

The first rays of the rising sun are just touching the parapet of the wall opposite my bench. I must have dozed off leaning against the mud bricks. Again. I could have stayed indoors, with the others. I didn't want to intrude. Anyway, I am used to sleeping under an open sky. Travelling does that to you. You lay your head down wherever you stand. Or sit. If you're lucky enough to own a tent, so much the better. I recall, particularly when travelling with Yeshûa, how we would pull ourselves out of the tent just enough to have our heads under the open sky. It got so that I could hardly fall asleep unless I felt stars overhead. A myriad of them. The N'har di Nur, the Bed of Ganges. It was like a familiar ceiling lulling us, him and myself, to sleep. At least, when we didn't talk till the early hours.

I find it odd, almost inappropriate, that the sun should shine with such carefree abundance. The morning air also seems particularly pure, reminding me of the desert. Even the gentle breeze adds to the pleasure of being alive. I wonder how many of his disciples had noticed.

I'd spent two interminable days and two even longer nights just sitting here. Here, and at the other two walls. A few times I went inside to ask if there were any news.

News?

What news could there be. He's dead. The dead stay dead. That's the way of the world.

Right now, we all feel dead. There is no desire for life in any one of us. Not one. The sun and the breeze notwithstanding. And yet, twice a day, one of the women brings me something to eat and some water. A force of habit, I suppose. Not much food. Not much water. Just enough to sustain me. To keep me alive. Should I thank Lord Vishnu? Or the quiet, kind-hearted women? I don't want to eat. They insist. I have no strength to argue.

There is an eerie silence around me. We are on the outskirts of town. There should be more noise. People-noise. Hustle and bustle of a new day awakening. There is nothing. Nothing has changed. For some reason the words of Yôhannan, of little Yôna, come back to me with nagging regularity.

"They say that he was the king who didn't make it."

What nonsense!

Yet the statement comes back to me with a sardonic force. I hide my face in my hands. Had I dreamt or just imagined last night? Were there eleven men devoid of life holding a silent wake for one who refused to fight back? One who had so much power....

I'd witnessed some of it. Yet now, or then, he'd refused to defend himself? Why? Yeshûa who couldn't hurt a fly. Yeshûa whom they murdered like a common criminal. My brother.

"How did he die?" *I'd asked Yôna the last time he came out to see me.*

"They crucified him," *he said and went quickly inside.*

No man deserves such a death. Certainly not one who is innocent. And surely, if anyone ever lived an innocent life it was he. And then I hear the same insistent voice I'd heard last night. Only this time I know I am wide-awake.

"Never have I suffered in any way, nor have I been distressed."

It is a voice I would recognize anywhere. In the desert, in the jungle, floating along the Nile, sailing the open sea. In my dreams....

"Never have I suffered in any way, nor have I been distressed."

It is a whisper. It doesn't make sense. Nothing makes sense any more. Then I hear it again....

"Never have I suffered in any way..."

I must be getting tired. How can that be? I'd only just woken up. Perhaps I'm going crazy. Can one go mad with grief?

"Never have I suffered...."

Yeshûa....?

Yôna comes back, again, to keep me company. He goes inside periodically, stays with his people for a few hours, and comes back. There is so much compassion in this man. He had a good teacher. My friend.

"It is not good to be alone," *he says.*

We sit together both lost in our own thoughts. But we are together. There is a strange easing of tension when you have company. There is more light. And then Yôna remem-

bers his Master's words. For the first time this morning he smiles.

"I am always with you," he says. Then he looks at me. "That's what he said."

I know who he is talking about. We both know. And then, we both drift off again.

As I look up I notice Yôna's eyes following a single cloud making its leisurely way towards the rising sun. It seems forlorn and lonely, like both of us. We all have company, yet the feeling of loneliness is overpowering. And then Yôna says something that moves me to the core. Somehow it imparts a responsibility on me that I have no idea how to discharge.

"'A time will come,' the Master said only for me to hear, 'when men will write scrolls about me. They will write of the words I have spoken but not one of them will understand what I said. Except for you, my little one.' He'd said those very words. And then the Master added: 'Except for you and Peter.'"

And then Yôna turns his head and looks at me with a strange light in his eyes.

"The Master gazed at me for some time and then once more he corrected himself. 'And Satya,' He'd added as though reaching into some long forgotten past. 'Yes,' the Master affirmed. 'Except for you and Peter and Satya. These three...' He'd said. And I detected a great sadness in His voice. Sadness of a Man who wanted to convey so much, yet there was no one who understood his words."

"Almost no one," I whisper. In two days I'd grown close to this young man. Young? Less than ten years my junior. Yet somehow there is a great innocence about him. "And just what can we do to help him?"

A cloud reaches the sun and for a moment hides its brilliance. Then the cloud passes on. The brilliance remains.

*I look at my new friend. He still manages a gentle smile.
He'd learned much from his Master. I suddenly realize that I
still don't know what it was that Yeshûa was teaching, these
last three years. I ask Yôna. He doesn't answer. I nudge
him gently on the shoulder. He remains very still. Then I
hear his words, seemingly from far away. It is both more and
less than a voice. A whisper? It feels as though he is drawing me into his memories.*

I hear... I see masses, mulling masses of people....

"People came from afar to see His miracles. They
came to be fed, to be healed, to be resurrected. Spiritually.
In their hearts they have been dead. Listless. He fed the
hungry, He healed the sick, He raised the dead. People
looked for miracles from Him. They didn't care much for
what he said. Or they would have acted differently. They
needed gods, kings at least, rewards, even punishment. He
only offered forgiveness. They preferred to punish the
guilty."

I dare not move. I can hardly breathe lest I miss....

*At first I saw a desert. A desolate place. Then a lake.
Tiberius? Then just masses of people. Multitudes. Suddenly
Yôna's eyes move over the distant hills. I recognize them.
They are the hills of Gallilee. Then more people, villages...
Cana, Tiberias, Magdala, Capernaum, Beth-saida... Many
others. Places I know. I've been there. I walked the deserts
and hills and valleys.*

*I continue to see through his eyes. How is this possible?
They come from afar. Masses of rabble, riffraff. Simple folk.
Ordinary people. From far and wide....*

"He didn't allow us to judge anyone. Lest we be
judged, He said." Yôna looked up. "Lest we be judged
ourselves."

Yôna's voice trails off into a near whisper.... "Tell me
more of his teaching?" *I encourage him as best I can.*

"Teaching? He only taught one idea. He taught me to
love the Lord my God with all my heart, and all my soul, and

all my mind. He taught all of us to do that. He also told me
to love my neighbour as myself."

*"Yes? Go on?" I prod again when my young friend re-
mains silent.*

"On? There is no more. This is all he taught us. All
the rest of his teaching consisted of illustrations, examples,
stories, parables, of how to put this single commandment into
practice."

*"That is all he taught you?" There must have been dis-
belief in my voice.*

*Yôna shakes his head as if coming out of a dream. Yet
his tone continues as before.*

"Love," he repeats as though to himself. *Then he looks
up at me, and smiles that wondrous smile of youthful innocence.* "Love, Satya. Just love..." *he repeats to me, in un-
qualified reassurance.*

*The next instant the sadness, which pervaded the house,
the courtyard, even the air we breathed over the last two
days, evaporates from his eyes.*

"That's all there is, Satya. That's where it all starts,
and that's where it ends. There is nothing else. Love is what
makes us one. All of us. Love is what unites us with each
other, with our friends, our enemies, the animals, plants,
flowers, the sky...."

*I press my palms to my face. After eighteen years of
study, day and night, Yeshûa came back to teach his people
to love. To love the God within themselves and within each
other.*

"And they killed him for that?" *I ask.*

*I shouldn't have asked him. It was unfair. The brief
moment of elation wavers and then it's gone. Yôna's smile
loses its innocence. He tries bravely to sustain it and then
gives up. Just its shadow remains. We are still here. Alone.
He's gone. I'm tired again.*

Wearily I lift my head. Past and present are all mixed up in me. I don't care anymore which is which. If only he were here. If only I'd gotten here sooner. Would I have made any difference? Was his future written in the stars? Or... or did he command the stars even as he'd ruled over the angry seas on the way to Kana?

He came back to teach them to love one another...

After studying countless religions of countless countries, delving into innumerable cultures throughout history, after dissecting social and political systems of vast empires that came and went across millennia... After endless hours, days and nights of meditation frozen in the sacred *Padmasana*, after giving up all comforts which life has to offer, he came back to teach them love.

There is a commotion inside the house.

Voices, which sound odd in the atmosphere of abject despondency, violate the hallow silence. They sound as though a bunch of women barged in on the disciples' self imposed tranquillity. There must be another entrance to the house. At the rear. The commotion is getting louder.

"Wait here," Yôna says rising. "I'll let you know what's happening." And suddenly his body responds to his youth. In three bounds he disappears in the gloom of the interior.

I sit back ready to drift back to the haven of my memories. He couldn't have been more than thirty, maybe thirty-three, thirty-four at the most. Four years ago we travelled to Egypt together. I'd heard that, after I'd left, Yôhannan, not my young friend, the other Yôhannan, had met him there. The man who later baptized people in Jordan. That's right, they called him Yôhannan the Baptist. Yeshûa and I had gone, together, as far as Memphis. That's where I'd left him. Yôhannan must have met him there. Later Yôhannan had returned to Judea while Yeshûa stayed on. For a while.

"I have so much to learn," he'd probably said, smiling. How can a man who has nothing, no house, no wife, no family of his own, no money... how can he smile? All the time?

My father had spent his life trading around the world. Sometimes I took the trip with him. Sometimes Yeshûa joined us. It wouldn't do to travel on your own. Not just for lack of company, but there were people who would cut your throat first and only then look through your satchels to see if it had been worth it. Such people led a nomadic life. And who could blame them? The Romans taxed everyone within a breath of their life. There were many roving bands. And not just the Bedouins. There were the Parthians who only got off their horses to rob you. The Kushans were no better. The world was full of rejects, of people disgruntled with their lot. Some had been searching for a better way, others were just surviving, living by their dubious wits. In Judea many had searched. For a better way. On my last visit to Jerusalem, I counted more than forty sects each one claiming to have all the answers. It reminded me of home. There are no two Hindûs who believe in the same god.

Yeshûa came back to teach them to love one another.

He and I had been so close yet, also, so far apart. So very far apart.

Yeshûa had absolutely no interest in money. He openly admired my father, he called him a fair man, but he said his own wealth lay elsewhere. He would stand on a hill, on an outcropping of rocks in the middle of a desert; his hands would sweep a vast arc, from east to west.

"All this is mine. Why would I ever need more?"

And he laughed. Only I knew him well enough to know that he meant it. He really thought that the world and all its marvels were no less and no more than a gift to us from an inexhaustible source. Later, after staying a few years in India, he believed that we have been unwittingly manipulating reality to mould it into such a form as we desired. Only most of us had no idea that we were doing so.

"If they only had faith like a grain of mustard seed...." he said a few times, in rare moments of sadness.

Or at least if they would learn to love the Lord their God. And each other....

They didn't.

The noise inside the house gets louder. There is shouting now. "I'll let you know!" Yôna had promised, but didn't come out again.

I hear a raised voice and shake the cobwebs from my head. Did Yôna call me?

A large, thickset man shouts something I don't understand to the men crowding in the doorway and runs across the courtyard. I recognize him as the man who denied their ability to aid Yeshûa. Who'd said one word to me: "No." It seemed like ages ago. A whole lifetime. Now he is running at full speed as though chased by an army of demons.

"Wait here," he throws over his shoulder. His tone is a command. I think he must be their leader now. Now that Yeshûa's gone. I have to find out what on earth is going on. In total contrast to the previous deafening silence, there is a veritable pandemonium coming from inside the darkened room. Everyone is talking at once.

"But I saw it, I tell you. The stone was.... "

"Don't be silly, woman. No one could move that stone."

"But he said he would...."

"No buts. I've seen that rock myself. No one could get into His grave. A dozen men would need long poles to pry it open. Did you see a dozen men? Or even some poles lying around?"

The women sound close to tears.

"But I did see it. I did. I really did!" Insists one of them.

"Don't you wish," another says. "We all suffer from wishful thinking...." This is a man's voice.

Then I see Yôna standing alone, leaning against the wall seemingly for support. Even in the relative darkness of the room, his face appears to have turned a few shades paler. His right hand is holding the edge of his robe, as though to wipe his forehead. The hand is trembling. His eyes are fixed on a point in the distance. He looks like a startled animal, not knowing what to do. I cover the room in three strides.

"Yôna," I tug at his elbow. "Yôna," I say louder. "What happened?"

His eyes slowly, still in a trance, find my face, then my own eyes. Something also happened to the pain. He is smiling again. The smile is in his eyes. That same smile, only now the serenity isn't forced. It is real, it is ebullient, hardly contained by the words he utters.

"He has risen...." he says slowly as though listening to his own words. "The Master has risen."

* * * * *

If we bring it forth from within ourselves,
that which we bring forth will save us.
If we do not have that within ourselves,
that which we do not have within us will kill us.

The Gospel of Thomas
Nag Hammadi Library

Logion 70

A word from the author

As mentioned in the Acknowledgment, had it not been for Edgar Cayce, this novel would not have been attempted. On the other hand, once Cayce stated that Jesus had visited "Persia, India, Syria and Egypt to complete His education," I felt motivated to imagine conditions in which such an education might have taken place. It is up to the readers to judge if the journey that the twelve-year-old Yeshûa had embarked on could have been such as proposed in previous pages.

Also, I had to suggest such learning opportunities as the times at the beginning of the modern era may have offered, and which might have resulted in the Teaching which later, between the ages of thirty and thirty-three, Jesus imparted to the world.

Readers familiar with my previous books will find this novel in keeping with the sentiments I had expressed formerly. Those who have not read my other attempts to explain my view of reality, might find it useful, if not edifying, to read at least some of them. They go a long way to explain the course that this book has taken. Either way, I wish to assure my readers that in writing this "memoir" I had no desire to offend anyone's sensibilities. If I managed to contribute a tittle to the understanding of the Master's teaching, then so be it. If not, then I hope you will find this novel at least entertaining.

Finally I would be remiss had I not thanked Madeleine Witthoeft and Meghan Nolan for their diligent editing, and my wife, Bozena Happach, who put up with being a grass widow for weeks on end and then gave me her insight into the underlying substance of the book.

Sincerely,

Stan J.S. Law

Lexicon of some ancient names and concepts.

atma	soul, as an object of contemplation, i.e. the individualization of Atma
Atma	the Source, from which all souls originate yet remain indivisible from It. (atman and Atman are the same concepts but personified).
Dimashq	the city later known as Damascus
Essenes	the followers of the strict observance of Mosaic Law as taught by Zadoc. The rest of information regarding this sect has been gleamed from Edgar Cayce.
Himalaya	mountain chain north of Benares, known today as the Himalayas
Kana or Kano	harbour on the Gulf of Aden, today known as Qana.
Muza	main port of the Himyarites on the southwestern tip of the Arabia later known as Al Mokha.
Palmyra	a trading centre in the New Testament times reaching its full growth around the 2nd century.
Pruyag	city in Northern India, present day Allahabad
Teberius	Roman Emperor from 14-37 A.D.. Also the name Romans gave to Lake Gennesareth. In the Old Testament time it was know as the sea of Chinnereth or Cinneroth. Elsewhere it is referred to as the Sea of Galilee and/or the Lake of Tiberius
Yeshûa	Since action in this story takes place in pre-New Testament times, I was compelled to substitute the original Hebrew name Yeshûa (also spelt Jeshua) for the later, Greek version, of Jesus. Yeshûa is the late form of Yechoshûa, meaning Jah is salvation. I applied this method for most names of people and places.

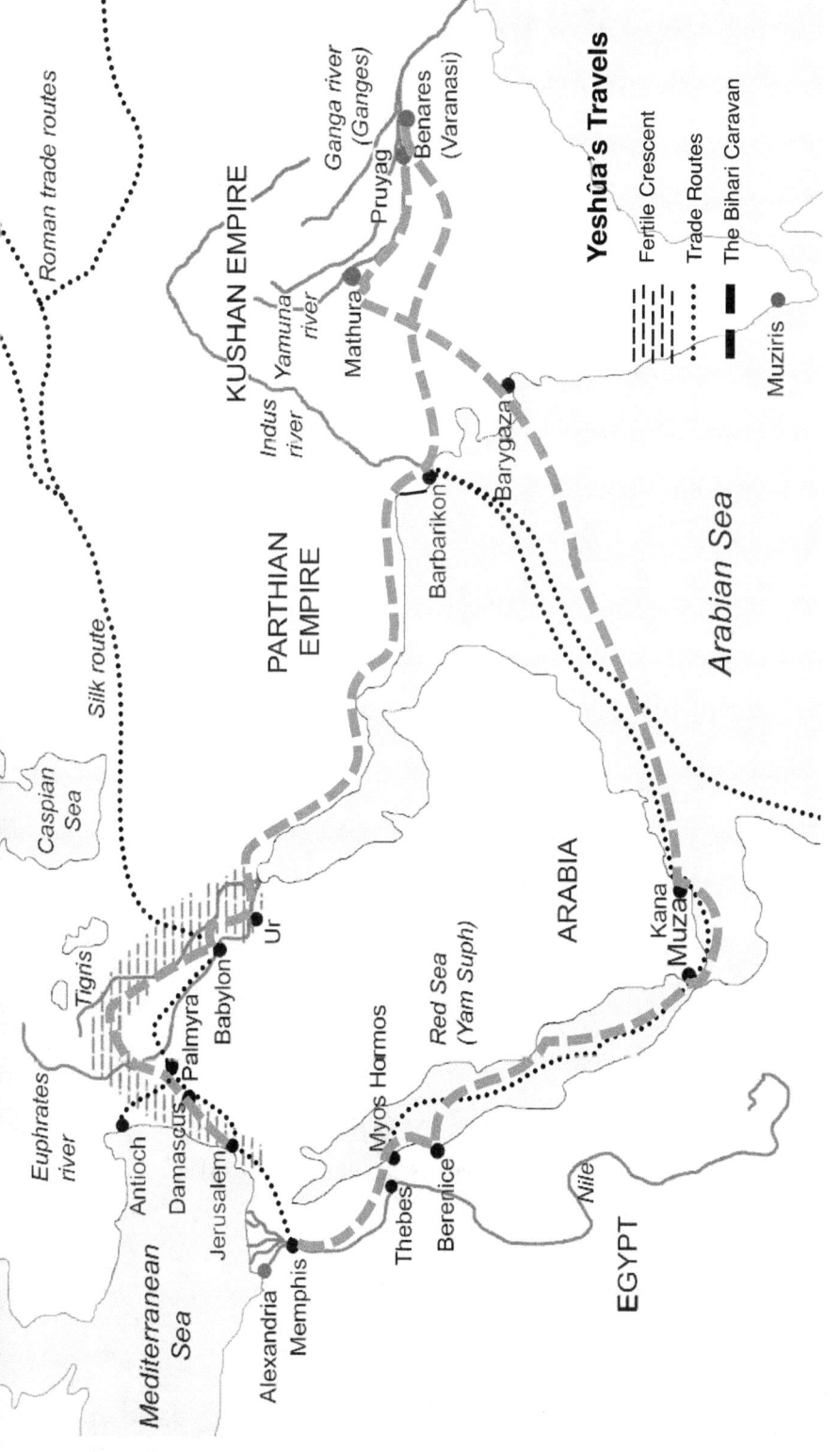

INHOUSEPRESS, MONTREAL, CANADA
http://www.inhousepress.ca

79,105

www.ingramcontent.com/pod-product-compliance
Lightning Source LLC
Chambersburg PA
CBHW072210170626
46813CB00003B/877